The Review Board: Dating in Dublin

The Review Board: Dating in Dublin

Orla Galvin

This book was published at a time when things were not quite right with the world.

Should this story book ignite a tiny trickle of joy in your heart, my wish for you is that it grows with every beat until your days are filled with blissful happiness.

To the ladies, Sarah Mc Loughlin, Rachel McKenna, Olivia O'Leary, and Stephanie Merrigan unknowingly inspiring strength and wisdom when things seem awkward at best, and impossible at worst, the world needs to clone you, or at very least capture and mass reproduce your positive energy!

To all of my friends and extended family, I thank you for all of your support! I look forward to the day when I can hug you all again!

Saving the best for last. Huge, MEGA, MEGA thank you to Mam and Dad for allowing me to take over your sitting room during these strange times. I love you both lots!

Table of Contents

Background

Well, it was certainly not a case of pathetic fallacy, I thought to myself. Unless you considered the blind rage that was bubbling inside me was being reflected by the heat of the sun, and that my inner calm felt as distant as the bright blue sky. Although, it was definitely a great day for a wedding! The sun radiated magnificently with only the odd feather cloud visible in the distance. Glory be to the Child of Prague, and to global warming-Amen! It was definitely at least 27°C, which oddly enough was much warmer than the Seychelles yesterday. Most importantly, I was definitely going to be in much better company than with the man with whom I had spent the last 5 days!

I couldn't wait to get to Cavan Castle for my favourite cousin's wedding! Who was I kidding?! They were all my favourite cousins! No matter how many seas or years were between them, once any of the cousins met up, their cheeks would hurt from grinning, and the words couldn't come out of their mouths fast enough. Best of all, was the belly ache and mild hyperventilation due to fits of laughter, conveying the physical reaction that you were among your own happy kind. These thoughts lifted my spirit, excitement began to brew, and honestly, I needed this escape. In spite of everything, this was a wedding I was truly looking forward to.

After the church ceremony, like moths to a flame, the cousins gathered in the sun outside the reception venue. The true heat of the day was felt when friendly slaps on the back burnt the designer gold T on my dress zip against my skin. This was mildly vexing, and I should have known better than to be out in the sun. The voice of my friend "The Doll" rang in my head; "avoid UVA and UVB exposure girls or I will be blasting you with Botox before you know it!" It didn't take long for me to spot glamorous Maria, single, 40 and holding the gaze of every man in the room - not that she noticed of course! Maria was my confidante, older, wiser and always ready with advice. I just HAD to bring her up to speed with recent events. A problem shared is a problem halved after all!

"Laura darling you look far too hot, and far too sober. Let's fetch some champagne for ourselves, and while we are at it, let's get one each for our sisters-in-law," smirked Maria. Our sisters-in-law were 5 and 7 months pregnant respectively, so I guessed that meant we were getting our loading dose in early. Before the first glass was downed Maria noticed something unusual.

"Is that a natural sun kissed glow I spy on you, madam, or are my eyes deceiving me? Don't try to hide it from me. I have spent the last ten years failing to persuade you, to try a spray-on developing tan, instead of that instant gunk you insist upon wearing. You know I can usually smell you before I can see you at weddings! Don't be shy on the details girl, you know I will get them out of you anyway." I took a dep breath and sighed heavily.

"I have been in the Seychelles with…," I leaned in, looked over my shoulder to make sure no one could hear, and started again half whispering, "I have been in the Seychelles with, himself, stepped back home off the plane in Dublin airport yesterday morning, never said goodbye to him, and I will never see him again," I said as plainly as I could.

Maria pursed her lips and glared for what seemed like an eternity.

"Look I am not going to say I told you so but, are you sure this time, it kills you every time you go back to him!?" exclaimed Maria.

"Yes, once I transferred him my share of the holiday cost, he TEXT to say he left my shoes and hair accessories that he accidently put in his suitcase, with….. the guy behind the counter…….at the grocery store…..beside my apartment."
I knew her jaw would drop and she would be speechless for once. This was a new level of low, even for him.

"Don't worry, he is already forgotten about, I have a date lined up for Friday," I assured her. Maria still hadn't regained the ability to comment, and I was glad. I wanted to say it out loud and then forget he ever existed.

"So, Maria, for my date do you have a top that would go with my polka dot trousers?" I asked, and Maria roared with laughter. It was a running joke at this stage - my polka dot pants as I called them, were my absolute favourite, and I wore them as "high fashion" to every event I possibly could, despite some fading!

"Hell no girl! You are not wearing those trousers AGAIN, especially not on a first date, and correct me if I am wrong but isn't there one butt cheek minus polka dots, faded through on them from how you sit? Where is this date?"

"It's going to be a care free fun date! We are doing something I haven't done in years! We are going bowling!"
Time ticked on and after the wedding meal, my very best friend Lisa arrived. Lisa was my replacement plus-one guest to the wedding, kindly stepping in at the last moment when I briefly informed her of the not-so-pleasant return flight from the Seychelles.

I was anxious to bring her up to speed on recent events. At this rate, the problem ex would be down from a problem halved, to a problem quartered. The focus was now on the impending new date, and funnily enough, work. At every wedding, catching up with aunts, uncles and cousins, the chat invariably goes to 'where are you working now, and what are you doing? And are you dating anybody?'

Work is something I love to talk about! I work for the International Therapeutic Medical and Scientific Approval Agency for Drugs (ITSMAAD), and believe you me, it's mad alright! Ha! We are constantly identifying new drugs for an array of diseases with our drug ranking table system. Lisa has also recently joined our team. Once you follow the method appropriately, it works perfectly first time, every time! After explaining for what felt like the seventh million time what a drug ranking table was, and confirming that yes I was still single, a new plan was brewing in my mind.

When the band finished playing, the DJ started and Lisa grabbed me for a few familiar dance routines- you know the ones they ALWAYS play at weddings! Cooling down with a couple of glasses of fizz later, that chatter was nineteen to the dozen! Fun was in the air and the final cog turned in my brain- my new plan was complete!

"Lisa, Lisa!" Was I slurring? The fizz sure was good! "Lisa, Lisa, Lisa!! I have a plan! You are going to love it! I won't be dragging you out last minute to any more weddings, I have a plaaaaan!!!"
Falling over each other in fits of giggles, I managed to explain my brilliant idea to Lisa.

"I just have to do a ranking table! A ranking table, just like I do at work! You know how at work we rank the therapeutic candidates (the drugs), in a ranking table, to find the optimum therapeutic for a particular disease?! That can be applied to dating! It's so simple! Why didn't I think of it sooner!"

"Slow down Laura. Go again, what do you mean exactly? How does it work?" asked Lisa.

"I've crunched the numbers....I just need to date 9 guys, go on three dates with each of them, rank the dates and the men against parameters that are desirable for a suitable plus-one-date for a wedding! It's so logical! Anne would totally be on board! Do you not seeeeeee Lisa! It's going to work!"

"Laura, you know I love you, and your crazy ideas! You are practically hopping with enthusiasm for this. Ha! I recognize that unstoppable excitement, and determination in your eyes. I know this is going to happen one way or another, so I might as well jump on board," said Lisa laughing and rolling her eyes.

When she recovered from laughing at me she began to gather her thoughts. "So OK, yes, OK, so…. how are you going to do it? I am totally on board with this grand plan! It's totally going to work! But what are the details, Laura?!"
"You are on board?" I asked delighted that she didn't think I had totally lost the plot!
"Yes! But give me the details, you need to flesh this out to me!"
"Oh my goodness, yes! Fantastic, you are on board! In fact, you are on THE board! THE BOARDS! The review board and the ethics board. You are on all of the boards for this experiment. We will have to have brunch tomorrow with the girls, I will fill you all in on all of the details then."
"No doubt they will be on board too!" grinned Lisa.

The Selection Process

The next morning, with just 4 hours sleep I woke up energized, or possibly still drunk. I was physically drained, but mentally on fire! I wanted to keep it that way. For optimum success I jumped in the shower, then filled a pint glass with ice cold water and dissolved a multivitamin in it. I popped a biodegradable straw in (watching my carbon footprint you know) and took a big sip. I wanted to get my plan down on paper for the girls to read before we had brunch. I meant business, I plonked myself down crossed legged on the sofa, pulled my laptop over, and opened a new word document. There could be no bias, I have to date more than just my usual type. Time to engage my brain, tell the inner lust to shush and focus like a scientist.

*****

Study Title: Investigation of Potential Candidates using
Online Dating Applications for a Plus-One to Cousin Michelle's Wedding

Start Date: August 14th
Target End Date: November 14th

Inclusion criteria are the characteristics the prospective subjects must have to be enrolled in the study:

Sex: Male
Age range: 28-35 years old (lucky number 8, 8 year gap right?)
Race: Any
Ethnicity: Any
Health Status: In good health

Height range: About 5'10 ish or taller (That's around a 180 cm + profile)

Psychosocial/ emotional status: Generally, sound, not too clingy, emotionally available

Mental capacity minimum requirements:

1) Knows the difference between girlfriend, friends with benefits, a lady you are dating and just a friend
2) Knows the appropriate actions that should be taken, and those actions which to avoid with regards to each of the above

Serious Factor: Sensible, a man with a plan, but doesn't take themselves too seriously

Fun Factor: There has to be a fair amount of giggles by the *second date (* the second date time point has been decided on for those who may have a nervous disposition on the first date)

Exclusion Criteria are those characteristics that disqualify prospective subjects from entry to the study:

Marital Status: For the period of the study in question, men with spouses currently (married), or previously (divorced/ separated/ widowed) are not eligible for enrollment.

Offspring: Candidates with children will not be enrolled for the study (and for the record, dogs do not count as offspring).

Pets: Pets are allowed with the exception of cats due to the primary investigator's allergic reactions to them.

Health Status:

Smokers will not be enrolled in this study.

Men who drink alcohol more than 3 nights per week will not be enrolled in this study.

Men in good health but with images of themselves at the gym flexing, or images of themselves with their tops off will not be enrolled in this study.

Men with 420 (indicating marijuana use) or any other indication of drug use on their profile will not be enrolled in this study.

Height: 5'9 ish or smaller will be restricted (lets be real here people, I am 5'10 and would potentially be wearing heels at the wedding, and I don't have a dress picked out yet. Depending on the design of the dress, if I brought a shorter guy to the wedding he might end up at cleavage eye level, and no one would want that- well except for maybe the guy!)

<u>*Points to query with the review board*</u>

You know there are people who drink neither tea or coffee? That just wouldn't really suit my lifestyle.

❖ Feeling cold? Solution: have a nice hot cup of tea or coffee.

❖ Need to talk? Solution: sit and have a chat over a nice hot cup of tea or coffee.

❖ The number one easy option first date is 'Let's grab a coffee?', should there be exclusion criteria on this point?

Although now that I think of it, the objective is to find a suitable plus-one wedding date, and whether or not the gentleman would drink tea or coffee would not impact on this. Ok, fine, consumption of tea or coffee should not really be an issue.....but seriously what do these guys do on sober dates? A date drinking a soft drink in theory is fine, but I think I would feel awkward sitting across from someone with their tap water while sipping on my lovely Americano. How many first dates are held in coffee shops?! Could you say let's go get a hot drink to keep warm while we walk along the sea front promenade on a cold, windy day? Maybe they could have hot chocolate, I guess.

While on the subject of drinking, you know how there are people who don't drink alcohol? What do you propose to do with those? Allow them in the study? For all the good intentions of not drinking alcohol, the health benefits and financial benefits, the always having a driver benefits; it does add a layer of complexity to the dating method. While it is not always the case, but with one or two drinks people usually become more relaxed and comfortable in themselves, and with their date. They may even become chattier, friendlier and seem funnier than if they were sober, not to mention better looking, but that's not the point in question here!

For example, based on my own experience, it was date number two, we had agreed to go for cocktails and dancing (although to be fair, maybe the dancing part was just implied in my head), and we arrive at the very nice cocktail bar HE picked out. We picked up the cocktail menu. It looked oh so good! I knew immediately that I wanted the porn star martini, so I asked him what did he think he would go for? It wasn't until that exact moment did he announce that he does not drink alcohol! I was gob smacked. I didn't know what to say or think! Except to wonder why on earth he selected for us, to go to a cocktail bar when he didn't drink them?! From there the date was doomed. I tried to be as chatty and friendly as possible but he remained his lovely quiet self- which unfortunately was no craic! I think for this study it is best to keep an open mind, but also suss the drinking habits of the guys out first.

My next main concern was to figure out what is important when bringing a guest to a family wedding. The answers to this would form the basis of the ranking criteria.

Note to the Review Board
Please find below wedding guest criteria to support scoring of candidates

An obvious first point is to know the person reasonably well, and not to bring a random guest for the sake of it. I think you should know your date well enough to know they will not embarrass you, or get so drunk they offend another guest, or do something stupid. It's a family wedding after all....we wouldn't want Auntie Rose bringing up the embarrassing shenanigans over next year's Christmas pudding!
In selecting your guest, ideally this is someone you are dating long enough to know that time spent together at the wedding will be time well spent, and a good time.

Good social skills are imperative, not alone for the purpose of a date for a wedding, but in general. I have no intention of dating someone who cannot string a sentence together or has no sense of humour. A person with a good sense of humour is desired, let's be honest here, someone who can give and take a bit of slagging would do very well indeed. He'll need to be able to hold his own with the Cousins. Within the topic of social skills, I guess it is important to remember that the chosen guest is a reflection of she who selected him. The guest is my selection, so I better choose wisely. "The chosen one" ha, ha, should not cause any drama, or have any pre-formed ill relationships with other guests that the investigator is aware of.

There IS a certain wedding guest etiquette to be considered. The wedding day and night are about the bride and groom. Their day should go as smoothly as possible. It is important that when the RSVP is returned that the plus one has a name, and that he shows up. Otherwise the bride and groom will have wasted money on the flakey individual who does not show up. (Of course there are exceptions, and people get sick and there are emergencies, but really the aim here is to invite someone, who when he says yes, will show up.)

Of course there is nothing worse than feeling like you have to babysit and protect a delicate little flower of a guest. On the contrary, the dream guest shows up, but does not hog the show! Ideally a plus-one can work conversations around the other people at the table without having his hand held along the way. While being sociable, the wedding should not revolve around your guest however, he should not draw THAT much attention to himself. Be sure he has a suitable suit, and not be the type of guy who thinks a white suit to a wedding, as a guest, is appropriate!

As with all my cousins' weddings thus far, the true sign of a good wedding, is directly proportional to the number of people on the dance floor, and the duration for which the dance floor is occupied. Individuals with poles shoved up their - you know where- who remain seated or propping up the bar are not desired. In terms of dancing skills, it is not so much skills that are required. The quality of the dancing does not need to be good, but the willingness to at least try has to be evident. God loves a trier and so too, do the Cousins.

Study Design:

The cohort of prospective candidates will form three phases. Each phase will consist of 3 individuals. Therefore, the study will enroll 9 prospective candidates. A ranking table will be created in advance of study commencement. The grading system is outlined below.

Each candidate will be marked out of a possible score of 50. The breakdown of this score is as follows:

Each of the dates 1-3 will be given an overall score between 1 and 5 by the investigator (yours truly). A score of 1 reflects a poor quality experience, and a score of 5 represents the best possible experience for that date.

In addition to the dates, the candidates themselves will be scored between 1 and 5 on the characteristics and qualities they display over the course of the three dates, and also on any communication from initial matching on the dating app to experiment completion. A score of 1 reflects low levels of the desired quality, and a score of 5 reflects the highest level of desired quality.

The seven qualities are described as follows:

❖ **_Good Communication_**: This quality refers to the ability of the candidate to express himself well, and in a manner that is frequent and consistent with good dating etiquette.

❖ **_Good sense of humour_**: This quality refers to the ability of the candidate to laugh at, or see the funny side to life's absurdities. The candidate himself does not need to be cracking jokes all of the time, but witty remarks will be rewarded on the ranking table.

❖ **_Willingness to dance_**: The candidate does not need to be good at dancing, or openly express a keen interest in dancing, but a willingness to dance if asked is acceptable.

❖ **_Confidence among strangers_**: This refers to the ability of the candidate to handle himself in a situation where he does not know the other people he is with. A good indicator of this is the confidence he expresses on the first date, at which point he is not yet acquainted with the investigator.

❖ **_Personality around alcohol_**: This refers to the ability of the candidate to drink sensibly where appropriate, and to remain his good natured self upon consumption of alcohol. (Too many people get angry, or cry with alcohol consumption. This must be avoided at all costs.)

❖ **_Trustworthy:_** This refers to the relative trust the investigator should have after three dates and good communication with the candidate. Of course excessive or complete trust at this point would not be expected.

However, another point to note is that if the investigator has any poor descriptions that oppose a trustworthy nature of the candidate, the candidate will score low on this point. Examples of poor descriptions include the use of the following words: liar, scum, sleazy, player, sneaky, snakey, obnoxious, idiot, fool, creep, leach, social-climber, parasite.

❖ ***Punctual:*** This refers to the ability of the candidate to keep good time. Anyone can be stuck in unexpected traffic, or be slightly delayed. In these instances, a text or voice message should be sent to the investigator to inform her of the new estimated time of arrival. Even with this notification, candidates who are more than 10 minutes late will receive low scoring for punctuality. It is important to remember, in attending the wedding, the bride should be the last to arrive!

If the Review Board are in agreement with these scores, the score remains, however should the Review Board deem a lower or higher score is more appropriate the final decision lies with them.

(Further detail on the Review Board members will follow the methods section.)

Methods:

Candidates will be selected from a variety of online dating applications. To avoid bias, the investigator should have no prior knowledge of the candidates selected. Each candidate will be given three dates. While the dates will vary in location and duration (imagine playing mini golf 9 times in 3 months-maybe I might actually get good at it!), at least one date will have to be an outdoorsy sober date.

No dates with one candidate shall overlap with another candidate. Overlapping communication with candidates by written, or oral means (such as video message, voice message or phone call), so long as it is not in person is permissible. This in part serves to use time in the most effective manner.

No physical interaction shall take place with any of the candidates beyond that of hand holding and kissing. Mental clarity is absolutely required throughout this process. Any comments or actions by any candidate which is deemed to focus too heavily on the physical side of courtship shall render the candidate immediately struck off the candidate list. If this happens on date number 1 the candidate may be replaced by an alternative candidate. If this happens on date 2 or 3 the candidate remains within the study with a deduction of 10 points. It is the responsibility of the investigator, i.e ME, to try to avoid such men in the selection process. The ability to "weed out the bad ones" should have been well established by now! Consider it a pre-established method.

Upon completion of Phase 1 and Phase 2, the study design and criteria may be revised in agreement with the Review Board. Study design and criteria may not be revised while any phase is ongoing.

*****

I saved the file to send it to the girls who would make up the Review Board. I created a new group chat "Dating in Dublin, The Scientific Method Review Board". I added Lisa, The Doll, Rebecca and Anne to the group and sent them a message along with the experiment details.

Laura:
Hi girls! I created the attached method for dating in Dublin with the objective of finding…not a husband…but a suitable plus-one date to attend a wedding. I am roping you in to act as the review board for this process, and maybe the ethics board too, though I'm not sure I need one.
All's fair in love and war right? Ha ha!
See you all at brunch later- the usual spot!
Puddles of cuddles, Laura xo

The Review Board

The sensible one, Anne, is single by choice as she firmly declares it to be an 'economically wise' decision. We all know, any effort in the beauty and fashion department which undeniably play a factor in dating, can range from a-wee-bit-pricey to extremely expensive. Combining this knowledge with Anne working in finance, no-one can argue with her on this point. Anne is super logical and always knows what the appropriate and sensible thing to do is. Anne remains true and unfaltering in her beliefs. She does not absorb any nonsense from anyone - she takes no crap and holds no prisoners. Anne is brutally honest, but borderline negative.

The wise one, Rebecca, is in an 8-year relationship and is engaged. This relationship has been going steady from the beginning, any potential threats of drama or issues are carefully diverted through the use of food. Rebecca navigates the relationship with ease and, as a home economics teacher, she has skills in the kitchen department. Rebecca practices what she preaches - a way to a man's heart is through his stomach! She is very accommodating, generally nice, extremely positive, and has good experience in approaches that work to stabilize a relationship.

However, she has only ever dated her fiancé, and does not quite understand the trials and tribulations of the current dating world. Her biggest issue is progressing the engagement to a marriage. This is a topic of conversation which became off limits after the first 18 months of engagement went by, and still no date was set. While methodically Rebecca is usually on point and displays dedication to following recipes or protocols to perfection, with her relationship background, her ranking may come from a mind that is more forgiving and naïve… but time will tell.

The excitable one, no-one knows her real name outside of her family and our friends group, as she doesn't believe her real name suits her profession, so she goes by 'The Doll'. The Doll is single but keeping an eye out. All of her clients (the "Botox Babes") know she is single and are also keeping an eye out. However, her start up salon has taken its toll on The Doll, in the first two years it completely ate up all of her time and all of her money. The Doll is all for romance, however being burned by love in the past has scared her heart. These days, The Doll just wants some fun, she works hard and plays hard, she has a risky spirit. The result of this is that in her rare down time, she has some fun but with her wandering eye it often lands her in trouble!

The balanced one, Lisa, is recently in a long distance relationship with one of her fellow yoga teachers in Italy. Lisa may be right with her theory, that in most cases men just need to be trained up, but is it really worth the effort of dating if they haven't been trained already? We are not teenagers anymore. First and foremost, Lisa is a scientist. Scientists have to be creative, innovative, logical and calculated (often described as engineers with imagination- ha, sorry engineers!) Lisa completely embodies this, in addition to being a super scientist by day, Lisa has set up a yoga class for people living with particular disabilities which takes place 2 evenings per week. This is a program that she is in the process of spreading across Europe, and one day hopes to leave the lab-based science world. Lisa herself is part of the upper class bourgeoisie, but does not act like it, though she does recommend The Doll's salon to her friends from back in the days at boarding school. Lisa is balanced, kind and an excellent listener. Lisa is very rational, gives the benefit of the doubt but slays when appropriate. Lisa is also the very best housemate!

Situated just off Grafton Street, the girls were sitting in our favourite brunch spot in the whole city, when I slid into the booth bedside them! Pancakes were ordered all round along with a skinny decaf cappuccino for Rebecca (Becks), a green tea for The Doll, a peppermint tea for Anne, a skinny late with sugar free hazelnut syrup for Lisa (she was trying to trick herself into thinking she was getting loads of sugar), and my usual, an Americano with room for milk.

After the usual banter of "oh nice top/ shoes/ bag/ did you get your hair done since we last met - it's lovely etc" I couldn't contain my excitement and decided it was time to lay out the plan for the girls.

"Ok ladies, firstly thank you all for gathering on such short notice!"

"Well you know the opportunity to have these amazing pancakes was the real lure in, not you babes" giggled The Doll. I pulled a face and she hugged me tight in consoling comfort.

"Ok, you are forgiven, because you are squeezing the oxygen out of me!!" I laughed.

"You know it's so true. These pancakes are mmm mmm mmm delicious carbs, we shall have to go for a walk after, but while I have you all here I want to ask if you would act as my, well, kind of my review board for a little social experiment. I am doing this, "social-experiment" to ensure I don't end up dragging one of you to my next cousin's wedding!"

"Ohhh tell us more!" they chorused almost in unison.

"Well, you know how sometimes it's easy to waste too much time on an idiot man, like how many dates is fair really before deciding? And, what criteria do we judge people on? What really matters? You know, how can we make a fair comparison?"

"Yes, go on" they agreed in unison.

"Well basically, I'm going to set up a ranking table for nine diverse gentlemen, no "type" in particular. I have set out inclusion and exclusion criteria which I have forwarded to you in the new group chat, based on wanting a suitable plus-one for the next wedding I have been invited to. I have drafted a ranking table for the dates themselves, and for the desired qualities of the optimum- (note I did not say perfect)- plus one."

"I've a question. Lots actually! How can you properly compare across dates without having them all engage with you on the exact same date, and if you are, would that not drive you mad? And you are already really busy, how will this impact upon your training for us walking the Dublin City Marathon?" inquired Anne, the practical one of the group.

"Oh God are we still doing that?" asked Becks, "like for definite?"

"YES!!" announced Lisa, The Doll, and Anne, laughing at all at once. "The DCM - Dublin City Marathon - is definitely a go!"

"I did think of that, and you know there is a way to solve the issue of comparing a similar date between men; and the issue of needing to keep up the walking for the DCM training. To be fair, with comparisons across individuals at least one of the dates with each man will simply have to be a really long sober walking date. Or some sort of activity to keep fitness up!"

The Doll raised her brow in a saucy manner with a crooked smile.

"No, not THAT type of activity."

"I didn't say anything" she laughed holding her hands up in defense.

"I would like you ladies to help me review the ranking table to make sure I ask the right one to the wedding!"

"We gathered that much from the group message but what about the ethics review board you mentioned last night?" asked Lisa.

"Ah yes, as my ethics board, I have one question to each of you before the study trial commences: do I tell the guys they are part of a plan, or leave them blissfully ignorant?"
Becks immediately piped up "Yes, of course, it's only fair that they know they have competition."
Lisa, Anne, and The Doll together disagreed, "No, no, no they don't need to know!"
The Doll simply said, "All's fair in love and war."
Anne had some deeper thoughts, "It might only bias their actions, and besides, they should know there is competition to win you over. Just remember, they have competition for them too. Also you must factor in, that whoever comes out trumps might not even want to go to the wedding, or go on another date with you Laura."
I did think of that. "That will be one of the criteria, I will have to suss them out for; willingness to attend weddings, or hypothetically ask would they dance if they were invited to a wedding!"
Lisa agreed with the plan in general saying, "Isn't it just a more structured way of dating. I think there is absolutely no ethical issue here. I nominate myself as chairlady of the board. All those in favour of NOT telling the guys the plan, raise your hand."
All hands went up, even Beck's!!
Anne as always had more practical questions. "So how will we know how the dates are going? Do we wait until the Review Board meetings take place?"

Lisa solved the issue with her suggestion of leaving a short voice note in the group chat after each date so the Review Board can hear immediately how it went. That way the information will be closer to the truth. You know how over time the story can change!

We all agreed with Lisa, I would definitely leave a short voice note. I would have to just stick to the facts of what happened on the date and not my observations and interpretations, that's for the Review Board to form opinions on, and note on the ranking table for each individual man. At the end of the experiment I told them I would pool the results together in a single ranking table.

Becks wondered what would happen if we were in stark disagreement. She was smart, and on-point for thinking like this. You know we are a bit of a diverse group, and are not likely to agree on the same guy, especially when there are going to be 9 of them. Becks also queried what would happen if the sum values for some of the candidates turned out to be equal? Although it might be unlikely, but what if, for example, there were four men who each have the highest score?

Eventually we agreed on a plan. We would have a process a bit like some of the talent shows on TV, where each judge (or in this case each Review Board member) could have a special nomination (wild card), whereby a bonus five points would be awarded to whoever the board member chose at the end of the process.

"That'll separate the men from the boys!" declared The Doll.

On my way home from brunch, I was enthused by the support of the Review Board for this experiment. I have known these girls for more than 10 years, since we lived together at university. As best friends we share a lot of common ground, however, each of these girls still bring their own unique expertise to the table. Our diversity no doubt helped us remain friends, but it also brings strength to all types of decision-making.

Now that I had confided in my best friends about my process to find a date for my cousin's wedding, I began to ponder the best and worst case scenarios. The worst-case scenario was that I would have documented and have evidence to show I had at least tried to find someone to bring as a guest to the wedding. I mean, 9 men with 3 dates each would total 27 dates - you couldn't argue with that for effort! In addition to the ranking table, each of the reviewers could give 5 extra points at the end of the process to the man they thought would be most suitable to attend the wedding. Surely with all of this, the best-case scenario would be the end result and I would find a great date for the wedding?!

The only way to know, was to get on with it! Step one, try not miss any more sleep before my first date with Candidate 1, Padraig, The Radiographer!

Phase 1, Man 1, Candidate 1, Padraig (The Irish for Patrick), The Radiographer

The first candidate was Padraig, pronounced *paw-drig*, and I had already agreed to meet him in advance of developing this structured, dating method. Sub-consciously, or not, he fit within the parameters of the candidate trial so we were good to go on our date!

His profile picture on the dating app was of him with three others in a fancy dress costume. The costume was from a film I had watched so many times as a child. Four men, one bobsleigh and a dream. It was one of my all-time favourite movies. It was that picture of him, in his fancy dress costume and a wig that sealed the deal, I was swiping right and that was it. He was just within my newly defined inclusion criteria for this process with his 5 foot 10 and bit height. Perhaps I had intentionally lowered what I would have desired in height, just to keep him in the running. He was not my type on paper, but the various colours in his pictures drew my attention.

I was excited about him in a different way. The conversation via the dating app flowed easily. He was my age, and he was a country boy from Galway. He was mad into hurling but he didn't play himself. That did not diminish his passion for the sport. He was witty and energetic and playful, and I knew within the first days of messaging he would be a pleasure to be around.

Quickly we switched from messaging on the dating app to exchanging phone numbers. This is the first real step towards securing a date. I learned we had gone to the same university at the same time. I was really such a girls' girl back then, and nerdy to boot. I didn't know a single guy (as in any!) when I was at university, except for the guys I lived with on campus in final year, but that didn't count.

He was quite scientifically minded, and had covered some of the same course material as I had back in the day. Some common ground is beneficial. One night we were messaging about how irritating it was to have to repeat experiments three times even when you knew it just wasn't going to work! He was just so warm and easy to talk to. He had shown such interest in everything about me and was so intrigued by my natural addiction to ranking tables, and my lists of favourite things. That night messaging, I came so close to telling him my plan for dating using a scientific adaptation of a ranking method for this 'plus-one wedding guest social experiment', but I persevered and the experiment remained a secret. Instead, we exchanged a few of our lists of favourite things over text. We dismissed our top favourite fizzy soft drinks, as we both agreed we hardly ever drank them anymore, our adult lives revolved mostly around water and coffee, and yes we admitted alcohol! We started with the basics- colour and why.

Padraig:

Alright Laura only because you asked so nicely, my top 5 fav colours are:

1. Yellow- because I think you look particularly cute in that yellow dress on your profile, Irish girls not the biggest fans of yellow. I thought you might have been Spanish when I saw you first.

2. Blue-because I am a boy and it brings out the colour of my brown eyes ;)

3. Red- No I am not fan of a red jersey wearing football team. I just think it can look sexy on girls, their lips and their clothes, lingerie ;) (oops maybe I shouldn't have said that) and fast cars too!

4. Black- because it is sleek and classy, again cars would be at the forefront of my imagination

5. Pink- because I love a good Strawberry Daiquiri

Your turn!

Laura:

OK Mister

1. Yellow- because it is my fav colour since time began, and now also because you like-y my dress ☺ making me blush

2. White- because it's pure, clean, striking and difficult to manage, but oh so worth it- a bit like me ;)

3. Black- because it is sleek, sophisticated and sexy, I agree with you on cars and for clothes too!

4. Green- because I am Irish, and it brings out the colour of MY eyes :-P

5. Lavender -because it soothes my crazy mind!

Let's revert back to the reference to alcoholic drinks...Strawberry Daiquiri?? Feminine much?

Padraig:

A real man like myself, is totally comfortable and can embrace at his leisure with his feminine side, now hush so I can tell you my favourite drinks

1. Strawberry Daiquiri- I lived in north Wexford for a while and suffered the commute, Strawberries are delicious and nutritious, and blended into the Daiquiri format brings about a pleasure unlike any other! No I am not gay or metro sexual, I just know what I like.

2. Cuba Libre- got used to drinking it in Rio after one of my trips to Cuba- tis nice.

3. Espresso Martini- well I mean who doesn't enjoy an espresso martini?

4. Cosmopolitan- because it is fruity and sweet and delicious, I would say there is not enough in it though. Can we get larger triangular glasses please?
5. The margaritas in the Mexican place on George's street –yum.

Laura:
Wow not a pint or bottle variety of alcoholic drinks in sight there! Mine are in no particular order, really, it depends on my mood or the event at which I'm drinking.
1. Prosecco- a girls second best friend, next to diamonds and I like both to be large ;-)
2. Espresso Martini- agreed it's a classic!
3. A good Argintine Malbec- especially on a winter night.
4. Pornstar Martini- you get the fruitiness accompanied by the bubbles of the prosecco- what is not to enjoy here people?
5. A good pint of Guinness- it's a classic, and counts as a meal, I rarely drink it, but when I do, I thoroughly enjoy it!!

Padraig:
Ah ok hold on, I may have misinterpreted drinks as cocktails, I guess I was hoping to ask you out for some ;)
So when the bowling date on Friday goes well, and we are on our second date which will be a night out going for cocktails, I know what to get you....and no it won't be a Guinness.

Laura:
Oh, mister confident! Though speaking of Guinness, I do love a baby Guinness.

Padraig:

OK Laura we have to do it- the favourite shot list! By the way, you mean mister positive, not mister confident! I'll tell you mine while you are thinking of yours ;-) I have some recovery on the strawberry daiquiri front to make up for here now!

1. Snakebite, it's whiskey and lime if you don't know- this counteracts my strawberry daiquiri right? ☺
2. Rusty Nail, yeah you are seeing me in a different light, I do shots like a real man baby!
3. Motor Oil, yes you read that right, are you imagining my muscular arms filling up my jeep with diesel? ;-) It's a blow the head off you drink- Jagermeister, Goldschlager, Rum, and Peppermint Schnapps. This one is for nights out when the girls aren't as pretty as you ;) Do I get bonus points for saying that, or am I laying it on too thick?
4. Hurricane Laura, just for you, dark rum, passion fruit juice, grenadine and orange juice.
5. Tequila Rose- seems delicate, almost too easy, sweet and smooth- to steal your line, it's just like me ☺

Right missus hit me with your best shot! :-P

Laura:
Oh the cheese is coming out now, big time! Right, apart from number 2 the rest of my selections are very sweet, almost desert-like, let's just say I learned the hard way that neat spirits are not really the shots for me!

1. Chocolate cake, made with Hazelnut liqueur, Vanilla vodka, and the shot glass rimmed with lemon and sugar- super delicious!
2. Sambuca, purely for the facial expressions after it! I should mention Sambuca of the non-flaming variety. I do have a Sambuca fire story- for again though!

3. Jamaican Dust, White Rum, Coconut Rum and pineapple Juice!
4. Baby Guinness, I know you know it!

   (Dare I type this next one I thought to myself, because of it's name!)

5. Blow Job, a layer of Baileys, a layer of Kahlua, a smaller layer of amaretto and whipped cream to top! Ha ha!

Did you like that?! ☺

Padraig:
HA! Oh maybe you are not as innocent as I think you are!

Laura:
Ok, calm down, cool the jets, so we know what we would be drinking. What if we watched a movie, what is your favourite film, is it the one from your profile picture?

Padraig:
No my favourite changes all the time but if there was an all-time favourite list it would certainly be on it. I haven't been to the cinema in a while but I watched an awesome musical with my nieces recently and you know what, it WAS the greatest show! What about you?

Laura:
My favourite changes with time too but usually contains a powerful female lead, kicking ass at a very high level.

Padraig:
What is your favourite place you have ever been?

Laura:

I travel a lot with work, as opposed to on holiday. California would be close to the top but honestly it's Inis Mór. I haven't been in years so maybe I have rose tinted glasses on when I think of it, but I love our coast line and that little island off it too! How about you?

Padraig:

I know; we have a great country for tourism when we have the weather. I'd have to say Cuba. I have been there four times! I love the place! The colours, the dancing, the food, the drinks I love it all! Will definitely go back there again next year!

Laura:

Wow you must really like it there!

I did note he enjoys dancing. I wondered what keeps bringing him back to Cuba though. Lots of cultures have colourful festivals, dancing, good food and drinks. I didn't want to ruin the moment by asking in case it was a previous girlfriend, or something like that, so I just told him I was up early the next morning and really had to sleep- it was true after all!

Laura:

Ok Mister, I'm going to have to call it a night, I have a date with some bloke tomorrow so I better get my beauty sleep in!

Padraig:

Me too, I am going bowling with some bird, she had better bring her A game!

Date 1 with Padraig, The Radiographer

Bowling! In my mind, it was a novel suggestion, I hadn't been bowling in years! On the one hand this made it exciting and fun. On the other hand, my hand-eye co-ordination beyond the micro-meter action of pipetting in the lab wasn't great. In fact, it was terrible! Tennis, badminton, volley ball, basketball, golf, I tried and tested them all, poor skills at best! The only hand-eye game I was good at, was pool. This was down to the years of babysitting by my older brother. A day in his care was often spent down at the pool hall, and ultimately it was of benefit to me. The amount of free drinks I won at the college bar through pool games was noteworthy! Thinking back of those thirsty college nights, and, well actually these days, that amount of alcohol would probably kill me off!

"Great timing young lady!" Padraig beamed at me.

"Not bad timing yourself good sir" I grinned back as we reached the bowling alley at the same time.

As we approached the door there was a huge sign, **BYOB (Bring Your Own Beer) Bowling**, we looked at each other and started to giggle.

Once we saw the sign we both knew we were heading for the off-licence. I was giddy, this was funniest man I had ever met! His stories were outrageous and his temperament endearing. This had made me so nervous, the good kind. So while I was getting ready, before walking to the bus stop....(dare I really admit this)...I tipped a couple of home measures of vodka into a bottle of diet 7 up, and chugged away on it on the bus journey in. The BYOB scenario wouldn't affect how I was getting home; the bus would take me directly back. For Padraig however, some additional co-ordination would have to be done.

This is where having the best housemates comes in handy. Padraig said he was going to take the car home, and his housemate would drop him back in. He gave me his order and money for the cans of beer he wanted from the off-licence. This meant I could keep the ball rolling while he made the return journey.

This was a perfectly good plan I thought, although as I strolled over to the off-licence, I wondered what on earth I was going to drink. I didn't like cider. I didn't really like beer, and besides I heard so many times that men don't like women who drink beer, especially not women who drink manly pints! That left spirits and wine. Spirits meant mixers too- that would be a bit awkward and a bit expensive and I would end up very drunk very quickly. That wasn't on my agenda. Wine it was so! Definitely white! It was still warm and sunny out, and a chilled white wine straight from the fridge sounded blissful to me at that moment.

My mind wandered to my first impressions of him. His vibe demonstrated he was at ease with the world, and I can't imagine how anyone could feel anything but comfortable with him. Having said that, there was definitely butterflies in my tummy. You could see the influence of the Spanish armada on the population in the west of Ireland in his features. His milk chocolate brown eyes were no exception. His wavy dark brown hair framed his kind face, he sure was every bit as handsome as his profile pictures suggested.

As I arrived back at the bowling alley Padraig's housemate dropped him off- again perfect timing!

Walking into the bowling alley we went straight to the reception to get our bowling shoes. He definitely asked for at least a size bigger than his feet wear! I kept my little chuckle to myself. For once I was glad my feet were small for my height. My feet were just about the only part of my body that seemed dainty to me. The next thing on my mind was plastic cups, perhaps Padraig was wise to this by ordering cans. Bottles would have required a bottle opener, spirits and a mixer or even my wine require a glass or something to put them in. Luckily the bowling alley had lots of paper recyclable cups for free.

He typed our names in on our lane and the competition began. I faired out OK at the beginning, more of a fluke, or beginners luck than skill. He was much better, of course. He was also super competitive.

The time went by so quickly, it was so much fun! We played sets of bowling with our weaker hands, and then with our eyes closed. It was all good, harmless fun. The drink went down too easy. Before we knew it the bowling alley was closing. I had only meant to stay out until 11pm! The buses were no longer running out to where I lived!

"I'll get my housemate Paul to drop you home, he'll come pick us up now" Padraig reassured me. I was also starting to feel a little bit hungry.

"Are you hungry?" he asked. "I am actually ravenous," I replied. I was delighted he practically read my mind! Either that or it could have been the gurgling noises my tummy was making though!

Once outside my giddiness spiraled, and though I couldn't remember quite what I was talking about, I found it very funny. Along came the giggles, and I literally, desperately, couldn't stop. I couldn't speak with the laughter. Along came Padraig's housemate and remarked about what a happy individual I was. Within seconds the hunger was encompassing me and the world around me began to spin. I stopped dead in my tracks, or at least that's what I thought I did.

"Whoooaaa, steady on up," Padraig laughed, and propped me up against his hip and shoulder, giving me a second to settle myself. He suggested we all go to the *Fast Food American Style Diner*.

"Are you ok?" he checked as we walked along the path.

"Yeah-of-course" I slurred. I had heard myself slur. I really should have eaten before the date, but I didn't want a bloated belly in my tight fitted top. A good way to redeem myself would be to speak coherently with my next sentence. Thinking hard, focusing on pronouncing each syllable properly and leaving spaces between my words I managed to say, "Food, yay! This is a great idea!" I cheered at the thought of the food to come! Off our trio went to the restaurant. I forgot to be a lady, to be reserved and delicate and fragile, and meek, when it came to ordering food......I had exactly what the guys were having! Oh man it was delicious. The burger, oh the burger and sticky melted cheese, this was definitely what I imagined heaven was made of. The boys gave me stick about how quickly I went from sober to completely ossified, and I started giggling at myself again.

Oh my tummy ached from laughing! This was a fun night! Oh, oh no, this wasn't tummy ache from laughing, this was tummy ache from alcohol, this could be alcohol poisoning! I felt a hot and clammy wave wash over me, I had to get to the bathroom quick! I made my excuses and walked as fast as I could, hopefully not drawing attention to my urgency to get to the ladies. Once inside I ran to a cubicle. I had never felt such relief from vomiting in my whole life. It felt good. I noticed how very hot I was getting again, it really was too warm, I felt clammy, oh no! Sick again!

Eventually it stopped, and I felt remarkably well. I felt more in tune with my mind too. Oh God I had forgotten my date and his housemate at the booth. A quick makeup-check in the mirror, wash of the hands and face later, and back to the main restaurant I went! How cute they were when I returned. I really did feel better. In fact, I was ravenous! I finished my meal and Padraig insisted his housemate dropped me home first.

They didn't know where my place was, and even when sober I was terrible at giving directions. I had to be in the car on a particular road to be able to tell a person where the next turn was. So the journey home was full of late stage recognition of where to turn, resulting in quick jolts, none of which was doing my delicate tummy any favours. Twice on the way home I had to ask Paul to pull over so I could hop out and be sick. The second time I was conscious they could see me so I moved further from the car. Padraig hopped out too, and started rubbing my back.
"You're OK darling, better to get it out."
"I hope I didn't get sick on the car."
"The car can be washed, just make sure you are ok, you mustn't have eaten before we went bowling, did you not? I really have never seen anyone hit the air and flip 180 like that!"
"Oh, don't look I'm going to be sick again!" I was mortified!

How sweet and caring he was towards me though, it must be the bed side training of his profession. I felt my temperature rise intensely, this time it was not to be sick, this time it was pure embarrassment. When we reached the gates of my apartment block I thanked them quickly, jumped out of the car and ran inside!

Beep, Beep I woke up and opened my eyes, it felt like my bedroom was spinning. I closed my eyes and clung on to the bed sheets for dear life. I reached out to my bedside locker. Thankfully I had the sense to pour a bottle of water last night. I drank a good half litre and drifted back to sleep.

Beep, Beep Cautiously I opened one eye at a time just in case the room started to spin again. It didn't. It looked brighter outside than the last attempt to wake up. I reached for my water and my phone. There were two messages from Padraig. A fresh wave embarrassment swept over me. I would need to take a shower before I was brave enough to read them! Cleansed of the night before, feeling a little refreshed, and with a coffee in my hand, I opened the messages.

Padraig:

Are you alive? You are some craic aren't you?! :-P You really went from sober as a judge to complete gaga giggle monster! You were saying something about wanting to do more active dates. Do you want to do an adult outdoor 10 km obstacle course (kind of an assault course) with me? I'll sign us up!?

That was not the absolute roasting of a slagging that I was expecting. Nor was it a message describing me as stupid and gross and all of the horrible things I felt about an hour ago. If anything it was positive, and instead of him seeing me at my worst and doing a legger, he wanted to meet up again!

Padraig:

So I was only joking when I asked if you were alive earlier, but now I am genuinely concerned, are you feeling OK Laura? Do you want me to bring you anything over? Ha, now that I know a really convoluted way to get to your apartment haha! I was serious about the assault course, you don't have to answer right away on that, but do let me know you are OK. Xx

Aw I almost cried. What an angel. This guy was the best!! Of course I had to reply!

Laura:

Ha oh Padraig, I don't know if I will ever get over such an agonizing mortification haha! Thank you so much for making sure I got home safely last night. You were right, I hadn't eaten before drinking-rookie mistake! This adult outdoor 10 km obstacle course sounds interesting- sure go on sign us up!

Padraig:

Ah don't worry about last night we had fun at the bowling and forget about the rest! Great about the assault course, I will have us signed up for Saturday! PS some people race it, I'm sure we will make good time!

An assault course. It sounded scary I had never done one, or know of anyone who had done one before. I had heard of an adult obstacle course and seen pictures online, and apparently it was a bit like that one. It was, I was told, like a fairly difficult obstacle course for adults. I wasn't at my most fit, but I was training on and off, a small bit, for walking the Dublin City Marathon with my friends on the Review Board.

People did this for fun, surely if people did something for fun it would be OK. Though people bungee jump, and sky dive, and B.A.S.E jump for fun. I strongly felt I was not quite the adrenaline junkie for those activities. It would be a really cool date to achieve together, it was the type of activity that encouraged team building, bonding and having a great story to tell.

Date 2 with Padraig, The Radiographer

Padraig picked me up from my apartment and we were both really jittery. It was more to do with the assault course than the date, I think. We both had sought information from friends of friends to find out more about it. We were telling each other stories we had heard from other people who claimed to have done it, and we really were bouncing off each other with excitement. By the time we got to the start line we were really pumped! We dived into the freezing cold water pit, and we were off! We really did work well navigating our way around and helping each other with a pull here, and a push there over the obstacles.

The race began to slow down, it was a welcome relief it must have been the mid-way point, we were both gasping for a drink, we had expelled so much energy! Oh goodness what my eyes saw next was heaven and hell. This was such a bad idea! What a sneaky cruel thing to do! While it might seem harmless, my body (which had been craving food and water at this point) could be rewarded with snacks and drink at the mid-way point, but it was immediately followed by a potato sack race. This race involved getting yourself into the potato sack which pulls up to your waist and then trying to either run or hop to the end point. Knowing what was coming next I only took one bite of the snack and sipped the water slowly. There was no way I was vomiting in front of this guy again!!!

The next moment we took to catch our breaths was when the course took us to the top of the mountain. The view was stunning. A momentary romantic gaze at each other, raised eyebrows at the view and confirmatory nods it was gorgeous, and we hit the trail again. The course finished in the best way possible- a water slide!! What a buzz! What a high! It truly was amazing! The experience of doing this adult assault course was SO good. I couldn't understand why anyone would want to talk anyone out of doing it! I would love to do the water belly slide at the end all over again! Everyone was all smiles! All around there were waves of happiness and shouts of "look how muddy you are!" and "take a look in the mirror!" followed by high fives.

The crowds drifted back to the end point where we could get our finishers t shirts, water and a shower. Now the showering part would be interesting. I hadn't known or even thought to ask what would happen at this point. By all accounts, it was a case of all in together to the shower area. That was the best way I could describe it. It was a cattle yard, with hose pipes in a grid in the air. I had never seen anything like it. In my mind the closest thing I could think of was an image brought to mind from reading books of Nazi Germany and Auschwitz. Jeez I really shouldn't have that thought now, not here, and certainly not on a second date with The Radiographer.

Uh oh, it actually had taken such a long time to complete the course, and the bottles of water at the end were so refreshing I easily downed two of them. Unfortunately, I couldn't see a toilet anywhere, and we were in a mob moving closer to our turn in the showers. I would just have to hold it. Think Sahara Desert, Sahara Desert, dry landscape. Oh God, I realised when I could see the people in the shower area, that with the urge to pee and trying to not think about it, I had totally forgotten about the undressing part of this.

I looked around to see what the other men and women were doing. Ok good, no one was completely naked, that's a good start. There was a high percentage stripped to their underwear- that wasn't really ideal, and then the rest just had their tops off, but shorts or leggings on the bottom half. I turned to Padraig who was following this latter trend, and praising the baby Jesus for this, I followed suit.

Oh God the urge to pee was returning and I didn't even have half the muck washed off. How could I be thinking of peeing in a large group shower that reminded me of all the books I ever read about Nazi Germany and Auschwitz, with a guy I fancied?!! I began to wonder were other people doing it? Is that why people were keeping their clothes on their lower half? I looked around, if anyone was going for it, I could not tell. The amount of mud and grass that was streaming off people, everyone could be peeing and no one would know. "Laura, Laura?"

"Sorry what" I had been so caught up in my dilemma that I wasn't engaged with Padraig. I really needed to pee, like I wouldn't be able to walk if I didn't pee, like right now.

"I was thinking after this, perhaps tomorrow we might need to go for a walk to make sure we don't end up too stiff, what do you think? Maybe a walk down by Poolbeg light house?"

"Padraig, that is a great idea, I will surely be stiff tomorrow, the walk sounds ideal!"

I really couldn't hold it any longer. Whatever about anyone else, I couldn't let him notice. I turned to face him completely straight on. I had to know where his eyes were for the next 30 seconds. Looking him directly in the eyes, I commented on the flecks of hazel in his, he loved that I was paying such attention to the detail of him. What I did next was against my better judgement and knocking back feminism God only knows how many years. Half swearing about how the mud and grass got everywhere, I started adjusting my bra, and honest to goodness there was mud there too. I knew where his focus was so I was free to pee as my hands and chest held his gaze. He looked me in the eye. His pupils were dilated. I knew he liked what he saw, and I got away unnoticed with my undercover mission. The girls will be in stitches when I leave the voice note about this date!

Date 3 with Padraig, The Radiographer

I had often seen the red lighthouse and wondered how to get there. This was going to be a great date. I loved exploring and finding new places! More than anything I loved the sound of the sea and I would be getting all of this on today's date! Padraig was so thoughtful! It really was a case of him seeing me at my worst, then my dirtiest, and still he was happy to meet me. I adored his cute smiley face. His twinkly eyes and he expelled such a 'can do' positive energy that left me hanging off every word he said.

"You have got to stop being so afraid of everything, Laura, or you will miss out."

That's what he told me during the assault course, when I climbed up a fence but was momentarily paralyzed by the fear of falling down the other side. He was so right about that, and many other things. I trusted his judgement on every climb, jump and I even let him catch me the far side of a 10-foot wall. I didn't feel like I needed to act in any sort of way in front of him. I was just myself. Completely open and at risk of heart break, but excited!

We were to meet at the Martello Tower on Sandymount Beach, and walk from there to Poolbeg light house and back. I was so excited to see Padraig again, and see how he was doing. I had acquired a few bruises and scratches, he said he did too, and was keen to compare with mine just so he could say his were worse, but that he was brave! Ha!

I worried frantically about the traffic, I really had no concept of what traffic was like into town on a Sunday via car. As a result, I gave myself way too much time. I arrived ridiculously early, so I parked up and looked around to find my baring. In the distance I could see a couple sharing a passionate kiss. I was walking in their direction and didn't want to be staring at them so I kept my chin down and sunglasses on, as I walked on by.

As I passed, there was something about the guy, I took a sneaky glance as the guy looked kind of familiar. Oh God, it was HIM, it was Padraig. He was with an exotic looking girl, she could definitely be from South America or Cuba. No wonder he kept going back there! I walked on as fast as I could, heart racing, trying not to run. A run would draw attention. I was almost twenty minutes early. I could walk 10 minutes in the wrong direction then 10 minutes back.

Once I was confident I was out of their sight. I stopped. I ducked around a corner and clasping a hand over my mouth I broke into….laughter. I was actually hysterical. I was so glad it was laughter and not tears. Ok this must be what people mean when they say they were in shock. It was so blustery and my coat was in the car. I was turning purple and my teeth were starting to chatter. I didn't feel cold though. I just felt numb. I could not let my emotions get the better of me.

I called on my logical brain to kick in. The part of my brain that would tell me to cop on. We had only gone on two dates. It meant nothing. He could have been on 10 dates, or be in a relationship with the girl he was kissing. I knew how attractive he was. If I found him attractive, a million other women could find him attractive too. I had no ownership over him. These were all true. These were all facts. I had to hold on to the facts or I was going to derail before the date even began. Telling myself to remember he was just part of the process to find a plus-one to a wedding, nothing more, nothing less. We were going on this walk today to make sure we didn't get too stiff from our exertion yesterday. My stupid emotions were feeling hurt for some reason though. God emotions were just getting in the way of everything.

The next two hours passed as an out of body experience. On cue I walked back to our arranged meeting point, stopping off to get my coat. There he was with his happy boyish smile. Same clean shaven face. No residue of his previous date on him. I checked for smudges of lipstick or gloss on his face. Either she hadn't been wearing any or he had easily wiped it off. He must be a pro at this stage. She was his 10 O Clock. I was his 11 O clock. He might have another at noon, or 1pm if he took an early lunch date.

In my mind I gave myself a pep talk: time to bring home the Oscar Laura, you just need to perform for an hour then you can have a melt-down in the car on the way home. Now is not the time for analysis. Walk, focus in on burning calories, stretch those long muscles, be polite, kill an hour and leave. Job done.

"Hey Padraig, how are you? I hope I haven't kept you waiting?"

"Nope, I just got here myself."

Liar. Did he even flinch saying it? I was going to scrutinize this man today.

"Ah great. It is so good to see you. Don't know about you, but my limbs definitely need a stretching! All aches from yesterday! Do you do this walk often? Ha, am I at risk of falling in?" I asked him trying to be as light in tone as possible.

"Ah I won't lie, I am fairly achy myself, can you smell the deep heat off me? I haven't been here since last summer. And," he paused taking my hands, "the only falling that is happening, is me falling for you," he beamed, or was it actually a smirk? A line he used on everybody?

Liar. Liar. Smooth f-ing liar.

I slipped my hands free. I pursed my lips attempting to do a bashful smile. I let him take my hand again and we began to walk. He was good, I had to give him that much. He stroked the back of my hand. Admittedly, it felt nice. Again I told myself to cop on and be practical, he likely did the same with the previous girl. I couldn't let his gentleness influence me. He was a liar and that was it. I switched on friend mode in my brain. You know what, it turns out I can be really funny, when I feel no relationship pressure. He was doubled over laughing at my stories. I paused. I hadn't made him laugh like that until now, until I began not to care about what he thought of me.

I wished someone could make *me* laugh like that. I laughed along at my own tales of near-misses and shameful disasters, and the Sambuca story. The night a group of friends at a house party decided to have flaming Sambucas in the dark. Which was fine until we all tried to do cheers across the table, and alcohol and flames went everywhere- and it seemed like 10 minutes before anyone could find the light switch. Thankfully no one was hurt! By the time I finished that story we reached our starting point once more. Out of breath from laughing we gradually came to a halt.

He took my hand and pulled me closer. I could feel the warmth of his body radiate towards me. My skin began to crawl. I had witnessed this move just over an hour ago. I tilted my head back and began to laugh. He giggled too he thought this was some joke, some game. I pushed him away.

"I have a sore throat; it wouldn't be fair to kiss you." Now I was lying. Is this what treatment by players did to me?

He pulled me in again and hugged me. He held me close. It would have felt so good only for I saw him kissing someone else earlier. He kissed my cheek, and I pulled back.

"I wasn't messing Laura, you are the one for me, I'm falling for you."

I looked him in the eye. There was nothing to suggest he was lying. Maybe he even believed himself. I certainly didn't. Apart from anything else, any logical person would know it was far too soon to be saying any such thing to a date. I was in shock with his brash and bold behaviour, did he actually think I would believe him? How dumb was I coming across for him to think he could fool me, trick me? He was smooth enough to have women to date round the clock. Why bother with me? I was so confused.

I laughed, touched my neck as if to say I really did have a sore throat, blew him a kiss, and walked back to my car without looking back. My mind was racing. What just happened?

Back in my house feeling a little bit stiff, and a little bit sore and a little bit sorry for myself, I picked up my phone to expel the dating experiences from Candidate 1. I left a voice message for the girls on the Review Board in the group chat and to Maria.

Then I began a new voice message to tell them about Candidate 2. Any confusion or doubt or annoyance from Candidate 1 evaporated talking about next Tuesday's date. Trying to keep things diverse, he certainly fit this effort. His name was Pierre, yes from France, from Strasbourg in fact. He was a baker with his own business. Not your usual bakery stuff, you know. He travelled around teaching artisan baking skills and techniques. I hoped he would be as delicious as he sounded.

Phase 1, Man 2, Candidate 2, Pierre, The Baker

In his profile picture he wore a stripy black and white t-shirt which almost made him look like one of those stand up boat rowers, you know the outfit the person who stands and rows with a single oar on a gondola in images of Venice, oh yeah, a gondolier? He looked very handsome, yet he wasn't a poser. I got the impression he didn't know how good looking he was. Or perhaps the French gene pool makes the majority of French men all handsome like that? He looked tall, lean, with dark hair, and dark eyes. His fine bone structure made him look oh so totally French- because as his profile states, he is. The only concern I had so far was not that he is French, but rather, that his work meant he travelled around a lot. I wondered how long he was going to be in Ireland for? If successfully selected, would he be present for the wedding? The best way to find out would be to ask, and the only way I could do that on this app, was to swipe right and see if it was a match! Happily, it was an instant match- that meant he had swiped right on me before I did on him. For some reason that was oddly satisfying.

Date 1 with Pierre, The Artisan Baker

His messages were simple, and succinct. He preferred to meet in person sooner than to be messaging a lot. That suited my agenda and we arranged to meet in the Temple Bar area. The bar he suggested looked quite dark, even though it was still daylight outside, hmm maybe it was a dodgy bar, with exception of Fleet Street I didn't know the area all that well. It was so dark, I had to stand right up against the window to see in. I thought I could see people inside. Once I saw my breath on the window and the imprint of my nose on it, I was really hoping I was the first to arrive, and that he couldn't see me peering in!

I tipped toed inside. The interior was beautiful, dimly lit in a romantic way. The lack of harsh lighting, particularly in contrast to the type you get in a lab, was actually a welcome relief, soothing, almost sleepy. *Beep, Beep*, I checked my phone, he was almost here, on his way. I went up to the bar to get myself a drink.

"Cash only love, the electricity is out."

Ah that explains it a lot better, the sun was going down and I sat in the romantic candle lit bar for my date to arrive. When he came in, it took me a few moments to recognize him. He didn't look like his photos, not better, not worse, he was just…hairier.

"Ellow, ellow, Laurrrah?!"

Wow he was really French, and his accent was strong. He was so handsome. There was no way he was going to fancy me.

"Oh hi, hi Pierre is it?" I said suddenly standing up to greet him and getting a bit nervous. He kissed both my cheeks (how European!) His voice was slightly shaking; he was nervous too. He explained the hairy face was to help him look older.

"Do you like, eh, the beard? Eh, people, they tell to me that I look so young when I am shaved the beard. I did not want you to think I am looking like a little boy when we meet. I am a man."

He made a face, a stern frown and flexed his arm muscles. He was smiling. His teeth were perfect, and his smile reached his eyes.

"You look good with or without the beard. Just be comfortable" I calmly replied.

"I like your answer. I like to be comfortable. In summer the beard can be too hot you know."

I felt myself smile, then laugh, he was funny, his English was not perfect but I completely understood him. He took the little laugh as a cue to continue.

"You know I am a hairy beast!" he smiled and I couldn't help but laugh again.

"In the summer I shave my chest too you know, not just the beard."

He rubbed his hands up and down his chest, "it is h-aero-dynam-eeek for when I am swimming." I was really laughing hard now, he was comical! The accent just intensified it!

We put our phones down on the table, and simultaneously realised, we both had pictures of ourselves with children as our screen saver. We both smiled and raised our eyebrows.

"Not mine. My one they are the nieces and the nephews, and you?" he asked.

"Ha same, they are my sister's children. This one" I said pointing to the first born, "is my god son".

"Me too, but the girl, this one, she is my god daughter."

Despite living in a different country, he was really close to his family. It was sweet.

I asked him what had brought him to Ireland- unsurprisingly, "I come for the work" was his response. "I am a master baker, you know, artisan, the bread, it is my specialty."

Well that was different. How on earth did he get into that I wondered. I doubted it was from years of stuffing his face with refined carbohydrates! He wasn't a big fella. Far from it in fact. Through broken English, and my half prompting him, and a painful amount of questioning because I just wanted to be sure I had the story correct, to be sure my ears were not deceiving me! I learned a fascinating tale of how this young Frenchman's profession unfolded.

"You know my training, my type of skill training was not at a university so much, you know the special artisan creativity training, to achieve, eh, the higher standard. Eh, you have heard of the Freemasons no? It is like this," he said.

When he mentioned the French Freemasons my mind swirled with a thousand historical conspiracy theories of a mythical cult. Did he really just say that? Was he part of some ancient brotherhood, with a reputation shrouded in mystery? I pressed for more information.

"So where did you go for your specialist training? Do you get a particular certificate of qualification from this? Or how does it work?" I quizzed.

From my understanding of what he said. The organisation he trained with has been around for centuries. He sometimes referred to his particular training as an "order" or the French word "compagnon". Historically he described it as a brotherhood and now more like a family. Much of the history and the inner workings of the system of what is today an international organization remains a secret. The "compagnon" have always valued the principles of freedom, equality, fraternity, humanity and tolerance.

"You know you say you walk the Dublin marathon for charity, I do also the charity. Through the compagnon but we do it in the secretive way. We do not put it on the social media. We do not bring attention to ourselves. How you say we act in a good way to avoid the lemon lights?"

Ha ha, aw his poor English actually made him even more adorable! "Oh I understand yes, you stay out of the limelight, and carry out charitable work anonymously."

"Yes, like this, that is how we do it!" he said.

"The students and trainers we live, eat and work together. We share the stories, sharing the experiences. All different skills in one big house, all in that region learning together." It sounded great craic altogether, almost like the way you learn at the Gaeltacht ha ha! From my understanding of what he said, all the trades in that area lived together, ate together, and a lady "mother" was always present to care of their well-being. How sexist indeed!

While it was true they followed the traditions of the medieval stonemasons and continue to use their symbols and rituals. He said it was not a scary thing, like the stories he had heard as a child. Nowadays, their symbols were more like a trademark, or a way of letting the world know the high level of skill and training that went into a piece of work. The central symbols are the square and the compass, which form the typical masonic logo. The compass is a circle which refers to the fraternity, like the brotherhood and family life, while the square represents the proper conduct of each member.

It was exhausting to get the story out of him, my brain was half drained and half totally fascinated. There was quite the air of mystery and fame surrounding this order. This is largely fueled by traditions of old which include passwords and secret handshakes that are still in use today. Pierre explained that these were established to preserve professional secrecy and prevent betrayal.

He told me to think of it as a professional training college for mostly trades and craft skills. It was an organization of craftspeople and artisans dating from the middles ages. Over the centuries a number of trades have become outdated and no longer in use, while others have been born. I was so intrigued I searched for it online, then and there. It was real and in 2010 the compagnonship was inscribed UNESCO, on the list of Intangible Cultural Heritage of Humanity.

Pierre was at the Grand Master level or so he claimed. He really did not look his age, and to me, this seemed like something out of a book! He was so interesting! If his story wasn't so unusual, I doubt I would have repeatedly asked him to go over parts of it. I felt fatigued though from patching together his English to understand him. He must have felt a bit frustrated too. The people he trained with were for him like a family, he spoke so positively about the paths they were taking. Historically this was magnificently intriguing. Although it could just seem a little bit like the FÁS schemes of old.

All-in-all it was very pleasant and interesting, if a little tiring date. I indicated I had to leave to meet my friend for an evening walk to get some practice in for the Dublin City Marathon. I received a kiss on the right and left cheek, and trusting my basic French, I replied with "a tout a l'heure Pierre, the hairy Bear- that is definitely my pet name for you!"

Date 2 with Pierre, The Artisan Baker

I was only in the door at home when my phone started buzzing.
Beep, Beep A text from Pierre:

I really enjoyed our date. Your smile is so big and so nice it makes me smile. Do you want to play some small golf game with me on Monday after work?

This was followed by a picture of flowers and a heart.

He was such a cutie, my own little care bear! Ha! My Pierre bear! That nick name for him was definitely going to stick! Although, I might have to explain it to him, I don't think he got it!

Laura: **That sounds like fun! Does 7pm suit you to meet there?**

Pierre: **Voila c'est parfait! Yes, that is great. See you soon my dear.**

Aww "my dear" such a cutie pie.

Monday afternoon Pierre Bear text:

I am being so excited to see you today. I hope I will win the game too. I will show you I am a man. I am good at the sport. I am strong and have lots of muscles. Ha ha!

Well now, there is competition, and then there is *competition*. This guy was all about show casing his manliness. Unfortunately, he was doing it in a rather childish way. I really did hope he was behaving like that just to be funny. Was it just me, or were there some early signs he was trying *too* hard to seem, as he put it himself "like a man" and not so boyish. Or maybe he meant it in a prehistoric Neanderthal man kind of a way. I mean it's cute, and it's sweet, and funny, but ultimately I don't know if I would really consider it 'manly'. I understand men have a bit of a need to feel manly, but, surely there has been some evolution in this space? Surely men recognize that women do not apply the same value to physical strength as they did thousands of years ago. Intelligence, integrity, ingenuity, and incredibly funny are the traits I am after!

Laura: **Hi Pierre, that's great, I'm looking forward to it too!**

Pierre: **I will send you some pictures of my muscles. I will send you some pictures of my cat also. He is such a nice cat. He is so soft. He sometimes sleeps on my bed. The cat, he takes over the bed sometimes. Sometimes it is his bed, he lets me know it is his space.**

Aw God, cats! They look real cute in pictures, but I am super allergic to them!! I better not burst his little bubble.
Beep, Beep
Oh he was serious; he is literally just sending me pictures of himself flexing his muscles. Yes, he looks like he has well defined muscles, but he looks really stupid doing this. This is hilarious!!

Beep, Beep

Oh a video. What pray tell is in the video I wonder. Oh he is speaking I better turn the volume up!
"A one, and a two, and a three, and a four, and a I can weight-lift the cat with one hand too, you know. Here we go, a one, and a two, and a three, and a four!"
With every number he raised the cat high above his head, first with both hands then with only one hand! The cat looked rather amused too. Ha oh ok, he was funny, in a 'laugh at him' kind of a way. So long as he does not request pictures of my muscles in return we are all good!

Laura: **That is a beautiful cat you have there, what is he or she called?**

Pierre:

His name is The Master. He is not really my cat. I call him The Master because he is in charge. He belongs to my neighbour who is my landlord. He comes in for me to rub his back and let him sleep in my bed. In the morning I find it hard to get up. He sleeps on me. If I wake him his nails, they dig into me if he is on my body. Or else he sleeps beside my legs and I have to move extremely carefully not to frighten him in the morning in case he scratches me, you know on my legs, or in between the legs!

When I arrived at the mini golf, Pierre was already there. He looked so happy and excited. We got our clubs and ball and I felt a spring in my step. Pierre's bouncing energy was contagious, truly it was palpable! Though honestly it seemed like at any moment he was about to start jumping about like a little puppy.

He was competitive alright. I was not too slick at mini golf, but I got a fluky hole in one, at a time when Pierre took three shots. He was genuinely disgruntled. Muttering away to himself in French, I really don't know what he said, but his face was grumpy in any language.

Halfway around the course we checked the totals of our scores. He was good at counting in English. I told him this, and he counted the scores up again- maybe showing off his English, maybe showing of his score? He was happier when he discovered he was in the lead by seven. Part of me wondered, what would his reaction be like if I was better than him at this little game?

We reached the final hole, and I must say it was an enjoyably time, however, the conversation did not veer from the game, and counting. It was easier that way. The final hole steals the ball back to the venue; we both missed the impossible last shot! Overall he was delighted with himself for winning, by nine points in the end. We left back our clubs and it was time to go. Although, Pierre was a little tetchy, and absolutely adamant that last hole was a trick shot, designed such that ball could not possibly go in the hole!

"Again with you I had a nice time Laurrahh" Pierre had his arms out, I guessed it was for a hug so I said "yes me too, it was lovely date."

I leaned over with my arms out too, and he went in for the kiss! Not the two cheeks kind! This took me by surprise so I ducked and embraced him in a quite a tight hug!

Ha! "Ah you prefer the uhhggg" he said.

"Oh a hug yes, a nice hug, and see you soon," I replied.

I felt so awkward. He was standing there, smiling and waving me off. Oh of course that was sweet, I guess. I just *really* was not prepared for there to be a kiss at that moment!

I turned around and waved back smiling too, he was such a nice guy.

"See you soon Pierre Bear!"

Date 3 with Pierre, The Artisan Baker

Ok so, I felt less exhausted after the second date. Maybe the trick with this guy was to go on dates with basic levels of language required. This of course meant the classic cinema date had to be next on the list! (Although you know, I really would have loved to go to a stand-up comedy night- the giggles are great! The risk was, however, that Pierre would be sitting there, not quite understanding and that would not be fair either!) I had agreed that I would go to the cinema to see whatever movie he had wanted. This was his prize for winning the mini golf game. Given the timing and how much I had blabbered on about one of my favourite actresses, I thought it was the new rom-com that was just out. I was **SO** looking forward to seeing it! He phoned to check I would get to leave the lab on time.

"Hey you, are you excited about the movie?"

"Yes, yes I am, are you going to tell me which one it is?"

"Bah it is only the greatest movie of all time- the very best story!"

Ok, that does not really sound like the new rom-com, I was already starting to feel a little deflated. I guess my excitment was more for the movie, and not him! Oops!

"Eh so what's this amazing story called?"

"Bah why it is the *Really Old Classic Animal Cartoon* of course! The cinema it is showing it you know, there is a special screening of it today. I am so happy. This is my favourite movie ever since I was a little boy."

Oh cool, that was interesting, I wonder why this film had such a profound effect on this guy? "So how did this movie make it to the high ranking position of your all-time favourite?"

"Ah it is an h-easy choice. The story is good, and the songs are good, it is a really, really, good movie."

"Oh ok cool see you later!" With that, I hung up.

Well, 'good' was a bit bland in terms of description, wasn't it? I hadn't really imagined busting my ass to get finished early in the lab to go see a cartoon. Don't get me wrong there are a lot of cartoon movies I thoroughly enjoy. I love the *Really Old Classic Animal Cartoon* story, but, for a date with this guy now at this moment, I didn't think it was going to do his chances of being wedding date material any good. Not to mention any chance of a fourth date. I don't particularly like going to the cinema to see stories that I have already seen. Oh no, I could feel my mood shift; I was turning into a such grump about this!

I began to feel guilty. It is more important that I spend quality time with this guy, it's about him, not the movie. Although, a cinema date is not really about either partner, it's about the film, right? You don't actually spend any sort of "quality time" together, or getting to know each other. To make it worth my while, I decided we would have to spend some time together after the movie. Some actual quality time. I phoned him back.

"Hi Pierre, do you fancy going for a stroll after the movie, down by the pier?"

"What is this, a stroll?" Oh for the love of God, my eyes rolled.

"It just means a slow easy walk. It won't be far, just down along the pier and back."

"Oh yes, a nice romantic walk, yes, yes."

"Great, ok, see you later!"

I was on my way for the clincher final date, on the N11 on my way to Dun Laoghaire.

*BEEP! BEEP! BEEP! * Ah no, I forgot to put fuel in the car this morning, I was too busy with trying to get in on time, to get my experiment started early, so I could leave at reasonable-o-clock! I was exhausted from all this dating; it was eating into too much of my time. Even though the dates were not over lapping, I was still keeping up my messaging of the other potential candidates, but as more time passed, this was becoming increasingly difficult and tiresome and mentally draining. Or maybe I just didn't want to meet this guy anymore.

"When you are sleep deprived, accidents can happen," I heard my father's voice ringing in my ears. I had the windows down, and the music blaring. I would get coffee now as I pulled in off the N11 south bound to fuel up the car.

Now to fuel myself up, I smiled as I savored the aroma of coffee from the machine as the Americano filled.

"Just this, and the diesel at pump number 7 please."

"Forty-euro petrol?"

"No, diesel, that one," I pointed to my car, "number 7."

"That pump has just been used for forty-euro petrol."

"Are you serious?" I couldn't actually remember which pump I lifted, black or green, oh no!

Lord only knows what expressions my face was pulling, I panicked.

"Oh my goodness, my car is not a petrol engine. What do I do? I am pretty sure I can't drive it?"

The shop clerk directed me to the accompanying garage, apparently they had the number outside in case of emergencies. I paid him for my useless, petrol. I went out and let the car roll backwards into a parking space. Thankfully the pumps were on a slant!

I rushed over to the garage. It was closed. It was evening after all. I rang the number anyway and I got it sorted out. The 'man in the van' would come and drain, and wash out the fuel tank. The trouble was he lived an hour away.

There was nothing I could do. I phoned Pierre to say I would be late, and asked if that was ok, or if he wanted to reschedule. He was so sweet, as always. This made me feel so guilty for all the negative thoughts I had about him. He was a nice a guy. He said it was fine and not to worry. There was a carnival in Dun Laoghaire and he was going to spend the time there until I arrived.

As I sat in the car waiting for the 'man in the van', I wondered if I subconsciously messed up my fuel so I wouldn't have to go to the cinema. In all my years of driving, I have never made that mistake before in my life! Maybe it was just tiredness.

Funnily enough there was a friendly soccer match between Ireland and France that day. He was wearing his French jersey and sent me a picture of it. In turn I too thought it would be a talking point if I wore my Ireland jersey. I also loved that our jersey was green- green was so my colour. The jersey was tight, it clung to my body perfectly. I had curled my hair too, just to feminise the ensemble. My mother always cringed when I curled my hair. It reminded her of the time many years ago, in the school play, when I played the part of a French gizelle called "Jou-Jou", presumably from the French verb "jouer" meaning 'to play', ha! ha!

*Beep, Beep! * A text! Oh, it was just Pierre bear again. I was hoping it was the petrol man.

Do you like coconut?

What a random text. Did I like coconut? Yes, coconut oil for cooking, coconut chips covered in chocolate, yes, coconut milk not so much.

I left him a voice note reply.

"Yes, why are you planning on wearing a coconut costume instead of a jersey when France lose?"

"Ha I am laughing so much at this idea Laura! Imagine that! A coconut costume," was his response.

Ok well I didn't think it was that funny, but whatever floats your boat!

"I have a surprise for you but it is not a coconut costume," he continued with another voice message.

Oh maybe it was a coconut body spray or perfume? That would be so nice.

Eventually the 'man with a van' came and sorted out my car for €200, I will certainly not mess that up again!

When I got to Dun Laoghaire I spotted Pierre's car. He had a cartoon character on his towel from his swimming hung over the passenger seat to dry.

I saw him at the carnival. His impeccable physique was evident and I was grateful for his love of swimming to enhance his shoulders to be broader than mine. Again my cavewoman notions kicked in, I really wanted to be finer, and more feminine than the man I was dating. This was stupid, and ruled out many wonderful men. This was not entirely my fault, the shorties are not exactly lining up outside my door seeking dates!

He spied me and waved. What the heck was that monstrosity he had with him!

"Ello, Laurrahh! Look what I-ee ave won for you! It is your very own elephant!"

"Whoa oh my goodness, that is huge!"

"It is, eh, how you say, life size?!"

"Yes, indeed it is life size!"

"Yes I play the basketball game and I won. I won for you. I am the best at the sport."

Oh, here we go again. The same phrases, the same tone. Yes, it's fun, and sweet but for some reason it was getting on my nerves. Fair enough, he loved sport. Anything that required strength and speed got his attention. We were polar opposites in that regard.

We went on the cup-and-saucers carnival ride, that was fun. The conversation was light. I felt like I was on a day out with my niece and nephew. Purposefully, nothing was serious. He did not ask about my earlier incident, of accidently putting petrol into my diesel car. Perhaps that was intentional on his behalf, to avoid anything difficult or negative. Maybe that was a good thing. Or maybe his attention was totally absorbed by the games and the rides at the fair ground.

I thought about what I was going to tell the girls on the Review Board about this guy. He was a sweet guy, he really was, but isn't communication key for any relationship, platonic or romantic? Communication is infinitely more important when it comes to cross-cultural relationships, especially where each person involved does not have the same first language. I couldn't really complain though, my French was terrible. In my defense, on the other hand, I wasn't living and working in a French speaking country, so maybe the onus really was on him to improve on his English.

As we whirled around being spun faster and faster by the man manning the ride, I thought back to my aim. The goal was to find a person to bring to my cousin's wedding. In my mind I suspected if I asked him he would say yes. I had told him I had many weddings to attend in the near future, and we had a chat about weddings in general. He was out-going. He loved meeting new people. He didn't have the Irish lad notion that going to a wedding meant we were "a thing". He was un-phased by attending a wedding. He was just happy for the happy couple. He knew exactly who he was and what he wanted. He was self-assured but not in a cocky way- again something that ranked him higher than most Irish men I had met. He knew where he was going in life. He had a path, a plan, and all of this was truly wonderful.

The niggling in my gut was that I knew I had the patience of a saint for all of 5 minutes when it came to people like him, who for some reason, just could not hold my attention with their repetition. Though he was such a kind man, and to an extent I could see how he could bring out the best in those around him. It is true, when you show kindness and goodness to people, it is returned. Unfortunately, I could not say the same about my family.

The girls would all love him of course; his looks alone would draw attention. Seriously, I have never dated anyone so aesthetically pleasing. However, it was really quite difficult to have a good conversation with him without putting in a huge amount of effort. No-one at the wedding would be willing to do that. People were away from their charges and duties and looking forward to fun at the wedding, myself included. Was his level of easy conversation always going to be this dim? He has been living in English speaking countries for over four years now. Were all the positives he had displayed enough to outweigh having to babysit and translate for him at the wedding? And every event should we keep dating if his English does not improve quite substantially? I believed in the ranking table, and trusted it would answer these questions for me. I picked up my phone and left a voicemail for the girls on this events of this date!

Phase 1, Man 3, Candidate 3, Laughlann, The Entrepreneur

I switched to a different dating app, variety is the spice of life, right? Oh this app was going to be interesting, there was a bit more detail in the amount of information you provide, and also, in the information you receive on the gentlemen.

The profiles on the previous app offered no information! To be fair, that's an exaggeration, more like it was really, really limited, apart from pictures and a name. The age of the person you were viewing was sometimes given, and sometimes hidden, but, you knew the age was within the range you set your search criteria to.

The very best of profiles on the previous app contained an age and a name, one or two random sentences, (on occasion the odd "Dad joke") and on the rare occasion a string of emojis the gentleman would issue about himself, or his life for you to decipher.

This app, offered all that and more. Included were the physical features such as hair and eye colour; height, not exactly your weight but how your physique could be described; how frequently you consumed alcohol; your profession; the longest relationship you have had; if you have or want to have children; if you drive or not; and the list goes on! The unspoken rule of thumb, is that the more information you provide, the more eager you are for the dating app to assist you in whatever the desired outcome is. This might translate to a person seeming genuinely interested in meeting someone with whom they could have a relationship with. This might translate as desperation. This might translate as an obvious attempt at hooking up. No matter what the intention is or may seem, you always have to keep your wits about you!

One thing that struck me as a little bit odd, was indicating how much you earn. Height, size and all of the other physical attributes, people can tell roughly at a glance, it is not exactly hidden. Earnings however, could attract the wrong type of attention. A bit like sending pictures of yourself nude, my thoughts are that it should remain private and completely unspoken until the point someone (usually the guy) requests it, and then at that point you could decide if it is something you are willing to share, or not. It can also help you to decide if you are happy to even consider dating someone who would even ask for such things. Would this really make for good future husband material? Would it matter if he was just arm candy for a plus-one to a wedding? What else would this say about his character?

Indicating earnings could prove misleading. The general reaction to this would be "Helloooooo Sugar Daddy! ☺" Though that works both ways. Many of us females are better skilled, better qualified, earn more, and look after ourselves better than a lot of men. Women live longer than men, while this is in part due to our biology, it is also due to our behavioural differences. So for those who want their other half to be with them until their dying day, my advice would be to look for a guy a few years younger!

Back to the issue at hand- earnings. To be fair I don't want some poor guy chatting me up for the purpose of obtaining a free meal or cushy lifestyle on the back of my hard graft. I want him chatting me up because he likes me- for me, and not my bank balance! Although by the same token, I don't want to be cat-fished by some guy pretending to be someone he is not. Maybe all should be fair and transparent in love? Maybe earnings are an important factor in dating? Maybe it's about finding he who earns as much as you? Though when financials are involved, it seems a bit more like a contract, no? The perks and pitfalls of dating apps are that you can enter as much, or as little, accurate or false information as your heart or loins desire.

In general, I liked how much detail about a person this app was providing, but to play my part correctly, it just felt like too much effort. It reminded me of work. There was also a huge surge in the amount of messages I received in the first few minutes of joining this app. I hadn't been prepared for that! The other apps require a match first. How on earth were you to sift through all those, where on earth was the filter settings? I should probably have done that first. For me, at least initially, this app was looking like a disaster! I decided to leave the review board a voice note, and compare all this swiping to a work task.

"Hi Ladies! You know when designing surveys, you have to be mindful of survey fatigue. You don't want the person carrying out the survey to feel burdened by the time it takes to carry out the survey. If it was a really long survey, people might just give up and not finish it; or, their answers might not be too accurate, they might just tick any box to get to the end.

Well, the same can be applied to these dating apps! On this occasion I definitely feel **SWIPERS fatigue**! My standards are going to drop if I don't find a suitable profile soon! This would not be good practice. I must maintain the equivalent of GLP (Good Laboratory Practice) or GCP (Good Clinical Practice), ha maybe GDP for Good Dating Practice! Ten more minutes and I am quitting for the day. Something will have to go into the methods development section on this point! Puddles of cuddles! Ciao"

After what seemed like an endless wave of men from the far West and far South of the country (resulting in a few minutes of swiping left due to distance), my finger hovered over a very pleasant face, the type of face you would say hello to walking down the street. This man's next photo was entirely different. Perhaps even more handsome. I flicked through his other photos, they were all him. Variations on a theme. Who knew over how many years these photos were taken. It didn't matter. He looked good in them all.

I knew the difference makeup could have on me. Ten minutes in front of a mirror with the correct cosmetics and I could instantly go from a two to a ten! A beard however, now that was the male equivalent. As evidenced by these pictures of this man, a beard could be transformative. A beard waves adios to the sweet boyish looks, and bon journo to the essence of rugged manliness.

Beards are not always entirely a positive thing though. When beards grow to big, long and bushy, as often they do, the beard can be the breeding ground for bugs, which eat the crumbs of food that can get lodged there! When this happens the beard screams 'lazy sod'! That extensive beard style, even when neat and tidy trimmed, in combination with the handle bar mustache was also a no-no. This hipster style is where I had to draw the line. I couldn't be dealing with the type at all, at all. The only exception to this rule, in my eyes, was during the month of November, or *"Movember"* when many men grow mustaches in all shapes and sizes for research and charity, often accompanied by beards. Unless the mustache is shaved early in December, any physical appeal to the man is gone!

This guy, plus or minus his beard, was from West Meath, not quite the far West or the far South, but not close either. The nuances in his pictures, that made him his own unique character before I had even met him, had an overriding effect on the distance issue. Therefore, I easily swiped right anyway, just to see what would happen. Dropping my phone on the sofa, I put on a windcheater (sweat-jacket, sure who needs a gym?!) and went for a walk.

I won't lie, I did think about him quite a bit on that walk. He was not working the camera, but just had a face that lured one in. I couldn't wait to get back to see if he had swiped right and matched with me.

This was the silly thought process that was developing in my brain. My neural circuitry was becoming accustomed to it. I would swipe right thus indicating I wanted to match with the man in question, but then, I found myself pondering the outcome if there was not an instant match. I really blame this scientific method for it. Ordinarily, I could easily not look at a dating app for weeks, or months on end. This method, however, had instilled a habit in me to check it daily. It was not quite an addiction, but it was certainly filling any potential need for instant gratification I might have had. I now had the notion that everyone should be on their dating app at all times.

His profile had a tag line of "My age and on a dating app – hmmm, I never thought I'd see the day!" Upon returning from my walk he had not matched with me, so I decided I would go on ahead and message him anyway. Gosh, would he smell how curious and needy I was to know more about him? I hoped not. Either way I had nothing to lose. Now what could I say to draw him in to conversation, there were some obvious things about his hobbies proven by photos (in a fishing boat, and sky diving) and his work (suit and tie at some presentation), but that is not my style, that's too easy and likely a very common initial topic of conversation.

I zoomed in on one of his photos, and if I was not mistaken there were tiny floral prints on it, they were so tiny I might be imagining blurred dots as flowers, but if I was right, things might go my way. Attention to detail is paramount for experiments to work appropriately after all!

Laura:

Hi Laughlann, you must have a certain confidence to pull off wearing that floral shirt, I like a man in touch with his feminine side ☺

Laughlann:

Laura, I noticed you on this app before, and I said to myself, should I ever match that girl, I will just have to convince her to spend time with me.

Laura:

Well there it is, that confidence again! So tell me more about you, you are handsome and a charmer, what else?

Laughlann:

Well now I am flattered, that someone like you, would compliment someone like me, you big flirt, I love that you are not just all about looks!

Laura:

The pen is mightier than the sword you know. Maybe I just want to be friends ☺

Laughlann:

Friends? Not an option when you have eyes as seductive as you do. I will have to work harder to convince you otherwise.

Laura:

Now, who is the flirt?!

Laughlann:

I don't need to be too flirty with you, I will win you over with a picnic of sushi in the Phoenix Park!

Now that was like something out of a fairytale. I would never have put sushi and the Phoenix Park in the same sentence, never mind as a date!

Laura:

Ha, a man from the Midlands on a sushi diet, now that's one for the books!

Laughlann:

I lived for four years in Goa, India, no doubt my practicing yoga will turn your head too?

Personally, I have not evolved into a yogi, I know of a few stretches and poses, but that's it. A great gal pal, who lives in London a few years now, is obsessed! Goes to at least 5 different yoga classes per week and practices at home too. Swears by it, and according to her, the guys who do yoga are SUPER FIT- like total dream boats, physically anyway. To the extent you don't notice their faces, just their awesome bodies. I laughed to myself remembering her audacious comment. I pushed that conversation aside in my head and replied to Laughlann.

Laura:

Interesting, you have succeeded in capturing my intrigue, for that I will grant you one reasonable wish.

Laughlann:

Meet me on Saturday in the Phoenix park at 3pm?

Laura:

You my dear, have got yourself a date- provided you can find me in the Phoenix Park!

Laughlann:

I will just go in the direction all the men are looking? ☺

Laura:

The summer must be hard for you? Ice cream wouldn't melt in your mouth would it, Laughlann?

Laughlann:

Laura, you will have to experience my mouth for yourself to answer that ☺

Laura:

Cheeky! Good night!

I put my phone away, it was late on a Thursday night, and my experiments were starting early in the morning. Was I mad in the head?! Was he really going to show up? Was he really going to come all the way from West Meath, for a date? A date in the Phoenix Park. Maybe HE was crazy. He probably wouldn't show up.

On date day, I began feeling uneasy when I hadn't heard from him since early the day before. His message had been positive suggesting he was looking forward to today but then he completely went off radar. However today was Saturday and it was now 1pm, and there had been no confirmation of meeting up. Surely a confirmation text was expected for a date that involved a journey. Surely a man of 32 would know that a simple confirmatory text was par for the course? Or should I take the hint, was it all just a big build up, to nothing?

Under no circumstances was I going to text him to confirm; that was not my style, I firmly believed that was his job. Unfortunately, this meant I didn't know whether to start getting ready, or not. Granted my journey was less, but still, you never knew how long it would take to cross the city on the M50. Sure there could be an accident or anything causing a huge back log of delays. I wouldn't risk driving through town. It was too hot, and the air would be gross and sticky.

It had to be at least 28 degrees outside, the car would be roasting hot. I would definitely need the speed of the M50 traffic to be fast. That way I could let down the window for air. It would be the only way to stop my makeup melting off my face! It would also keep my hair light and fluffy. At all costs, the hair had to be prevented from falling slick against my scalp, and face, and from going dry and frizzy at the ends.

Finally, I decided I would just get ready. The worst-case scenario was that I would have my makeup done, and body all a glow for a night with the girls later instead. *BBBZZZ, bbbzzz, bbbzzzz* was that a blue fly, or a wasp? *Bzzzzz, bzzzz, bzzzz* Oh no it was coming at me! I ducked under the ginormous wasp in flight, or was it two? Were they on top of each other? Do wasps have sex? *Bzzzz, Bzzzz* Frig no! No!
Oh please do NOT let them go into the kitchen, my makeup bag is in there! No! *BBBZZZ* Ah!

I ran out of the kitchen allowing the door to slam shut behind me, with the makeup bag and magnifying mirror left on the table.

Ok, ok, was the kitchen window open I wondered? Maybe they would fly out? My phone was in the kitchen too. Tough luck Laura, I said to myself. I began to try to calm down with a few deep breaths. Feeling a little more in control of the situation I grew brave and began creaking the door open just a little. *BBZzzzzzz! Bzzzzz!* Oh my goodness the wasps were crashing into the door!
I closed it tight again. Ok, I told myself, I'll give it a minute and try again.
BBBzzz, bbbzzz followed by *bump, bump* against the door. They were actively keeping me out! The little feckers!
Beep, Beep! That was my phone! I had a message! I wonder if it was Laughlann? It probably wasn't from Laughlann. It was probably from my mother. Was I going to risk getting stung just to check my phone? No. Risk heart break over a boy? Sure, that is something I seem to be open to, but getting stung by wasp? That would just be stupid.

The best thing to do was to shower, just shower, get all fresh as a daisy and then try the kitchen again. With any luck my housemate would be back by then too, to help. Good fortune was on my side. While I was in the shower, Lisa arrived home and saw my sticky note on the kitchen door informing her of the frisky wasps inside. Calmly Lisa opened the window and shooed them out! Not a bother to her! She is definitely the embodiment of a woman 'at one' with nature. To my pure delight, the message on my phone had been from Laughlann, he was getting himself cleaned up, and would soon be on his way! I thanked Lisa most graciously and promised her an ice-cream upon my return, as a thank you!

Date 1 with Laughlann, The Entrepreneur

Crossing the city was no mean feat. The quickest way was to drive from Sandyford over the M50 to the Phoenix Park. I wondered what my Dad would think of how I was using the M50 tag he got me for the car. Both the tag and my Dad were brilliant - automatically paying the toll. I imagined he got it for me because he felt responsible for all the times I had to pay going up and down home to visit. What he definitely didn't feel responsible for was all the times I forgot to pay the toll by 8pm the next day, and wound up with more fines than I could remember! This time my northwards trip wasn't homeward bound. This trip was to the Phoenix Park!☺

I got there 15 minutes early. I text him to inform him of the gate I had entered, that would give him a clue to my location. That was enough of a clue for him. There were crowds of people lying out on the grass, some eating ice cream, some drinking chilled cans or mixing soft drinks with whatever was in their sneaky naggin's. I was wearing my trusty polka dot pants, and a lacey white crop top. Curvy legs and bottom, but abs of steel. This was my go-to look, first time, every time. Though I had noticed a paunch on occasion recently. Why is it when you live abroad you are your best self? You are fit and healthy, lean, toned and fitting into your clothes perfectly; and then upon returning home the carbs just take you hostage!!

The grass was calling me. So I decided to risk it, one butt cheek was minus polka dots anyway, and the chances of having a green grass transfer was very low given how dry the ground was.

Beep, Beep It was Laughlann:

On my way, will be there in 30 min

Thirty f-ing minutes! This guy was taking the biscuit! I would need to apply more sun protection. Gone would be the instant tan replaced by streaky orange lines. Streaky orange lines on a super sexy, lacey, white top! No, that was not allowed to happen. I didn't really care what my date thought of how I would look with streaky lines. However, I **absolutely** did not have the domestic goddess skills to get fake tan stains suitably off, a lacey white top!

Where could I take shelter? The car was exposed to the sun, so sitting in it, I would melt. Maybe if there was an umbrella in the car I could use it as a parasol…. but no such luck I had taken it out weeks ago! The only other option was to find a tree no else had already had the sense to take shelter under. So with sunglasses on to protect my eyes, I was on the lookout for a free tree.

Just as my warm body was threatening to break into a sweat, I found one! Thank goodness! This avoided the return journey to the car for additional deodorant and perfume, which I was keen to avoid because:

A) My tree could be stolen,

B) There was actually a good chance if exposed to this heat, the deodorant can would explode, and finally

C) I would be too sweaty by the time I got back to the car, the damage would already be done!

Finding an appropriate tree had killed some of the time. *Beep, Beep*, oh it was from Laughlann. It was a voice message.

"OK I am entering the Phoenix Park. We are going to the zoo. I will find you near there because your phone's GPS is on, and sounding like a stalker….. girl I am going to track you down."

I felt my temperature rise again! We were going to the zoo!!! Oh I was in love with him already! No risky sushi spills on my white top, and I get to see all the animals. I shrieked with excitement. It's ok, only the tree could hear me!

I had been crazy to wait that long for him to arrive, but it was a fab day, I was not going to let anything spoil it! The air started to lift, it felt spectacularly fresh with a slight breeze.

I spotted his vehicle while I was listening to his voice message on the phone. In a video clip he had sent to me (while he was driving days earlier- shhh don't tell the police) I had noticed the symbol on the steering wheel. I don't know if my sharp eye is a curse or a talent. Knowing the brand of the car, combined with the WH (indicating West Meath) on the car registration plates meant it was a no brainer. The man inside that vehicle was here for me. He stepped outside and turned around. I ducked behind the tree. Then phoning him I said "OK stalker boy, I can see you have exited your vehicle, oh that made you smile. You might have GPS on me, but I have my eyes on you."

He laughed, I could tell he was impressed or at the very least amused. I stepped out from the tree and walked towards him. He smiled and took his sunglasses off to show me his handsome face. (Later, Lisa said this is a clear sign he was trying to get a better look at me. If there was a ranking table for friends, Lisa would definitely be top place!)

So what were my first impressions of this self-proclaimed entrepreneur?

He was tall, definitely more than 6 feet, I believed his profile on this point, which indicated 6ft 3inches (190cm). He wore full length tan trousers, with a brown leather belt and tan boat shoes. His white shirt was tucked in. The detail on his shirt was exquisite. Tiny burnt amber, and gold floral prints decorated his torso beautifully. This shirt should have looked feminine, but on him, with his sleeves rolled up to show muscular working man's arms, it was the polar opposite. This man knew the colour scheme that worked for him, and he was on point! His auburn hair was slightly wavy, the intense ginger colouring more apparent in his beard. He lifted his sunglasses as he made his approach to reveal hazel brown eyes.

Jeez, I wondered when would I ever have an outfit that also coordinated with my eyes? My outfit seemed a little inferior now.

He was very handsome. Unfortunately, I was too sticky with the tan and the heat to approach him. So when he leaned in for a hug hello, I promptly stuck out my hand for a good old fashioned hand shake instead. Yes, 'weirdo Laura mode' was kicking in. This was a sure sign I fancied him!

I looked at my watch, we were going to run very short of time at the zoo, because he was so late I might add! So we walked quite quickly to start. We noted and nodded at the various animals we saw, and sections of the zoo we could tick off as having viewed at record pace. It actually became quite fun, and turned into a game of sorts. How many animals and sections of the zoo can we see before it closes? Bells began to ring indicating it was time to leave.

Everyone was going in the opposite direction to us. Deeper and deeper into the zoo we ventured. We ducked and dived out of view of the zoo staff, or pretended we just needed to put something in a nearby bin. This tactic bought us a good extra 10 minutes running around the zoo. Eventually our luck ran out, we couldn't stop laughing, the zoo keeper however looked less than impressed. We were definitely the last to leave.

Back outside the zoo, with an air of mischief about us Laughlann's stomach made some gurgling noises.

"Laura will we get food?" he asked very directly.

Now, the sensible thing would have been to pop in somewhere close and handy. However, I was too sticky from running round the zoo, mixed with the heat of the day and instant tan, I was actually on the verge of disgusting. I had waited on him, and I was going nowhere without a change of clothes. If he wanted more of my company it was going to have to be on my terms.

"Honestly Laughlann, I need to change my top I am far too hot. How about cooling down with some sea air and maybe sea food?" I responded.

"Sea food?" Laughann winked, "Sounds perfect."

I laughed "And, I can change my top with a quick detour on the way."

"Ideal," he said "when we stop I can make a quick work call. Sure we are all about the compromise. Look at us, already working as a team. We have this dating thing mastered!" Laughlann beamed proudly.

We hopped in our cars and hit the road.

A change out of sweaty clothes, and a phone call that went on FOREVER later, we were on our way to some fresh Dun Laoghaire sea air! He drove, we agreed two cars just wouldn't be sensible; it would be bad for the environment too. This thought was quickly followed by another, that sitting next to him in the car, would get us a little closer, and that would not be a bad thing! ;-)

We went straight for food and just one beer. While we were deciding what to order he declared that after food, the responsible thing to do would be to go for a walk and get ice-cream. This would allow even more time for the alcohol to be out of our systems before driving again. I couldn't have agreed more! Waiting on the food, I looked at him properly. I took him in.

This man exquisitely well-groomed and polite, was also an animal. Being exposed to his all-consuming manliness, built like a machine, made me feel like an animal too. He caught me looking. He was definitely in a flirty mood. He was working his eye brows, *a lot*, in a playful way. There was a giddy air about us, I switched from feeling like an animal to a teenager again.

I loved watching him eat. It has been said, that the way to a man's heart was through his stomach. The chemical and biological reactions begin with just the slightest scent or sight of his food. Laughlann was most definitely your textbook example of this. He assessed his food approvingly with his eyes before tasting it. Satisfaction evident as his eyes closed, and mmm he moaned with it hitting the spot. His flirtation continued, saying my name with his surname after it. It had 4 syllables, quite the mouthful. I was fascinated. He said he liked the sound of our names combined, and asked what did I think. All I could do was laugh. He was trying to be smooth. The only thing I knew for sure about him, was that he was hungry. He was hungry for food, hungry for success and wealth, the question remained however.....was he hungry for me?

We walked, got ice cream and stared out to sea, but work was certainly playing on his mind. His conversation was all work, *his* work-related chat, which for now was new to me and seemed interesting. The sun began to go down and there was a chill in the air. I called it home time. I hopped in his car. As he began to drive me back home his phone was ringing the whole time, and he tried his best not to pick up.

His effort waned when we stopped for fuel on the way, and he was on the phone again. He was still on the phone when we reached my place. I mouthed thanks for the lift, and waved. He put his hand out and said wait, he told his business partner on the phone he had to get off the line immediately as a beautiful woman was about to walk out of his life.

Yes, he had the lines for sure! Cue warnings! Mr. Smooth will always be too sweet to be wholesome. Lucky for him, I have a sweet tooth! He was granted another date.

He phoned every night thereafter. The chats were good, I knew this was a good sign, it was more personal than a text. More than that, his voice was everything, it was better than music to my ears. It was a real man's voice, deep, rugged, country-but-cultured, and definitely manly. He had a soft side too though. When he spoke about his family, an element of his potential to be a caring family man shone through. This didn't come via the phone calls but the texts and picture messages he sent.

And no, he did not send dick pics. Instead he sent pictures of his nephews, he took them camping! Of course he took them to do a macho activity! My personal favourite however, was the picture of the 5 nephews all lined up. Standing eldest to youngest, tallest to shortest, most to least freckly, and diluted shades of his familial dark red hair to a strawberry blonde. The littlest one, only 3 and a very important half years old, with a big black eye. This was received from the 4 and half year old "play fighting", and was well able to retaliate by all accounts!

Date 2 with Laughlann, The Entrepreneur

Our second date was to be a dinner date on Wednesday after work. We were to have one drink then go for food. I still couldn't fathom why anyone from outside the city would agree to an after-work date in Dublin. Traffic would be mental. In fact, I was sure the single-dom of the Irish population, particularly in the city, was largely due to bad traffic and the inconvenience of it all!

We were to meet at 7pm in a bar near Stephens Green. Knowing how late he had been for the previous date I decided I wouldn't get there until 7.30pm. Plus, he really wasn't absorbing my insistence that traffic would be bad. Dressed to impress in a little black number and floral blazer, with my highest heels, I was feeling pretty good! Oh how I loved dating a man I was shorter than in heels!

I ordered a coffee flavored cocktail which happened to be both our favourite that day. It's always a delicious treat, but goes down way too easy! Sitting alone at the stylish bar was a far cry from sitting alone in an old-man pub. I felt amazing, and unless my imagination was running away with me altogether, I was getting a few admirable glances. Perhaps instead of swiping I should just perch at a bar looking fabulous? Could a woman really get a date for a wedding that way? Perhaps this could be an experiment for another time!

I began to wonder though, who were these men in the bar on a Wednesday. I certainly wouldn't be out drinking unless it was a special occasion, or a date. Was after work drinks still a thing, so early in the week? Surely it was more acceptable on a Thursday or Friday? Perhaps they were all waiting on their dates. That's how it should be, the gentleman awaiting the fair maiden to grace him with her presence.

One cocktail down, I promptly ordered another, I would be in fine spirits when my date arrived. It never dawned on me that he wouldn't show up. You see, for Laughlann and his line of work, his word was his bond. I knew even if he was an hour late, which by this point he was, he was always fully intent on showing up. He knew what he wanted no matter how many miles he had to go to get it! He may have been an absolute scoundrel, but he was an honest one!

Laughlann burst through the door, at speed. I couldn't help but laugh as he stumbled down the steps into the bar. I knew from my position he wouldn't be able to see me. Dating him seemed very cat and mouse. I enjoyed watching him seek me out, his head twisting left to right, eyes wide open searching. Just as he reached into his trousers to pull out his phone I messaged him.

Laura:

Your two o clock the other side of the bar ☺

Laughlann's smile widened ear to ear, as he slowly tilted his head to see me. We had one more drink there but Laughlann was really hungry and verging on hangry, so we headed off to the restaurant.

The restaurant was busy, we would have had to wait another 45 minutes so we kept walking to find another one, where we were truly lucky to get a table.

"Did you not book somewhere?" asked Laughlann, his face deadpan.

"You have got to be joking me right?" I glared back.

"Well if you were to come all the way to West Meath to see me, I would have booked a restaurant like."

Ignorant swine, I thought.

"You do realise you showed up an hour late, right? What time was I supposed to book for? If you are twenty minutes late here, you lose your table and your deposit. Might I politely remind you, you were *THREE* times twenty minutes late."

"Miaow! Easy tiger. You are a feisty little madam aren't you?!"

He gave a little laugh, not sure how to take my criticism, and mentioned the need for the loo. He jumped up to the waitress across the room to ask where the toilet was. He was such a flirt with her, touching her arm too. She started to laugh. It was only dawning on me that he might actually be a bit of prick too, but I was a little too tipsy to care. I had busted my ass in work, and it was going well. Tonight, a Wednesday night, I was letting my hair down, and was going to enjoy this dinner date one way or another!

He came back with a glint in his eye. His pupils dilated, always the give-away. He was chuffed with himself whatever he was up to.

"I just got off a call with one of the lads in California, I can run a US based part of my business from there and make about five to seven million in the next two years."

I loved how excited he got when he spoke about his work. Passion is an attractive thing. Someone with fire in their belly is definitely a quality I desired in a partner. Unfortunately, this fire was blazing on another continent. I was genuinely excited for him and his grand ideas. I knew at this moment he was not the one for me long term, or short term for that matter, with all his flying around!

We discussed how we each had work in various parts of the world. Our favourite cuisines, climates, and ways of life. Dublin itself boasts a glorious mixture of ethnicities and this was apparent everywhere, even in the restaurant we were in.

Our waitress had an unusual accent, it was very hard to place. We decided to play a game. We had to get the waitress to tell us where she was from without directly asking her. I was in the mood for fun, and a little competition. The loser had to pay for the meal.

The waitress arrived with some drinks on a plate, how unusual. This is what he had been laughing about with the waitress. He had told her he had some making up to do for being so late, and hey presto, a delicious cocktail for the lady with macaroons placed in a heart shape was presented as an apology. I giggled, it was a bit mushy but I was loving it! He was good at making up it seems! Was he trying to get me drunk? If he was, he didn't have to, with the two cocktails due to his tardiness, I was already there!

"OOhh this is tangy and light, very refreshing! What is this drink called?" I asked the waitress.

"Yes, it is good right?! It is a secret, I make it myself, I used to work in Cyprus and this was a favourite there!"

"Oh were you there for long?" Laughlann piped up.

"No, I just worked there for a year," the waitress smiled, "enjoy your drinks."

Our dinners arrived and they looked and smelled so good. The hunger beast from the drink was alive and well in my tummy, and this was just what he ordered.

"Two steaks, one medium and one medium rare."

"Oh your accent is lovely where is it from?" this could be borderline cheating but I didn't care.

"Ah my accent is from everywhere, Cyprus, Amsterdam, and my boyfriend is from London so I picked his accent up a little bit too."

The waitress returned to take our plates away.

"Would you like to see a dessert menu?"

"Well there is no harm in looking, now is there?" Laughlann reckoned he could charm the waitress to telling him more about herself. I was beyond caring. With his lack of punctuality and this tactic of showing how smooth he could be to another female, in my presence, there was no way I was paying for this dinner, whether I lost or not, even though it was my turn.

"Oh lah lah" I cooed, as a little pot of creamy fruity scrumptious-ness went by to another table. "What is that now?" I asked the waitress.

"That is the best dessert in the house!"

"Oh really why is that?"

"That is a layered rye bread, with cream and fruit, it is a traditional dessert from Latvia from where I am from."

My eyes beamed wide open, I had just won this competition, my smile grew big and toothy, I was totally doing the horse smile. My horsey smile was the natural full on grin I did, when I was beyond delighted with myself. Ordinarily I hated this grin that displayed my full set of teeth and gums, hence my description of it as my horsey grin! For losing the bet, Laughlann graciously paid for the meal and we hopped in separate cabs, me to home and him to wherever the night was taking him. Let's just say the date didn't end romantically.

Date 3 with Laughlann, The Entrepreneur

I did agree to meet him again the next night for a sober, chilled out date, maybe some mini golf or an easy cinema date were thrown out by him as suggestions. As I was leaving work he messaged to say he would be late again! Oh my goodness, I couldn't tolerate this, could anyone? The only good thing was that I had anticipated it this time, and had scheduled the date at a large shopping outlet, very near to where the mini golf was, and also the cinema.

Detrimentally to my bank balance, there were a number of shops with clothes and shoes there that caught my eye! Nothing like retail therapy to calm myself down before he arrived. I knew full well he would show up, but the question of how late he would be, was any one's guess. I figured I had at least 20 minutes before he got there, so I could have a quick nosey in the shops and perhaps get a new top, which was fairly essential at this point.

You see I had spent a huge amount of time not sleeping the night before. I was too perplexed about whether I should meet him again or not. There was no doubt that he made me excited, I absolutely felt the elusive 'spark' but could my brain tolerate how reliably late he seemed to always be? Knowing I wasn't getting enough sleep then made me worry that I would have dark circles under my eyes, and as a result I would not be looking my best for the date. This in turn did not help with falling asleep. It was a vicious circle. Not the best at getting up exactly when my alarm goes off at the best of times, I had made a mad dash into work that morning.
Thus, I had forgotten my makeup bag, my tooth brush, and my lunch.

At least I had my bank card in my wallet, and thinking I was a genius, I bought a yoghurt at lunch, so that nothing could get stuck in my teeth of course! The only trouble was, in opening the yogurt, it totally splashed on my top, ruining it. No amount of water helped, if anything it just made it worse!

With a new top purchased and with Laughlann 30 minutes late at that stage, I felt tired and I decided I really did not want to see him. I left him a voice note to that effect and headed home. By the time I got there, he had sent two texts and I had a missed call from him.
He left me a voice note:

"Look Laura, I know you are not answering because you think I'm a dickhead, and you're right. I am. But I don't want to be. I don't want to be a dickhead to you. I know what I should be doing, you know. I should leave work on time and take Laura out for dinner and keep my phone on silent. If you stop talking to me I'd miss our chats. I'd miss your funny accent and your funny stories. You know you sound like you are from all over the place?! That accent just can't consistently be attributed to any particular location. I am sorry. Let me make it up to you. Don't think I haven't seen how you look at me eating. I know you like me just a little bit. Ha or at least you did. I'll be driving for a while now so my darling Laura please give me a call."

I reckoned he just wanted company on the phone while driving. It's the constant communication that gets addictive. Having said that, he was incredibly handsome and somewhat interesting. He was part of the overall experiment and a third date was a requirement for this process. He was also right when he said he was in fact a dickhead. However, he knows the mistakes he has made and he knew himself how to correct them. This in itself was a bonus.

So many men think they are perfect and don't seem to know how to behave, or treat a lady. One guy once told me he was the most eligible bachelor in his home town. I didn't have the heart to tell him that was because no one wanted him!

Perhaps the third date could be Laughlann's greatest redemption ha! I decided to call him back and see what we could arrange. When I phoned, he picked up immediately. He was really happy I called. He said almost slyly that he had a suspicion that I would call but that he was delighted. He said with his optimism and his suspicion he went ahead and booked a restaurant for Saturday night. This was no ordinary restaurant. On the first Saturday of every month the restaurant in question held a special event for various charities. This Saturday his work was sponsoring a very unique dining experience. He had said he wanted to show me off.

He said he selected this restaurant, and this occasion for a very particular reason. He had noted that he had not given me his full attention on our previous dates, but that he was going to make up for this, and, go one step further. This restaurant was going to allow us to communicate better with each other and with our senses. By removing one of our senses, our vision, we would be forced to rely on our other senses for communication and interpretation. Yes, we were going dining in the dark!
 I was so intrigued I had heard of this experience before but I never engaged with this myself. The dinner was booked for 7 pm and he said he would meet me there. Of course I agreed, I mean how can I resist his voice, and his earnest efforts, combined it's my weak spot.

Moreover, I was intrigued by the dining in the dark experience, how and when would it begin. Was it on the arrival at the restaurant? Or was it after you were seated at the table? Was it for one course or was it for all three?

I decided to wear a red dress, plunging neckline and killer heels, if he wasn't going to get to see me for the whole night during the dinner, I might at least seize the opportunity to wow him at first glance. His outfit no doubt would be on point as always. He promised he would be on time. I arrived at the venue 10 minutes early, this was on purpose. I absolutely wanted to see what was going down before we took part.

I was a small bit nervous about what the evenings events would be. I wanted to get there early to ask at the restaurant what the process was. I guess you could say there is a small element of a control freak within me. I didn't particularly want him to see this side of me. I also didn't want him to think that I was a chicken. There is an element of fear or maybe the element of the unknown that leads to fear, when you are in total darkness.

Unsurprisingly, that was part of the charity night to raise awareness and funds for those with sight loss. So not only were we going to have a good night ourselves, but we were doing good for others too. We knew what table we were booked to sit at, his lucky number 7. The night was busy and the restaurant manager began to call out table numbers to bring the guests to the dining room. It had just gone 7 pm and the manager was calling out number table number 5. I was giggling and talking to those around me, there was an air of nervousness with everybody is seemed. The manager called table number 6 and those individuals followed on through. "Table number seven for eight people. Table number seven please come along."

I looked over my shoulder to see if anyone else was coming in the door, there was still no sign of Laughlann. Here I was chatting to his boss and he was nowhere to be found. Typical, so much for his night of redemption. I pondered for a moment if I was going to actually go and sit at the table with these people, his people, without him, all while dining in the dark.

"Excuse me miss, excuse me are you with table number seven, please come along."

I sighed and nodded my head and began to shuffle along the corridor.

"Allow me take your coat madam." I handed my coat to the manager and he said that once we round the corner we would be in complete darkness and guided to our seats.

"You are missing one of your party I believe."

"Yes," I said "there is one more gentlemen to arrive. Will he be able to get in if he is late?"

"Yes he will. But the event won't wait for him, we will commence the evening with a small toast, so you can have his drink if you like, since he is late hahaha!"

I laughed along politely. I was really annoyed. Once I rounded the corner a member of staff gave me a blindfold and goggles and pointed to a room that was in complete darkness. I put on the blindfold and the goggles. A staff member asked me to stick out my elbow to be guided to my seat. We shuffled along, I giggled nervously, but within a number of seconds I was seated. Briefly those at my table stop speaking, they were conscious of the new arrival.

"Hi" I said "I'm Laura, I'm supposed to be here as Laughlann's guest but I think he's quite late."

"You deserve to have a good night one way or another. Not known for his time keeping is our Laughlann, but he is a good man," said a male voice from across the table.

A speech was made at the start of the night about the needs for continued research, funding and resources for those with sight loss. A toast was made to the organizers of the event, and it was champagne all around. Two for me in light of Laughlann's absence. The waitress came around the table and began to ask us if we wanted red wine, white wine; and also steak, salmon or the vegetarian option which was a risotto. Given that Laughlann had prepaid the tickets for the event, I decided I was going to go to town on everything, I ordered salmon and white wine for myself and red wine and steak for his empty place. It was no time at all until the starter arrived, it was a goat's cheese salad. The conversation at the table was all introductions of who we were, and why we were there. By the time they were clearing our starter course plates, we were all in agreement that Laughlann was no good at dating.

This was rather unfortunate for him, because as the final plate was lifted, we heard a rattle from the corner of the room and man calling out.

"Laura, Laura, I'm here, I'm sorry. Man can we shuffle a bit faster here please?"

This was followed by a heavy thud, as Laughlann practically fell onto his seat.

Thinking I was sitting to his left, Laughlann clasped the arms of the man next to him, and began to apologise. The startled man sitting there said "it's not me you need to apologise to!" The whole table erupted laughing, myself included. Laughlann put his arms around me and pulled me in for a hug and kissed the top of my head. Pulling off his goggles and mine and flashing the torch of his phone between us Laughlann began again.

"I am so sorry Laura, I am so sorry I got held up at work, just as I was leaving a man came into the office and then I got stuck in traffic. Laura you look stunning! I am so sorry! I am such a fool for being so late again!"

The waiter came over and told us we had to put our blindfolds on and to switch off the torch. Obediently we did as we were told. I was strangely enough having a good night, with the random individuals at the table. I wasn't exactly missing Laughlann. I was too pleased with my independent self at that moment to feel any ill will towards Laughlann.

With the champagne already downed and goodness knows how much wine, I was feeling a little bit tipsy. I told Laughlann I'd ordered him steak and red wine, he was pleased with what I had ordered. He said I was too good to him, and that 'many-a-woman wouldn't have ordered him anything'. I told him that the thought did cross my mind to let him sit there without food or drink. In the end I knew I would be glad whenever he did appear. He kissed my cheek and I think that sealed the deal, there was to be no argument.

The main course arrived and after a few bites our table got rowdy again. Poor Laughlann, he got a lot of abuse for turning up so late, but I was loving it. He was well able to take it, and you know what, he took it in stride. I was a lot more drunk than I thought by the time we got to the desert course. It was only at that point I realised I wasn't fully aware of when the wine glasses were being topped up. I could hear it but never sure if it was my glass or the person next to me, or across from me. I definitely had consumed more than one glass, but, I couldn't see how much I was drinking, or how much was being refilled into the glass!

I could feel the alcohol heat rising inside me, and absolutely everything was more amusing than it should be. The table was a lot of fun. There were a lot of giggles. We also noticed we spoke a lot louder, as we didn't have the visual cues to allow us to know if someone was hearing, or understanding what we were saying properly.

Apart from the bit of smudged eye shadow and mascara from the blindfold, I reckoned I would leave rather unscathed. It was great craic. At one point, it was clear Laughlann had greater drink consumption than food consumption, and he blurted out loud that he knew what he would rather being doing with me in the dark! This would have been fine only other people I'm sure could hear!

I obviously couldn't see anyone reacting, but there were a few, not so faint chuckles which were in time with them hearing him! I very quickly and politely reminded him, that although he couldn't see people, they were there, and they could hear him!

The chocolate-y scent of dessert arrived. That is one thing I do have a good nose for! It was creamy, sweet and delicious with a hint of dark chocolate in there somewhere. Apart from that, I've no idea what it was.

By the end of the meal everybody was without a shadow of a doubt beyond drunk.

I leaned slightly over to my left and whispered, "Em Laughlann, give me your hands, I just want to check something."

"Oh Laura, are you getting all romantic on me now?" he giggled.

"No, no," I whispered, "I was just checking to see if the hand on my lap was yours or not! And it is definitely not."

I leaned slightly over to my right and lift the man's hand on my lap by the wrist and politely told him "I know we had great chats tonight, but I believe this hand belongs to you, and it probably was meant for someone else's lap!"

With half a snore, it seemed as though I had woken him, the hand lifted immediately.

"Oh, oh my God, I am so sorry, Mary, Mary which side of me are you? Oh Christ I am so sorry, I am so full and so sleepy from the dinner I, I." His voice was rattled. He seemed genuinely embarrassed and apologetic. I think it was a genuine mistake, though you never really know.
"It's ok, no harm done, just be more careful in the future. Imagine if it was a man's lap your hand landed on, or worse, his you know what!"

We were escorted away from our table to get our coats, and then we could remove our blindfolds. Adjusting to the light it was quite stingy to our eyes. Most people's eyes were actually quite bloodshot, though this is probably due to the alcohol. For some reason I felt a little bit hungry, so too did Laughlann.

At the end we were shown how much of our food we had eaten, and how much wine we had drank. This was an experiment to see who were visual eaters and drinkers, and who were not. Apparently the majority of us are visual eaters stimulated by the sight of our food, thus ate very little. Similarly, we rely on our visual cues to know when to stop drinking wine.

Because we hadn't realised how much we were drinking visually, the majority of us just kept on drinking and drinking. It really was quite an interesting experience, and one I would never forget.

Outside when we were alone and could speak privately Laughlann had a glint in his eye.

"Wow Laura you look sensational in that red dress. You've gone all out for tonight. There must be someone special in your life?" He sounded smug.

"Yes, I thought I might dress up for the special occasion, but," and I smiled up at him to show I wasn't actually angry, "once again you were almost an hour late. You know, I really enjoy your company, and our chats are great, but you have the worst time keeping."

"I know. I know but I'm changing. Just give me one more chance, and to be fair I haven't picked up my phone all night." On cue his phone began to ring, it was his business partner, and because it was late he said it was likely to be urgent, and that he had to pick up. I nodded my head, and said "fire away."

As far as I was concerned I had my mind made up. We went on to Fade Street to have a couple of drinks and a sneaky kiss but that was it. At midnight I called Cinderella O Clock and said it was time for me to go home. He looked a bit confused while I hopped in a taxi waving goodbye. On the way home I left the girls a voice note. I told them what an amazing man Laughlann was, with his business acumen and his super-hot body, not to mention his voice just as seductive as chocolate spread on hot toast, but he absolutely could not be relied upon to attend a wedding. He would surely cause a scene arriving much later than the bride. It had been a great night. Definitely one that gave me great memories, but I knew it was time to say, next candidate please!

Phase 1 End Message from the Chief Advisor to the Principal Investigator

I had filled Maria in on this dating experiment. She thought I was a mixture of half crazy, and half genius, and wanted to be kept informed. Of course that would not be a problem, so I bestowed upon her, a very specific title for this process. With her seniority in the dating game, she was dubbed Chief Advisor to the Principal Investigator! With her positive, perky attitude, and advocacy that happiness is personal and not dependent on a man, there was no one more appropriate for the role. As Maria was a lady who never seemed to be anything other than blissfully happy, and glided through life with an air of graceful elegance about her, it was very difficult to argue against her beliefs. It certainly worked wonders for her!

From the few times the girls on the Review Board had met Maria, they adored her, and like most, were in awe of her charisma and success. They were more than happy for me to include her in the process, and for her to interject if she ever felt it was necessary. Throughout the experiment, Maria received the same voice notes on the dates as the Review Board. I decided I would speak to her in advance of meeting with the Review Board, just to hear her thoughts. One of the many great things about Maria, is that she absolutely always, *always* answers her phone. Even if she is on a call with someone else, Maria puts them on hold to inform you that she will be with you in just a moment.

When I phoned Maria I gave her my breakdown of how I felt about the first three guys now that Phase 1 was complete. I asked her for her thoughts, and prepared myself for whatever opinions she might have. Another great thing about Maria, is that she never sits on the fence, she processes the data then takes a firm decision on things, whether you agree with them or not.

"Ok so The Radiographer lured you in, and you fell hook, line and sinker - big deal, it happens to the best of us. To be fair, from what you said, you had absolutely no reason to doubt him, so please stop feeling stupid. And perhaps to his credit, it was he who just had the edge on you, with his ability to trick smart women, versus your ability to identify him as a man who is up to no good.

I like this dating method, it really helps to serve the purpose of just forgetting one guy without being too invested, and moving on to the next. I'm glad you dusted yourself down and got straight back up on the horse. The Frenchie sounds like he would be great for a fling, are you sure you don't want him? I could take him off your hands no problem- o. Do you still have a picture of him, from what you have said it seems as though his looks were all that were going for him? Ha- I am joking, but you know the language issue might have just kept things nice and simple, no difficult chat, just fun! But I know you, and simplicity is not really what gets you going. You are more the type that requires a bit of a mental challenge from someone in order for them to earn your respect.

And as for mister late- well I can only imagine how absolutely crazy that drove you. You are used to planning experiments to the minute, and sometimes even the second, so how on earth a character like that was going to fit into your life would be beyond comprehension. In all seriousness, how did you tolerate it, at all? No offence but you are not patient by any stretch of the imagination, he must have had a lot of physical appeal for you to let that go on for three dates. P.S I love my title of Chief Advisor to the PI. Looking forward to my next installment of this science saga!"

The Ranking Table and Phase 1 Interim Report Review Board Meeting

Once again, the Review Board and I were meeting in our favourite restaurant just off Grafton Street at 10.30 am on Sunday! To me this was a more appropriate time to have brunch, you know between the typical breakfast and lunch feeding times of our girl group. However, this was slightly earlier than our usual Sunday time slot of noon, and a certain lethargic member of the Review Board (Rebecca) left her disgruntled voice note in the group chat the night before. The disgruntled reviewer indicated she would be late, because sleep was more important.

As the principal investigator, I responded with my most gracious appreciation of the reviewers' participation. The reviewer quite amicably responded with the suggestion to order the pancakes for her because she would be there by the time they reached our table. Of course I agreed, it was splendid idea – every scientist knows, it is wise to keep your reviewers on board after all!

I got up that morning a tiny bit hungover from my final date with Laughlann. With myself rehydrated and topped up with multivitamins, and chart music on the radio, I got a little bit giddy. This was actually the fun bit of the experiment. I wonder if this is how team-sports commentators feel about post match analysis?

Being the primary investigator can be isolating at times, but the inclusion of the Review Board meetings not only added value to the experiment, but I didn't feel alone in the process. It was time to get ready to meet the girls for the brunch-time meeting! Energy bubbled inside, radiating down my hips and legs, and before I knew it I was swaying and tapping my feet to the rhythm of the music as I searched for my sports bag.

A good gym session was put in by all (except Rebecca), in advance of the plate of golden carb-a-licious pancakes that would be presented to us! For the Review Board meeting I had created a score chart in the form of a table for each guy. I inserted the points for each date, and for the candidates' qualities along with a general comment. I sent this scoring system to the Review Board, and was going to get their additional comments today. Their job was to ensure I was not over reacting, or under scoring, and being fair to the guys, and in particular not being misled by any compounding factor.

For example, I may be more lenient on a man who was more aesthetically pleasing than another. The Review Board would also need to override points given to a man who was too sweet to be wholesome when I was blinded by love, and you know well that by love, I mean lust! (You can't seriously love someone after three dates, can you?!)

"So Phase One is complete, and I have been swiping away on the dating apps, and have the Phase Two candidates lined up. In fact, I will commence dating Candidate 4 later today! You know I have taken on board your comments that I have been playing it safe and standard with the Phase One guys. With Phase Two, I am expanding the mix of types," I laughed and continued, "this next dating Phase will introduce me to the number crunching brainy type - an accountant, the ever abundant type - you guessed it - a personal trainer, and, a man who works with his hands, skilled at hammering, nailing and screwing."

"I like the sound of him!" teased The Doll. Laughter erupted at our table!

"All innocently of course," I assured her, "he's a carpenter!"

"Furthermore, now brace yourselves for this" I said holding my hands up, palms facing them signaling calm, "the Phase Two guys are all non-drinkers according to their profiles!"

The ladies pulled their faces back, dipping their chins and looking under their eyes at each other, as if this was a bit of an unusual state of affairs, said nothing at first.

"So if they are not drinking, does that mean you are not drinking?" queried The Doll, "because that would be like, a total bore fest!" Laughter erupted again.

Anne brought us to attention with a somber, snippy comment to The Doll.

"Sounds like you have a drink problem, hun." At that we raised our eyebrows and smiled trying to keep the giggles in. We were all well-accustomed to Anne's ways. Anne followed this by instructions to the group not to run away with ourselves, and to focus on the task at hand. We had three score charts to discuss before we could tuck in to our lovely brunch. Love her or hate her, Anne keeps us on track!

Table 1 Padraig, The Radiographer

Candidate 1	Marks
Date 1	4.5 /5
Date 2	5.0 /5
Date 3	4.0 /5
Good Communication	4.0 /5
Good sense of humour	4.5 /5
Willingness to dance	4.0 /5
Confidence among strangers	4.5 /5
Personality +/- alcohol	5.0 /5
Trustworthy	4.0 /5
Punctual	5.0 /5
Total	44.5 /50

General comment: Excellent potential for whoever he ends up with, shame you can't believe the guy! He ticked all the boxes. Totally fell for him, but seeing him kiss someone else was really gutting!

Wedding guest suitability: High

"Girls, this one completely knocked my socks off! I was totally falling for him! I was blinded by the sun shining out of his bottom! Ha, no seriously though, it nearly killed me seeing him with that other girl. If I could just detach my emotion from this, it would be grand. He is perfect wedding guest material! I did my level best to detach, to objectively allocate scores."

Lisa was first off the bat, "Hmm, I get what you are saying. He does seem to have that bedside manner to make the ladies go weak at the knees. He is also a lads-lad, that makes him a good 'all-rounder' (she indicated the inverted commas with her hands), and he treats you impeccably well. You even seemed to shine more yourself the more time you spent with him. It is a pity about the other girl. Would you not just ask him about her, and see what the story is? Maybe it was a break-up kiss goodbye?"

"A break-up kiss good bye?! What planet are you on?!" exclaimed The Doll, with her perfectly made up eyes hopping out of her head with disgust and disbelief at such a suggestion.

Anne objectively stated, "You two are not an item. You have not spoken about exclusivity together. He is well within his rights to date whom so ever he chooses. Do not forget your objectives here. You are looking for a wedding date, not a husband! He is the best candidate, in my opinion, of the first three candidates - don't forget there are six more. You completely over-reacted to seeing him kiss someone else. That did not warrant the low score of two that you were originally giving him for trustworthiness. Did you forget how tentatively he took care of you when you were a drunken mess, and how he didn't let you fall down or hurt yourself at the adventure obstacle course? You will note I left a voicemail to increase the trust score from two to four, and I am glad to see you have accepted my suggestion, and I hope it remains at a respectable four."

Rebecca agreed with Anne. "Yes, a score of two would have been unfair. He would be an easy plus-one to bring to a wedding. Smooth without being smarmy, you wouldn't have to worry about him, with the added result that you would enjoy yourself more too. Going on the voice messages, out of these first three candidates, he would be top of my list too."

Rebecca continued, "It seems to me he is the type of dessert that is the whole reason you go out for dinner. He is the ultimate chocolate fudge bownie Sunday. The perfect mix of a cool trio of salted caramel, vanilla and chocolate ice-cream, with warm chocolate fudge brownie pieces and hazel nut sprinkles mixed throughout. Finally, this piece of heaven is all drizzled with warm chocolate fudge and caramel sauce."
"Luckily we have the pancakes to satiate us after that description, I am practically drooling here Becks!" Lisa said licking her lips. "I agree with the girls, Laura, trust ME, ha, he is a four out of five not a two!"
"Fair enough, fair enough, you are all right I guess, that's fine. I'm still annoyed but that's fine" I conceded. "Right let's move on to Candidate Two, Pierre-Bear."

Table 2 Pierre- Bear, The Artisan Baker

Candidate 2	Marks
Date 1	4.5 /5
Date 2	4.0 /5
Date 3	3.5 /5
Good Communication	3.0 /5
Good sense of humour	3.0 /5
Willingness to dance	5.0 /5
Confidence among strangers	4.0 /5
Personality +/- alcohol	4.0 /5
Trustworthy	4.0 /5
Punctual	5.0 /5
Total	40 /50

General comment: Attractive to look at, extra interest in him due to cultural differences, language barrier evident, a wee bit too childish

Wedding guest suitability: Low

"Ok this time girls, this man was adorable! However, I cannot have a grown up conversation with him. He just doesn't understand me. He comes across as very childish too, which makes me think he might not be too clever. To be fair, I don't understand him when he does make an effort to have a mature chat. It is just such hard work. I would have to babysit him if I brought him to the wedding."

Lisa chipped in, "Oh I am a biased here. Aa someone who has dated an Italian, I do understand the challenges you face. Despite some of the difficulties in language though, he HAS communicated some interesting stories to you. Perhaps give him the benefit of the doubt. I would have to say I am on the fence with this guy."

Anne, assessing the situation logically noted, "You will never be happy with someone if you don't find them smart. In time you would definitely lose some respect you have for them."

The Doll not wasting time summed it up nicely, "He is a ride! But yeah, you can't bring him to the wedding if he can't have the chats like! Next!"

Becks looking completely bored and un-phased simply explained, "It seems to me he is like a Latticed Cherry Pie, decorative to look at, sweet to taste, not a challenging recipe, quite simple in fact - not the dessert for you."

"Well that's that settled," said Anne, "on to Candidate Three we go!"

Table 3 Laughlann, The Entrepreneur

Candidate 3	Marks
Date 1	**4.0 /5**
Date 2	**4.0 /5**
Date 3	**4.0 /5**
Good Communication	**5.0 /5**
Good sense of humour	**5.0 /5**
Willingness to dance	**3.5 /5**
Confidence among strangers	**5.0 /5**
Personality +/- alcohol	**4.5 /5**
Trustworthy	**5.0 /5**
Punctual	**1.0 /5**
Total	**41 /50**

General comment: Lovely, lovely guy! Physique of Michelangelo's the David! Distance is a nightmare! Exhausted trying to meet him and that was only 3 dates!

"You know I want to say more than that about him. Him and his stories they were exciting, interesting, but he was chronically, extraordinarily LATE. He is honest though a little too smooth, and totally driven by money. Furthermore, he indicated at one point that wouldn't be caught dead dancing, but then conceded that anything could happen when a few drinks were in.

Wedding guest suitability: Medium to low

Lisa was straight in with her comments. "Axe him, I just split with Francessco. The distance will suck the life out you. I want a human not a face on a phone."

Anne turned to Lisa "Are you OK? You really liked him."

"I liked him in person, conversation dries up when you don't see each other properly, and you know I can't do small talk for long!"

Anne tried to stifle a smile "We are not built like that!"

The two girls began to giggle; it was a long standing joke that they were hopeless at small talk. They were happy to be bad at it. To them it served no purpose. Just a waste of time. Unless you were genuinely interested in something or someone or their health - then don't ask! Unless there is a lightning storm, hail stones in summer or a heavy snow drift - the weather is really not a hot topic!

Anne reckoned this guy had potential. "He seemed fun, listen back over your voice message about him, you will hear yourself laughing as you talk about him. Apart from not getting to you on time, I don't think you really had any issues with this guy. I know timing is important but do you think maybe you are weighting it too highly? And I have to say, how cute was his gesture of the cocktail with love heart treats. Now there is a man who recognizes when he was in the wrong and made a bit of an effort to apologise. I wish all men were like that!"

The Doll answered for me. "She was laughing on the voice message because it is utterly ridiculous how late he was. He must have made some impression on you though Laura, to wait so long for him so often. You were always confident that he would arrive, never concerned that he wouldn't show up. There must be an earnest vibe about him."

"Absolutely" I agreed, "he just came across as a very trustworthy person, fun and light hearted, I would trust him with everything except to show up on time, and that is fairly critical for attending a wedding! I don't want him bursting through the church door *after* the bride!"

Rebecca concluded, "It seems to me like he is a lemon meringue pie - a little bit of a sweetie, provides a fleeting bit of fun which is light to enjoy for an afternoon treat, but no substance. Not the one for you."

"To hell with sweet pie," said The Doll, "Laughlann is a man who knows what he wants, he has got drive, ambition, determination, it's hard to pin down a partner when you are so busy. I definitely give an A for effort to Laughlann, he is getting my golden Wild Card 5 points!"

"So soon? Would you not be worried you are missing out on giving the 5 extra points to someone more deserving?" asked Anne.

"Ha, I guess it is a case of when you know, you know! Especially being an entrepreneur myself, it's a risky business, this 5 points is an easy risk I am willing to take, sure I have nothing to lose! He's not going to be my date!" explained The Doll.

"Fair point, well made," conceded Anne.

By that point, I was only half listening, my mind was no longer on the first three gentlemen. I was contemplating the next three candidates, and I was so glad to be going on sober dates.

Dating was expensive. With exception of coffee first dates, another very common first date was to go for "drinks in town". If that approach were to be taken for all three dates, with each candidate, I would end up broke! Not to mention the effects on my liver! At least by going on sober dates, you could drive anywhere. This would eliminate the expense of a taxi home of a late night.

I decided it was time to call the Review Board meeting to a halt so we could enjoy our brunch. We all agreed to meet for more walks for Dublin City Marathon training. I said my sober dates would help, and that I would totally be dating in athleisure wear!

The Doll raised her brows when I said this, looking somewhat concerned.

"Let me tell you what a girl at work told me...first things first girl, we have got to get you shopping. This does not mean that I am saying you look bad."

We all looked at her stunned. Apparently one of The Doll's clients out of concern for her, was trying to insist that she wear fancier clothing while doing her house calls. This would apparently help her to get more male attention, as she goes about her day-to-day business. In this case, The Doll's concern for me, was that if my sober dates were all action dates in my gym wear or equivalent, that the dates might not go my way.

"All I am saying is your gym attire and workout gear are a little… unappealing to the eye. Your date night clothes and important work day clothes are all totally fab. The clothes you usually wear to get your sweat on, though, well, they do absolutely nothing for your figure. And mustard, Laura, who looks good in an oversized mustard hoodie? You live with Lisa for goodness sake! Have you not seen how much better our bodies look in yoga clothing? Stretchy, and fitted to every curve. We want you looking bootilicious, and not like an old pair of boots!"

Rebecca was nodding. "It is so true, we have to be on our A game all the time it seems. I went shopping just to get kitchen supplies without makeup last week, and bumped into one of the other teachers at my school, who was also out shopping. She suggested to me that a trip to the makeup counter wouldn't go astray either. It nearly seemed to be out of politeness. Her exact words were, "I'm not quite sure what your makeup routine is. Do you even have one? Let's go have a girlie day, and ask the experts what can be done to make us look our bouncy, youthful selves!"

Lisa chimed in with advice that was given to her. "I was told us single ladies should have a night out, that's how you really attract the men! You have to be with a group of really good looking women, this will attract the men over, and start talking to you."

To me, this was all getting just a little bit ridiculous.

"HOOOOLD UP! Hold up! Hold up! Hold up! WE (I gestured to our group with the exception of Rebecca) are ALL single. We **all** go out together. We NEVER get chatted up. Are you trying to tell me that we are not getting chatted up because nothing about us looks good? Are you telling me that in addition to new face, new clothes, new attitude we also have to get new friends?!"

They all rippled into fits of giggling, how disastrous and unfortunate it all sounded. Though we agreed, the fools imposing their opinions had only made those suggestions out of an ignorant concern. Even coupled up Rebecca admitted a brunch as part of a fabulous five was more fun than a dull duo.

Anne summed up what we were all thinking. "Love yourselves, isn't that what is always preached at women and men everywhere. You have to love yourself first before you will let love into your lives. Unfortunately, that is frequently followed by the accusatory 'You're too fussy,' 'Noone can live up to your expectations,' 'Your standards are unrealistic, don't you know no one is perfect.' I am not sorry, and I will not lower my expectations, I don't need to!"

And we all cheered in agreement!!

On my way home from brunch I began to wonder, how quickly upon turning 30 did the sound track to our lives change? Why are the lyrics of all the best songs not still belted out fiercely to us? I decided to make a list of my top ten 'strong women' songs.

1. Destiny's Child "Independent Women" (totally an obvious choice)
2. PussyCat Dolls "I don't need a man"
3. Katy Perry "Roar"
4. Christina Aguilera "Fighter"
5. TLC "No Scrubs"
6. Alicia Keys "Superwoman"
7. Shania Twain "Man I feel like a Woman"
8. Ariana Grande- "God is a Woman"
9. Beyoncé- "Run the World (Girls)
10. Arethra Franklin "Respect"

These songs as well as 10 more I could think of, were going to be on a new play-list, my pre-date getting ready sound track. These songs would remind me society was not going to put me in a box. More and more reports of the longest-living, healthiest, happiest women in the world were single women, who avoid stress, and live with everything in moderation, keeping physically and mentally active, and while friends, social life and human interaction were of course important, a man, however, was not on that essentials list!

My song list made me nostalgic to a very different time in my life. First I thought of "Scrubs", it was the pre-drinking house anthem of Tuesday nights out during second year at college. The house was called "The Castle", full of six friends living together, all budding medical scientists from all over the country. Our favourite TV program had the unfortunate scheduling of coinciding with deadline night for experimental reports, due weekly on Tuesdays at 11 pm. This meant Tuesday nights had really strict deadlines - because you know, spacing your work through the week would have been far too practical back then. From 8 pm to 9 pm the girls took turns having showers. The beloved TV show was on from 9 pm to 10 pm with us girls huddled together on couches and sprawled across the floor, half watching TV, while completing the easy parts of the reports. During the add breaks, we were a team trying our best not to wildly plagiarize each other and reaching submission in the nick of time.

The next and most important deadline of the night was being dressed, with perfect makeup, and on the last bus into town at 11:30 pm. Scrubs would kick start the "getting ready" process at 11 pm, and be played again as the count-down to get out the door and race to the bus would commence.

The song "Superwoman" reminded me of every interview I have ever had. I played it on repeat prior to my PhD interview a time when nothing seemed impossible, and since then it has been my lucky interview charm.

I was brought back to present day with a reminder on my phone to be on time for my date with Raj. I would have to leave reminiscing about the songs on the playlist for another time!

Phase 2, Man 1, Candidate 4, Raj, The Accountant

Raj, what a cool name I thought to myself, looking at his profile. He looked quite exotic, almost dreamy, and happy. Definitely happy. His smile reached his eyes in every picture. You could tell he was self-conscious of his height though. In his group pictures, you might notice he was aware he was the shortest of his friends, as he wore his hair all spiked up; it gave him an extra inch. By comparison in other photos of individual selfies, he wears stylish hats and caps. He didn't have information about his height on it, but he looked like he would just about fit the 5 feet 10 ish criteria. He did have one gym photo, but I could let that slide, it was a joke. It showed Raj using only one hand to lift an absolutely huge hand-weight, with 200 lb written on it, while he appeared to be busy on the phone with the other hand. Ha, multi-tasking! It made me smile.

His profile indicated that he was religious. How religious however, there was no way of knowing just yet. It crossed my mind that he may follow Islam. All I really understood about this was, no alcohol and fasting during Ramadan. I wondered would a guy who followed Islamic ways be interested in a girl if she followed Christian ways (to a certain degree)? I had no idea of any of this, and I had nothing to lose, so I swiped right, and we matched!

We messaged a lot over the next few days. He asked me where I saw myself in 5 years' time. What did I think of living in Dublin? Was I going to stay in, or close to the city? Or did I fancy living back at home? He said he was asking because a lot of girls he knew were keen to move back to their respective places of origin. That encouraged me to ask about *his* place of origin.

He was from Dublin, (well not really a surprise) but his parents were from Pakistan. So that explained his gorgeous skin tone. His older brother and sister were married and they were living in Birmingham. He had a lot of family there. His little sister was still in University in Dublin, she was studying law and by all accounts, she was spoiled rotten, mostly by Raj! He was so family orientated, maybe a little bit of a mama's boy, but everything about him was oh so endearing. I asked if he was thinking of moving to Birmingham.

He said he gets asked that a lot because he loves spending time with his friends and family there, but his answer remains a constant and firm "no." His parents fell in love with Dublin and wouldn't leave it, not for all the money in the world. He said they love the little island of Ireland, and go to a different part of the coast every summer for two weeks. He would not leave his parents (though I suspected this was more to do with his mother).

Orla Galvin

He was passionate about his accountancy work for sure, and even did some pro bono work for a charity, helping the elderly in his community. Would I be good enough for this saintly man? Though he wasn't all about the balance sheets; he was interested in holistic health. His Mam suffered badly with arthritis and was pre-diabetic. Raj explained she was trying to manage her pre-diabetic state through diet and exercise, and he was really focused on helping her with this. He had heard about the thrifty gene hypothesis and became concerned for his own health. The proposed hypothesis suggests that certain populations possess genes predisposed to diabetes called "thrifty genes". These genes were historically of benefit to enable people to store fat during periods of food abundance in order to provide for periods of food shortage. However, upon these populations migrating to western regions and becoming exposed to western diets and environments the genes that offered protection now posed health risks.

As such he begun to up his gym game, and although his Mam cooked everything from scratch with the most nutritious of herbs and spices, he began to take note of his food portions too. After a week of messaging, we decided we would go on date to Dun Laoghaire, on Sunday, to the food market. Raj said he was going to give me a food education. Now that did sound intriguing!

Date 1 with Raj, The Accountant

We walked along the pier first, to build up our appetite. It wasn't long before we began to speak about food. The smell from the market was luring us in! It also wasn't long before Raj began to speak about his mother. Raj admitted to eating mostly dinners prepared by his mother, but he was learning a lot. He told me lots of things about his mother, and lots of things about food.

He explained how Pakistani cuisine was a blend of Central Asian and Indian cultures. He told me that in recent years his mother was particularly happy with her slow cooker. This was a point he was keen to get my opinion on too. Now, not being a slow-cooker-owner, I couldn't comment first hand, but I had heard great things from my friend Rebecca who, of course, had one.

He made me laugh trying to claim the slow cooker thing started in his culture. "Dum Pukt" was his traditional technique of slow cooking meat and vegetables over a low flame, which always left him satiated with how the flavours oozed. His absolute favourite, however, was Chicken Karahi- or a Pakistani chicken curry if you like. His mother's recipe was his favourite. She created the fragrant dish to awaken all the senses with a blend of ginger, garlic, turmeric and cumin.

He was learning about the health benefits of each of these ingredients. He explained to me, that he understood that food could be your medicine or your poison. I was loving him already! I listened as he enthusiastically described the rationale behind the constituents of this dish - there was a scientist in the making with him yet, I thought!

He was so cute. A furrow developed in his brow as he carefully recalled the benefits of turmeric lowering the risk of heart disease, cancer, brain conditions, and even relieve arthritis symptoms. I agreed it sounded like a wonder food. I had tried sprinkling it on a stir fry before, it tasted nice but stained everything yellow! Even when I thought I had scrubbed the wok to the extent the water ran clear- my tea towel somehow still had yellow stains on it! Raj had a counter argument that a little yellow stain was a small sacrifice for the anti-oxidant and anti-inflammatory benefits of this spice.

At that point we were walking passed a bakery stall. The cakes looked delicious, but I was craving something savoury rather than sweet. I pointed out the ginger bread men who appeared to have dungarees on them, and were positioned beside ginger bread farm yard animals. It was a farm house bakery, so the theme fit! How cute!

This prompted Raj to return the conversation to food and his Mam. He began to bore me when he launched into his ginger knowledge. He told me ginger is beneficial to the digestive system and may also alleviate symptoms of arthritis, he explained this particular benefit could help his Mam. He recited his learnings of how cumin too may help with diabetes, improve blood cholesterol, and may promote weight loss and fat reduction. In a matter of fact tone, he explained how all of these things would be of benefit to his Mam as well.

My eyes rolled, he didn't notice. I was running out of the capacity to say "OK", "right", "oh that's good". Thankfully he stopped in his tracks talking about his mother, his expression changed. I think the new expression on his face was one of 'OMG I have not asked you anything for ages, and, have blabbered on about my mother no end!'

He smiled, paused and looked at me from underneath his long black eye lashes. I doubt he knew the power that action had on people, he was too pure of heart. Then proceeded to say,

"Of course you know the molecular rationale behind the use of garlic, little miss scientist?"

I smiled back raising an eye-brow. He took the hint to continue.

"The garlic was used to repel any vampires or evil spirits! He laughed, "but it has ALSO been long associated with warding off the common cold!"

I laughed, mostly because he was cute, not because he was funny. Our focus returned to the food to hand. In the end sweet won over savoury, we got hazelnut spread and strawberry crepes. We walked some more, and he asked if I would meet him again.

Overall I had a nice time. Though a little less information on food and his mother would be great! I thought quickly, the following weekend I had planned to visit friends on the Friday night but really needed to fit two more dates in with this guy, and soon to keep up with the experiment. So I agreed and asked if he wanted to meet for some mid-week mini golf. We agreed on Tuesday at 7.30 pm.

It was very easy and simple planning, we both headed off chuffed with ourselves.

On the way home I reflected on this date as a whole. It was a pleasant date; he was such a nice guy and wandering around the stalls was enjoyable. There was no flirting that I could pick up on, not even a bit of slagging. It was only the first date, perhaps the chemistry or the elusive spark might become apparent or ignite on the next date?

Perhaps in the long term it might be a good thing that he wasn't a brazen flirt. His mama's boy ways gave him a solid respect for women, so perhaps this was what I had been missing in previous courtship? Although, really, after just one date, all this was outlining to me was how he could be friend zoned. My gut was already starting to think he would be a really good friend - but anything more than that? Time would tell!

I was convinced dating Raj was going to be easy, too easy in fact to hold my attention. However, on Monday night my plain sailing notions hit a tiny iceberg when he messaged to say:

Raj:

Hi Laura, my Mam is not feeling very well so I just wanted to let you know, I am only 50 /50 about meeting up tomorrow. She does not like to be left on her own when she is feeling poorly.

Laura:

Oh sorry to hear that, sure just let me know tomorrow, no worries, hope your Mam feels well soon!

No reply. I wondered if he was giving me the brush off. It had only been one hour since I had replied. It was a nice reply though, if I had received a reply like that, I would definitely have said thank you!

Tuesday morning first thing I checked my phone. There was no message from Raj. Lunchtime Tuesday I checked my phone. There was no message from Raj.

At 5.05 pm *Beep, Beep* went my phone. It was Raj.

Hi Laura, I'm just finishing work and received a message from my mother, she is starting to feel better but asked if I would make her some chicken soup. So I was wondering... if I was lucky enough for you to be free to meet for the mini golf tomorrow instead?

Hmmm, I wondered if I should say yes straight away. To have another date with him would be great, but I was still a bit miffed at his lack of reply until now. Still, my options for tomorrow were to go on the date, or go to the gym, and I could always go to the gym after if I really wanted to. So I replied:

Glad to hear your Mam is on the road to recovery! Sure, tomorrow would be great if we can meet at a slightly earlier time, say 6pm?

Raj:
Great! It's a date ;)

Wednesday morning, I checked my phone on the bus on the way in to work, I had a message from Raj that morning.
Raj:
Morning gorgeous, looking forward to seeing you later! ;)

A big grin was plastered over my face all morning. How simple was I?! Reacting all girlie because Raj thought I was gorgeous!
Beep, Beep went my phone at 1.15pm, it was from Raj:

Hi Laura, I'm sorry to mess you around like this, but my Mother asked me to bring her home some lemon and ginger tea. She is very insistent, I guess she is just not a good patient, so I'm afraid I won't make it to mini golf this evening, I am so sorry.

Ah for the love of God - at least I could still get my gym session in. I would need it in advance of going to my friend's birthday party Friday night! I was already feeling like Raj may not be ideal date or wedding-plus-one material, part of me just wanted to let him go. However, I had an experiment to complete and the view is better from higher ground. They are the only reasons I bothered to reply.

Laura:

No problem at all, you are very good to your mother, she raised you well! I hope she feels better soon!

Raj was quick to reply:

Laura, I really am sorry, I really would like to see you again, are you free at the weekend? I know you mentioned going out Friday with your friends but how about Saturday day time?

Laura:

OK. Saturday we can do something, let's avoid any more attempts to play mini golf though!

Raj:

Saturday, we should have some fun! Have you been to that huge theme park outside the city? If not let's go, there!?

Laura:

Never been! Actually quite excited for this! That's a great idea!

Raj:

Perfect- just like you! I will pick you up at 10.30am sharp!

Ha '10:30 sharp', I laughed to myself, he was early for our first date, so I had no doubt Raj would definitely be on time! Unlike with Laughlann, this meant there would be no wriggle room with time for getting ready, I would have to time it to perfection!

Date 2 with Raj, The Accountant

Dating a non-drinker meant that this guy knew how to have fun the old fashioned way. His suggestion of going to an amusement theme park was brilliant! He was joking how his cousins in England were slagging him off about it. They told him us Irish were so obsessed with our potatoes, that our major theme park was named after a variation of our best known food! They seemed like a funny bunch, and were Raj's third most frequent topic of conversation, after his mother, then food.

I was excited to go to the amusement theme park, I had never been. The only thing was, I had a little bit of a fear of heights and of falling. Yes, I know that was a little dramatic. Still, no-one wanted a fear of pooping in their pants with anxiety on a date! Strategically, when we arrived, I suggested we do the tour of the food factory first, then go see the animals. By then it would surely be lunchtime, after which we could catch a bird show. It was a little bit chilly, and with any luck (it being Ireland) it might start to rain, and I could escape the giant, big rollercoaster under the pretense of not wanting to get wet!

The teeny tiny goats and donkeys were adorable. I couldn't stop gushing over them! I wanted to bring one home. He thought they were a little bit dirty. He did gush over the little children playing in the park though, openly stating he wanted a big family. I laughed not quite certain how serious he was.

A thorough wash of the hands later and we were off to lunch.

We assessed the menu, and looked at the carvery as it was being dished out. We looked at the food the adults were getting. We looked at the food the children were getting. The children were definitely getting the better deal. I nodded at the chicken goujons and chunky chips as if to say, that will do me nicely. Telepathically he understood and said "Yep, I'm getting that too," and we both laughed. Approaching the cashier, we were the chuckle couple as we ordered our juice with our kiddies meal deal.

"With any luck people will think we have children sitting over there somewhere, and we are getting it for them!" I whispered.

"And maybe one day we will," whispered Raj in return. His face blushed, he really was cute, and it was a fun day so far for sure!

We ate and chatted quite animatedly, both eager to speak, and both eager to listen to the other. Our thought processes were so aligned. I began to wonder would we end up as one of those couples who never EVER fought. Often people said there was a name for couples like that; divorced. Surely one or other party was holding back on opinions, but so far with Raj, this all felt real and legitimate. We were united across all topics.

As we finished lunch I checked the schedule, we would make the Bird Show if we went that way now.

"I'm excited to see the bird demonstration; I was at one before over near the Aliwee Caves. Have you ever been to one?" I asked.

"No, not yet, I have no idea if it will be any good or not."
"Ah it should be!"

We took our seats on the top row, but little did we realise it was right under a post for the birds to take flight, and land. The wind began to rise, and we felt a little chilly so we sat closer together; for the warmth of course. The first bird out was a secretary bird, neither of us had ever seen anything like it! It was hard to look at it and not laugh. Mostly a terrestrial bird, it had long legs like a crane and awkwardly stalked about on them with the body of an eagle looking for food from the demonstrator. The hair style of this bird is what caught most people's attention. It looked so funny, the bird gets its name from its crest of long feathers that look like the quill pens 19th century office workers- SECRETARIES- used to tuck behind their ears.

The bird show was entertaining and educational, there were eagles, owls, vultures and falcons from all over the world taking part in a free-flying demonstration. It was open air seating arena, and we felt the extra whizz of wind as eagles flew past during aerial displays.

When it dawned on me that we were immediately in front of where the birds walked, I was frightened. I put my hood up to shield myself from any poop, but also from any attacks. Knowing the world's largest eagles and fastest birds of prey were right behind me at times, and also flying overhead, I was genuinely petrified. Raj was a little scared too, but it seemed the more anxious I got, the more of a protective alpha male he became. I liked seeing this side of him. He put a protective arm around me. I felt warmer, and safer even though I scolded myself for thinking his arm was going to halt an angry bird at speed. Have you seen those guys fly!!! Of course we were never at any risk at all, the demonstrators had them totally under control!

It had not occurred to me before that moment, but being sober really heightened the way in which I experienced my emotions. The highs were really very high! Perhaps when October comes around I will go 'Teetotaler' for more than just Sober October!

After the Bird Show we wandered around some more. The water ride looked harmless enough compared to the huge roller coaster. It was really windy and cold at this stage. We got in line, but quickly reverted back to the shop for the poncho when we saw how wet other people were getting off it!! The ride was super splashy and a lot of fun. The cold water and the cold weather had my teeth chattering. This made it all the more unexpected when Raj planted a kiss on my cheek when we finally made it out from the last dive into water! We both began to giggle, it was so childish and funny. Thankfully there was a human sized cave which was really an air drier to stand inside, and get warmed up. It was pure heaven! Just at that moment, the rain kicked off and neither of us wanted to get wet again. We agreed it was a good time to hit the road. It was such a fun day out, and Raj was a total gent throughout, and also a smooth driver it must be said! A lot of people in the city do not drive. I do understand that it is not a necessity, but, it is nice to have the freedom and luxury to be able to have these types of random adventures!

We agreed to meet again on Monday after work for some tea and cake. Dating Raj was a breeze! That was until Raj's mother phoned while we were in the car on the way back. She was livid with Raj for having left his phone in the car while we were in the theme park. There was nothing wrong, but she was worried when he didn't answer. I overheard her say to him, how a nice girl wouldn't keep a son out of touch from his mother. I could see his face flush, but he didn't defend me, he simply apologised to his mother.

Date 3 with Raj, The Accountant

Monday ended up a long experimental day in the lab for me. Raj had a long day of audits. We moved our date first from 5.30 pm to 6.30 pm, and then to 7.30 pm. We were both exhausted by the time we got to the quirky little café in Dundrum. We both ordered coffee and cake; mine was a tiramisu and his was a lemon cheesecake.

The conversation was silly, and we were giddy with over-tiredness. Raj's phone was buzzing away. I told him he should answer it. He said it wasn't important. A few minutes later, the colour drained from Raj's face. I turned to see what had got his attention. I knew immediately that it had to be his mother.

"Raj, there you are, why are you not answering your phone? Did SHE put you up to it?" Nodding in my direction but not looking me in the eye.

"What is that you are eating?" She continued "I hope that is not the Baileys cheesecake. Is SHE making you take alcohol without you knowing!?"

I sat in silence. Genuinely gob smacked. He sat in silence too, and let her rant on. When she finally drew breath Raj said,

"No, Mam, this is the lemon cheesecake with no alcohol. No alcohol at all. What Laura is eating is tiramisu and there is only alcohol flavouring in it. She is driving of course, so of course no alcohol."

I could feel his mother's eyes boring into me. Ordinarily I would have stood up and greeted her, but at that point in time, I didn't know what to do. We sat in silence with her glaring at him, then me, on repeat for what felt like a lifetime. Eventually the shock passed and I remembered how to speak.

"Hello my name is Laura, please to meet …"

"I know who you are, keeping my son out all day at the weekend and now look at him. He needs his rest. He has a very important job and works hard at it. Raj I will be 15 minutes in the grocery store and you will drive me home, thank you."

And just as quickly as she arrived, she was gone!

We sat in silence. I let a whole 2 minutes go by, before asking Raj if what happened, had actually just happened! I said it was clear his mother had an issue with me, and I wanted to know what it was. If he knew, I wanted him to tell me. I asked if it was my faith. He said no. He said his mother was happy for him to marry any woman who believed in one God - that meant the Jews, the Christians and the Muslims were all fine. He then said, that his family however had been helping his younger sister find a husband. Apparently, they found a very suitable man for her, from a wonderful family. However, this family did not approve of partners who did not follow Islam, and that Raj dating me, was putting his sister's marriage at risk. His sister had met the man once and said he was ok. If she was crazy about him, Raj would stop dating me. However, he insisted that his sister spend some more time with the man to be sure.

"So Raj, when were you going to tell me any of this, if your mother had not made her grand appearance this evening?"

"I don't know. I was kind of hoping my sister would not really like the guy."

"That is a pretty lame answer. You also did not really defend me in front of your mother, who was quite rude to me."

"I know. I know but she is my mother."

"OK. Well you better give your mother a lift home."

With that, I got up and left. I was baffled at Raj. I was impressed with the power his mother had over him. Most of all though, I really just wanted my bed! I was done with the drama, and he was more friend than boyfriend material anyway. I really needed to get my sleep in. I wanted to get a good work out in the morning before meeting Candidate 5 the next day. He was a Personal Trainer and Nutritionist. As soon as I got in the door, I left a voice note for the girls on the Review Board, mentioning the need for a modification to the selection process to eliminate men with interfering mothers, and fell into bed!

Phase 2, Man 2, Candidate 5, Andrew, The Personal Trainer and Nutritionist

We matched on the 'limited information' dating app. His name was Andrew, and according to his profile he had studied at a north side university and was just home following 3 years in New Zealand. He looked a little preppy. He was possibly a little on the short side, but perhaps that was just due to how bulky he was. He definitely knew what items not to stand beside, so no one could quite ascertain his height. Perhaps he was a pro at advertising himself, or was this a sign he knew his camera angles. Serious camera angle trickery always makes me dubious - what could he be hiding, is he a conman?

Over a few evenings messaging I learned he was from Cork originally. He had previously lived in Dublin and his brother and sister lived there too. Thus, he said it was a natural progression for him to move to Dublin upon returning from New Zealand.

He didn't drink. He was a non-drinker, a teetotaler. Why did this feel strange? I was OK with it when it was for religious reasons. Surely it was good thing he didn't drink. I wondered if he ever drank? Or maybe he was drunk driving and was in accident, and something serious happened, and so he swore never to drink again? Maybe that's why he moved to New Zealand? Maybe he lost his drivers' licence and had to go away until he could drive in Ireland again? Or maybe he was drunk and got into a fight with his best friend, and he swore he would never drink again until they made up? Or maybe he was a closet gay and was too afraid to drink in case the truth came out? I didn't want to be a beard!!! Or maybe.....or maybe I should just ask him?

So I asked about the non-drinker side of things. He told me it was not the complete truth but that he had two reasons for stating he was a non-drinker on the dating app. The first, was that in the past he had encountered women who just wanted a night out on the town with him paying for expensive cocktails.

(Can I just say that whoever those ladies are, need to give the rest of us ladies lessons in this! A few free drinks would be great! Though, thus far however, it has always been a case of taking it in turns to buy the drinks. I have yet to receive a night of free drink! I always feel bad if the guy pays for dinner, then I insist on either splitting the bill or buying the next one - even if I didn't want another date - the guilt would just eat me up.)

This Andrew guy was not into plying the ladies with drink, or at least he was not into that anymore. (Ha, or maybe he used to be cash rich and loved to flaunt it, and now he was a poor, tight, git, perhaps I could investigate?!) The second reason was because he was a personal trainer and a nutritionist. Now don't judge me, to be fair with the number of them on the apps it was impossible to avoid!

I do think with regards to his argument and rationale for stating he was a non-drinker; he should have led with the health issue! I told him as much, and he actually thanked me for my feedback. Yes, he used the word feedback. Was I engaged in a survey I was not aware of? Was I market research tool? This guy was already entering the difficult to like zone, but, he was very handsome and we were approaching the one week of messaging mark, surely a date was imminent.

Thankfully in his photo's he didn't look like he was a sunbed user, or flash himself as one of those body builder guys greased up on oily tan for competitions. He also wasn't all THAT muscular, in the sense you know you wouldn't need to test him for steroids! A little shy on leg day too it would seem.

Photos on apps can leave you perplexed. The guns of steel flexed in photos suggesting arms of lead, can be confounded by the next photo where mysteriously appears an abdomen of lard, a.k.a, the beer belly. This look is often completed with pasty white chicken legs (sure you just can't skip leg day-ladies, am I right?). My mind wandered to the Irish rugby team, now they were men who knew about not skipping leg day!

It should be noted, far from perfect am I, on more than one occasion I have pulled out the "flowy top" to hide a less-than flat stomach. I would be highly surprised at this stage if all genders have not received the same online dating app photo advice: Insert photos that are flattering but not filtered, along with everyday photos of your current activities. The hope is the person you match with has done similar. That way you recognize the person who shows up on the date too!

There was also no way of telling what his natural hair texture was like. To achieve that quiff, there was a lot of gel and/or hair spray required. He was an image man. Not many image men were also intellectually challenging men. Extreme time on image did not often allow for full intellectual development - I am biased of course, and so that is why I must date him to find out!

He was keen to meet up soon. The reason behind it could be good or bad. There was only one way to find out! We agreed to meet at Stephen's Green after work, and get some steps in walking. If the walking went well, we agreed to have dinner at a roof top restaurant with a swing! With his nutritionist obsession with food, at least one conversation starter could be the macro content of the meal! Was I awful to think that perhaps I could use the information I had learned from Raj to impress this guy too?

Date 1 with Andrew, The Personal Trainer

The evening before our date my mind began to wonder about the passage of time, men and dating. I wondered if men who worked with human bodies for a living such as doctors, nurses, physiotherapists, and personal trainers paid extra attention to a woman's physique when dating? Or, perhaps they were desensitised?

Women and men are not the same, but will there ever be equality unless it takes women and men the same amount of time and effort in preparation for a first date? Goodness knows this dating business was really testing my time management. No matter how early I got up in the morning to do my hair and makeup, there was no way I could possibly arrive to the after work date looking blemish free, with dewy fresh skin, and bouncy, shiny, stylish hair!

I would be wind swept as a result of the journey in to work alone! Any attempt at sultry eye makeup would be wasted, and the risk of smudging the makeup around my eyes was high! This was mostly due to my boss and his newly adopted cat! I like cats - but I don't love them, mostly because I am super allergic to them. The slightest proximity to their hair makes my eyes itchy and watery, and my eyelids swell like I had done 10 rounds with Katie Taylor. (Realistically I couldn't last even one!)

My boss was besotted with his cat and religiously spent his mornings before coming into work feeding, playing and photographing the cat. This was evident by the hair balls on his work clothes, and by 9.15 am I could feel the itch begin! No point doing the makeup in the morning, I would just have to get dolled up after work.

I would have to pack a backpack tonight to bring to work in the morning. The one thing in my favour was that tomorrow was a data analysis day, so I could wear nice clothes in the office without worrying about anything in the lab or on my lab coat getting on my dress.

First, I would need my makeup essentials: moisturiser, primer, concealer, foundation, blusher and blusher brush, bronzer and bronzer brush, contour and highlighter chubby sticks, eyeshadow palette, one singular blending brush and the greatest thing since sliced bread, my double ended mascara. One end lengthened and the other end volumised! Speaking of volume, I would also need a small comb, large rollers and hair spray; and, deodorant, perfume and of course my heels!

Hmm maybe I should pack some Vaseline to rub on my heels and my baby toe just in case the shoes hurt after a while. Prolonged sitting during the day, combined with heels, and alcohol if I was tempted to have just one, was surely a recipe for cankles (calves that run into your ankles with swelling) and once that happens blisters have potential to form. No man was worth that! I packed the Vaseline!

Lastly I packed a few lip liners and lipsticks in reds, pinks and nudes - because it was getting late and I just couldn't decide. Reds make your teeth look white, pinks make you feel more girly, and nudes were quite chic and trendy. This was definitely a tough call - one for tomorrow! Does everyone pack their makeup bag in the order they apply products I wondered?

Thankfully the next day I got in early and checked my emails to discover I would be in the shared office alone that day, even the technical lab staff were on a training day so there would be absolutely no interruptions. Fantastic! I practically ran down the corridor to the bathroom with my squishy rollers in my bag. If I was quick enough, no one would see what I was doing and no one would ever know! I set my hair up in my large rollers, spritzed a bit of hair spray for extra hold and darted back to the office without being seen.

5 pm arrived quite smoothly, I pulled my rollers out and proceeded to pursue operation transformation in front of the bathroom mirror. After 5 pm there was always a bit of competition for the mirror in the ladies' bathroom. All my time spent watching makeup tutorials online was paying off. I was pleased with my artwork in the bathroom mirror, even though the mirror was serious high spec, and displayed every flaw with high resolution. This, in combination with harsh bathroom lighting made me even more delighted with my look when I eventually felt half decent, because I knew I would look even better in literally ANY other lighting.

With a half confidence about me, I headed off to meet my date! Though the sun was shining, it was quite blustery. I spotted him from quite a distance away. He was wearing a navy and white peaky cap. This was a planned part of his outfit. He had informed me he would wear it to help me find him in the park. This was in case I was too obsessed with his body and forgot what his face looked like, he said! What a cheeky confidence! In return, just as promised, I was wearing my third favourite scarf which was a delicate bright red beauty.

A millisecond later he recognised me too, and while I couldn't quite make out his expression at first, I could see a big white smile forming. Ordinarily this would have made me feel at ease, but then I realised his blindingly bright, white smile was packed with big false veneers. I was hoping he was not the type who was in pursuit of perfection. Maybe he was just an insecure guy who thought a new smile would give him confidence.

He was in fact, tall and handsome. So with his mouth shut, he was definitely my type on paper. His accent was so strong. Apparently those years in Dublin and New Zealand did nothing to his vocal chords. I reckoned those years away in Dublin were really 10 years of 'Monday morning to Friday afternoon' in Dublin, then it was straight back to Cork boi! This man is all the evidence I need to believe that the further south in Ireland you go, the accent picks up in pitch and pace! The comical nature of his high pitched accent was masked by his evident maturity. He asked all the right questions, I don't think I ever felt the effort with which someone was trying to make me feel comfortable so quickly before. As soon as I realised this though, I began to wonder if he was actually a shark leading me into a false sense of security. Time would tell!

Physically speaking you would definitely not put us together. Objectively, I knew I was physically less fit than he was- by a mile! Yet, that did not seem to be holding him back. He seemed to be very intrigued by our conversation. We were talking about how we got to where we are in our careers. I guess meeting up straight from work meant talking about it was inevitable.

He asked so much about my work, my background and education. Some of this was on my profile. His eyes opened wide with delight when I assured him that yes I did have a PhD. Yes, I explained further that I understood how drugs and food interacted with the body on more than a basic level. He was so impressed. He asked about my colleagues, and my friends and what areas they worked in and were interested in. There was an edge to his questioning though. I couldn't quite put my finger on it. My uneasy feeling was more than just irritation at his fixation on earning more money. He saw his role as earning money through the need and desire for people to look good. It seems that was what "health" meant to him.

People say your health is your wealth, he was all about lining his own pockets, to him, your health was his wealth. He was all about the money, or maybe he wasn't explaining himself very well. He had the cheek to ask me how much I earned!

I explained to him that for me it wasn't so much about ambition or money, rather I loved to learn and challenge myself. Learning something interesting is what motivates me, understanding new methods and processes to serve the greater good and if I can help the more vulnerable people in some way while doing it – all the better!

He was certainly keen to let me know how ambitious he was. Last year he qualified as a personal trainer and was in the process of writing a book on his methods for optimum training for lads to get the ladies. I didn't quite like his tone on this topic. He was clearly new to the PT world and this was becoming a saturated market, but maybe his borderline objectifying, misogynistic ways would get him attention. Maybe his approach was that there was no such thing as bad publicity?

While I was happy he was so enthusiastic, I wondered to myself about his potential for success, which, unfortunately to me seemed low. This was not because I had social circles of personal trainers or dieticians but based on the dating apps alone. Every third or fourth guy was a personal trainer. The pictures were mostly great to look at. Health and fitness is certainly topical and trending, and important. To make a break for yourself however, you would need a different approach, something that was unique, and an added extra that no one else, or very few had. Standing out on your own in that profession would be difficult. In particular, my concern was that he did not seem to be very well connected or even know his competition. Although he was only too delighted to take on board areas he should be addressing from a business perspective.

"We'd make a great team!" he told me with a wink and a laugh.

"I'll stick to the day job of what I know, thanks!" I laughed back.

Our chat went straight to the benefits of walking, and how our generation of office workers were a little on the sedentary side - bring on the desk-exercise!

We were in agreement; at our age we should be smarter than to lead inactive lifestyles. We have access to so much information online and through various media platforms regarding our health. Surely we owe it to our present and future selves to take healthy action now, to preserve life-long health?

His theory was that we don't stop exercising because we become older, but rather we become older because we stop exercising. To be fair, he had a point! This is something the Review Board and I work together on with our hiking, and our training for the Dublin City Marathon. He believed what most people struggle with is diet, he was another individual presenting diet as your medicine or your poison. I chuckled when he described that concept as hard for people to *swallow*, and adhere to. At this point, feeling a bit guilty, but with the need to interject stronger, I reminded him eating clean all the time is easier said than done. When the pastries are presented at meetings, and a glass of wine with the ladies turns into a half bottle - all we can do is try!

The chat was interesting, no sign of any real chemistry though, just good intellectual conversation. We were just straight out of our respective offices so smart work chat was bound to happen. I guess it would only be fair to go for dinner if he suggested it. Telepathically he looked a little sheepish and asked,

"So, em, Laura, this is going well as far as the chat is concerned, so I was thinking maybe we should go get food, get some nourishment?"

I was not expecting him to come across so shyly.

"Of course Andrew, sure we have to eat, right?"

At the entrance to the restaurant we couldn't pass the famous swing! We took turns sitting on it to have our picture taken, all I could see were his teeth, oh his teeth were just so, so white. He asked for a selfie with him, of course I agreed making sure I smiled with a half pout of pursed lips. I was not letting my nashers be compared to his! He looked at the snap of us and then he looked at me.

"Do you wear glasses?", he asked.

"No, why?"

"I think you would look extra super smart, and sexy if you did, you know."

I wasn't sure how to respond to that statement, and was quite happy to switch topic as the waitress came and took us to our table. We selected the two course deal. Usually my temptation would be for a main course and dessert. Following the conversations around diet, of course the only option was to have a starter and a main, what a pity!

He selected the wings as a starter. Correct me if I am wrong, but the wings in combination with the associated sauce must have close to a thousand calories in it!! A sorbet desert would have been much less calorific, and please don't tell me it was all about the protein content of the wings! It surely was not!

Having gorged on his chicken wings, he proceeded to horse his dinner into him. The food went in so fast, I doubt he tasted it. I thought at one point he was choking for a split second on a fish bone. This was before I realised he had a cough, and proceeded to cough with the worst cough etiquette I have ever seen. No, he did not cough into his elbow, or his napkin, or even his hand. Instead it was an open mouthed hack to the side of the table. I said nothing, my face said everything, he didn't notice and continued to chug back his water. I just thanked my lucky stars he didn't cough in my face!

So apart from the grotesque coughing incident, I could really only say at best the date was ok. He was inquisitive and interested and very present, except while eating. Having only encountered reasonably good dates during this experiment I wouldn't mind if there were no further dates with this guy. I was not going to flirt or show any further interest. If he wished to pursue things further I would for the sake of the experiment, but the dinner really put me off him.

Date 2 with Andrew, The Personal Trainer

Ladies, isn't it always the way?! When you are not interested in someone they make a lot of contact! Andrew was no different. Before I made it home I had received not one, but two essay type text messages from him. In summary he thought we got on really well, that our conversations were high level and that he suspected I didn't meet many men who could hold those types of conversation (hello mister cocky). When he finally finished blowing his own trumpet, he got around to saying he wanted to meet me again on Friday.

For our next date he decided he wanted to break his rule of not drinking and said we deserved a night on the town.

It seemed to me that he was falling into a category in between shy and sly. I didn't like this territory of no-man's land. This is where you could get tricked. Tricked into a false sense of security when no man's land veered towards shy; and at risk of totally writing someone off when no man's land followed a demeanor towards sly.

The date started well, the bar I picked near Baggot Street was busy. There was good music and a general buzz after the rugby game; Munster, his Province, had been playing.

In an attempt to get to know him better, I decided to ask if he or any of his family were into ruby or other sports. I thought this would be met with a resounding yes for at least one sport given his chosen profession! He completely shut this topic down. He didn't talk much about family apart from early text messages about his siblings living in Dublin. It was clear discussing family was a no-go area, which was to me a red flag, a bad sign. Family is personal, and in my experience if you do not talk about family on your first few dates that was (not exclusively but) often due to two reasons.

1) He was disconnected from his family. This was the least terrible scenario. This could be for any number of reasons. However, I knew I wanted a person who was as connected to their family as I was with mine. 'Baggage issues' were not on my agenda. Surely it wasn't wrong to wish to attract a clean and clear-cut guy as my plus one. Drama was not something I was ready to welcome into my life - not yet anyway!

2) He was a player. He was closed. Inaccessible. Not interested in anything other than - well, you know what.

The sensible one on the Review Board would say the majority of men were like that, and, in general, I might be inclined to agree with her on this at times. However, there were a plethora of men who at least *tried* to hide the fact they had a priority agenda, and at least *made the effort* to make you feel special.

The next pub was his selection. I didn't get to see the name on the way in, the street was so jammed with people. Jeez! Was he trying to put me off him?! Three breaths into the building and it was **definitely** a man's pub. Good grief! I had to peg my nose! The air was different in here. My super expensive (only for special occasions) perfume would surely be drowned out in here. There was not another female in sight. A slight, or more frail woman would not be caught dead in here! Or rather, the only way a woman would be found in here, was dead!!

He said it was usually a quiet pub, but with the rugby on it was jammers. He suggested we try a different street, Dawson street - and my heart, mood and smile lifted! I always had a good night on Dawson street. Dawson Street meant pub crawling, singing, and my absolute favourite - DANCING!

He didn't strike me as a dancer though. This would be interesting. I was chatting away to the barman having a laugh. Man the music was good in this place. OOOOOHHH and I bagsied myself a seat in a booth. There was another girl on the other end, plenty of room for us both to sit at the table and have our men, remain manly and upright.

The girl was really friendly and chatty. We got on like a house on fire. Unintentionally Andrew and I were matching in maroon and black outfits. Likewise, my new best friend forever in the booth, and her partner were in matching outfits too. She was in checkered mini skirt and her man in a checkered shirt. How funny, I thought, it was like a double date. The girl noticed we were a little 'matchy, matchy', which just made it easier for us to be instant BFFs. The kind you meet on a night out and never see or hear of again! We ended up singing into pretend microphones and laughing uncontrollably. This was followed by shots and dancing! There was frig all interaction with Andrew.

Although at one point he did seem to make some sort of …well I guess you could call it a move. He complimented me on my jewellery. In particular, he complimented the ring on my left middle finger. He removed it for a closer inspection. Then taking my hand he returned it to my index finger, before slowly taking it off and sliding it half way down my middle finger, then grinned again removing it, and placed it on my wedding ring finger, and told me that was not the only ring he would be putting on that finger! Of course I found this sweet, cringe worthy and hilarious all at the same time.

Apart from that, even with drink on board, he was minus craic! (You know that is when quantifying the level of fun, he was sub-zero!) I was having mighty craic, entertaining myself and those around me. I just had forgotten how much fun I could be, even solo!

He began to get a bit slimey, you know all the B.S. men throw at you when they want to try take you home for the night. Apparently I was so pretty, he couldn't imagine waking up to a more beautiful face. I'm sorry mister but you would have to come up with something more original, and witty to even get me to kiss you, the state you are in, I thought to myself!

He began twisting his head from left to right in search of something before shouting in my ear. "Hold on I'm just heading to the smoking area for a fag I'll be back!"

What the heck! I thought to myself, so much for mister healthy. Mister fraud more like! I watched him go, thinking he would have to bum a cigarette off someone, but nope! He had a packet and a lighter in his jeans pocket! I started to think all his positivity and health crap was really his best attempt at a sales pitch.

When he came out from the smoking area he spotted a friend of his, by the looks of things in the same trade as he was. Andrew beckoned me over with his arm, as if he was doing a breast stroke with one arm. I slowly walked on over.

"Simon mate this is DOCTOR LAURA, she totally gets why we need to keep people fit and healthy. She is going to be my new client, the face of the brand. Hasn't she just got such a pretty face."

I laughed along at these two knuckle heads, before saying "No, no, no, I have nothing to do with whatever he is up to."

We all were laughing. The eyes on Simon suggested he wasn't really on planet earth at the moment, and I doubt he would remember anything Andrew said. So I left the bar and headed to the Shelbourne in an attempt to shake him, unfortunately Andrew followed.

I think I had brain fog as a result of Andrew's height or something. This has always been my handicap - I could never tell on the initial date or two if a tall guy was attractive, physically or personality wise, or if he was just tall? Gosh it would definitely take another date to begin to draw any sort of real conclusion. Even with drinks on board my gut told me he was absolutely no good.

I was getting annoyed at myself. For all my education and all the years of human evolution how had this cave woman concept remained? Even when I was consciously trying to avoid it! It was baffling. This idea that a man bigger than myself could somehow protect me in this day and age, was ridiculous! Protect me from what I wondered?! Never the less I would need to take time to assess his face and personality properly, up to this point his height could have tricked me into more dates, even if his face was the male version of the female "butter-face". From the get-go his teeth were too much. His voice interrupted my thoughts.

"Laura, Laura, seriously though with you backing me, you know we could be great. Have you plans to change your body? You know, get fitter. You would need to be *really* thin for this to work best. Then maybe get a boob job? A picture of you with glasses on would totally add to the image!"

That was it, I knew immediately that even though I was nicer than him, smarter than him, earned more than him, made him laugh way more than any polite half laugh I gave him out of sympathy, did not judge outwardly his complete lack of business acumen, comment on his snobby attitude and lack of anything to back it up, and while my face satisfied him no end - unless I ticked the stick thin profile, and resultantly needed a boob job for the fat loss in that area - he was going to think of me as "less than", or "not what he was after".

Perhaps I should have been upset, or mortified by the fact we had gone out for dinner and how he had watched me eating, when all the while he was thinking was that I was too fat for him and his plan? Yet he wanted me to go home with him? Yet he wanted to see my pretty face when he woke up!? Yet he wanted *my* title, *my* merit, *my* knowledge, and *my* social circles to support *his* **stupid** idea, that let's face it was doomed to fail.

I was annoyed at him for being a prick, at myself for thinking he could be anything more than that, and most of all I was annoyed with the stupid surroundings for being so uppity that I could not cause a scene. Like it, or lump it I thought to myself, I didn't like the situation I was in, but there were 20 taxis lined up outside to take me wherever I wanted to go.

And they did not care what my body plans were!!!!

Date 3 with Andrew, The Pri**, oops Personal Trainer

Even though I gave him zero attention since our night out, he wanted to go on another date. He even had the nerve to attempt to scold me for not giving him enough attention at the start of the night. I did my best to hold back from telling him, that the reason for that was mostly because he was a boring old fart. This is a comment I have about a lot of men. Do you ever find yourself being the life and soul of the party, even if it's just a party of the two of you? Yes, it is great that the person you are dating thinks you are lots of fun, and really entertaining, but who is entertaining you? Are you always the provider of the giggles? I think the man who ultimately wins me over will have to be able to make me laugh, and this guy really doesn't.

Andrew insisted he had something to chat to me about that he thought I would really want to hear it. My initial thought was, well of course he is going to apologise, but then I realised, he was not well mannered. I wonder what else it could be. It had mostly all been career chat really, so far. I had described him as worse than vomit to the girls on my last voice message to them. They all insisted I didn't have to meet him if I didn't want to. I said I was only going to see what he had to say out of curiosity and amusement.
This guy was a nobody, going nowhere. He didn't even have an idea about an idea.

We were to meet at Stephen's Green again to do a couple of laps and then eat our lunch outside. He was sitting on a bench chatting to someone on the phone. I overheard him say "Yeah, I'll run the idea by her now, she will be eating out of my hands."

"Those hands?" I said out loud sitting beside him, I had a half smile on my face but I knew he was talking about me when I saw the colour drain from his face. I had only come to hear the apology, then I was leaving, and I was happy with my decision. Anything he had to say beyond that was going to be entertainment value purposes only. So I waited for him to get off the phone and let him speak first.

He attempted to give me a peck on the lips but I presented my cheek, and asked what it was he was so keen to speak to me about. He told me he would speak to me about it over food and proceeded to unpack his lunch. He ate like a skinny girl on a skinny girl diet. This made me feel really uncomfortable. I had not noticed this on our restaurant date. Was he actually counting his chews before swallowing?

He began to chat all about his new product that he was giving his clients to lose weight and gain muscle while working with him as a personal trainer. It was his secret formula.

I didn't need to wonder if he only matched with me online to try recruit me as a client. Of course it would be good for his business to transform me into a fitness fanatic. My Dr title backing his method would surely be good for business. I admired his ingenuity, but I was not going to allow myself to be used. More to the point, I already thought he was a failure. "So what is all this about your secret formula? Do you mean the routine of workouts you specifically design for clients' individual needs, combined with a diet plan for them based on their body mass composition, lifestyle and health needs?" I asked. This was standard issue material.

"No, no, I don't believe in that at all." That was my first confirmation that he was climbing up the wrong tree. "It's very simple, all the best ideas are simple you know." This he said as if he was trying to convince me of something.

No, mister, I thought to myself, *you* are simple. To be honest, the seeds of doubt were well planted in my mind already. A lot of people like to sell the idea of things being simple but I decided I would hear him out.

"Ok, so if it is so simple and no one else has come up with it, then you could help a lot of people right? That does sound exciting!"

"Yes," his eyes lit up with delight when I agreed with him. "And make a lot of money!"

Oh now I did not like that his primary focus was on making money. When money is the driver behind a so-called 'passion', it really did not sound too good.

"Right so what is the secret formula?"

"How about we do a deal Laura? You are my secret asset! We would make a great team! I will train you and give you a fake tablet to take for 12 weeks? You will train hard, not eat, and be a lean, mean, green machine by the time I am finished with you! Think about it, with you, and your background promoting me, I will be destined for success!"

This guy was a joke, a bad one, he didn't make me laugh not even once. All he was trying to do was use me to be some sort of brand ambassador for himself. While simultaneously trying to get me to be his client and change how I looked! No way could I sit through another lunch with him.

Another date, or evening, never mind attendance at a wedding with this type of guy would be an uncomfortable and horrible waste of existence. I knew he would be another "Mr step of the plane and never look back" kind of guy. A guy who loved everything about me on paper, loved how well I reflected on him, but would always nit-pick and try to change me.

After I left a calm voice note to the girls on the Review Board. I informed them of the full conversation exchanges I had with Andrew over the past two days. Nothing was omitted, I did not say how any of the conversations made me feel. I was in pure scientist mode. Record and report the facts and move on.

As soon as I stopped recording the voice note, I began thinking about my ex, and then The Radiographer. If either of those had to have behaved better, I would not be in the position I was in now. I felt my bottom lip begin to quiver.

My mascara was on point so I would be damned if I were to let the thoughts of any man ruin it. There was 20 minutes left on my lunch break, I picked up my phone, found Maria in my contacts and hit dial. I needed to convert my upset into anger before I went back to work. Upset leads to moping and slow sluggish sorrow, but anger, anger can be converted to a fiery energetic wave of productivity, and Maria would sort me out!

Phase 2, Man 3, Candidate 6, Daniel, The Carpenter

Two days after the final disastrous date with Andrew the PT, I took myself off to the hairdressers. You can eat all the good stuff, do all the exercise, but nothing really sets your heart on fire like a well done mane! Ordinarily this was a task that I dreaded. Too many times the hair dresser chopped off more than requested, or added layers thinning my hair, when all that was coveted was thick luscious locks! Sometimes the "colourist" packed the high lights so tight it looked like a block colour. Please do not get me started on the blow dry, that left my already naturally straight hair appearing glued in a flat line against my face. How could anyone think that was flattering?!

"A man's crown in glory is his woman, and a woman's crown in glory is her hair!" These words like so many from my Auntie Rose were the key to a happy life, or at least, in this case happy hair! Getting the style just right was not an easy task, but essential. Yes, these were first world problems, but it was my first world, hard earned cash that was paying for it! This time was different, and one full head of low-lights later, I was a rich, warm, chestnut brown! Gone was my blonde look, it had taken two years to get used to, and Brunette Laura was back! The joy of how well, and how shiny my hair turned out, was only slightly marred by the thought I was turning into a total cliché of "New Man, New Hair, New Me!"

Date 1 with Daniel, The Carpenter

Would my date freak out, I wondered, since all of my photos online were with a slightly different look? Apart from that, I had no nerves at all. This was a simple next candidate date, and if it went well it would help to oust the negativity Andrew had left behind.

We were to meet at the top of the West Pier in Dun Laoghaire. That was something that didn't sit right in my head. Dun Laoghaire was on the East Coast of Ireland so why was there an East and West Pier? Surely it should be North and South depending on which one was further up or down the coast? Who am I to question the sea bearing ways! As it turned out, the more southerly pier was the East one. I parked the car, and checked my makeup in the mirror.

West Pier was quite different to the East pier; some middle aged folk were swimming in the sea, and even with sunglasses on, the sea glistened. There was a tidy neat cut grass area with wooden picnic benches, and tables to sit at. A man and his dog finished their snack and I seized the opportunity to perch at their table. Despite the calm the rippling waves brought, a trickle of nervousness crept in. Then I saw him. Dressed in sports clothes, he was tanned. His clothes were not tight, but you could tell he was toned. He smiled broadly at me and my nerves disappeared. He was lean, clean shaven, and blonde. He had an altar-boy innocent look about him; similar to how he looked in his photos.

He walked right up to me and said "Hey, I'm Daniel" and gave me a hug. We walked to the nearest coffee chain store, got our coffee to-go and began our first lap of Dun Laoghaire.

"The passenger in that car is oogling at you and winking," he said, "who is?" I asked, but before Daniel had time to answer, I heard the roar of the three-cylinder gas engine, battery assisted all-wheel drive belonging to the white and blue BMW i18. I was briefly distracted while I recognized the national treasure, that was the MMA champ spinning around in his toy on his way to the yacht club, and his passenger was cute!

Daniel was flattering me of course, though until that point I hadn't been able to tell how well he liked me. I wondered if it was the sun, that kept his pupils tight, if he fancied me they should be dilating, right? That's what the magazines say anyway. Making a mental note to google reasons for pin point pupils after the date, I kept on walking and talking.

Granted he was the first mid- thirties guy I dated, but I wasn't quite prepared for all the future planning questions he was throwing at me. He commented on how women his age would always ask about settling down, and how many babies they wanted. Suddenly I felt under prepared. In my mind I would find a boyfriend, then after some time talk about marriage and babies and dogs, not on the first date! Was this something that happened once you turned thirty? Were you just supposed to switch on maternal and wife-y instincts?! The baby thing was bugging me, I was still on the fence for many reasons, but I wasn't going to get into that with him yet! I wished sensible Anne was there to rhyme off the litany of reasons not to procreate. For now, all I wanted to do was keep my mouth shut and let Daniel do the talking on these topics.....my gut was telling me he had more to say on the matter, and he did.

What was this intrigue with the number of babies I might want, I wondered? Was he forward planning his finances? Did he already know he didn't want any? Maybe he couldn't have children? My mind wandered. It was cool that he was interested in my work asking questions about blood, but he was like a man possessed, he even asked about my blood type.

I only know my blood type because I am a blood donor. I remembered feeling a bit ordinary when I learned I had the most common blood type, O positive. When I told him that he smiled. He said he wanted to have a number of children, but his ex- girlfriend was rhesus negative, and while a first baby would be fine, there was a high risk for any babies thereafter.

I couldn't help but immediately ask if that was why they split up!? He assured me it was not, but now it is something he was aware of, he was going to ask women this before taking dating further. I thought about asking why he was aware of it but to be honest, I just wanted to get off the baby chat.

As that conversation came to a close, he pulled me in tight, to rescue me! A bike went swerving past us almost knocking us over! A push bike at that! He had really gathered some speed! "Look, look! The speedometer for the cars is picking up his speed, 42 km per hour!"

"Ha, I wonder does it pick up pedestrian speed, or does it not detected below a certain threshold? Or maybe it doesn't detect movement below a certain size or shape? Like it hardly picks up the speed of the dogs running by? Or *does* it?" I asked. Nothing like a near-crash to get the brain juices going.

"Only one way to find out!" Daniel answered raising his brows.

He handed me his keys (many), wallet (chunky), and his phone (unscratched). He was either ridiculously trusting of me not to run off with the lot, or more likely he knew that if I did, he would easily catch me!

We walked back along the road for him to get a good run at it. He began to run, and the speedometer reached 15.6 km per hour. He was holding his head up at a funny angle to read the speedometer while he ran. I reckoned he could go faster, and told him so.

"Ok I'll run straight and not look up, no distractions, and you tell me how fast I get to."

We moved back even further to really let him get a fast sprint at it.

On his approach I told him, "Ok you are past 15, past 16, holy cow 18.3 km per hour it went to! That's fast!"

"You better believe I am fast," he flashed me a wink and knowing grin.

Ha, he was a cheeky devil. Eventually we returned to the benches where we sat straddled and facing each other. The chats had been great, but the evening grew chilly. I decided it was time to go. We had traversed 8 km of Dun Laoghaire, who would have thought it! I had not expected this date to go this well. Well, that was until he leaned in for a kiss.

"Oh I don't kiss on a first date" I said, and his face grew cold. He stared at me with a big dirty frown. I edged back. He took a deep breath like he was calming himself, it was so strange.

"Ok, cool," he said, "I get it, you are playing hard to get. I like a challenge."

I really wasn't, the date was good but, I had no idea about him really or what germs he might have had. I gave him a flirty smile and waited to see what else he might say.

"Let's walk again, tomorrow, indulge me?" With his alter-boy face, sure how could I say no.

Date 2 with Daniel, The Carpenter

I think the cunning of my previous candidate had hardened me to this process. My heart was closed but my mind was open. This was a second sober date, also at the seaside, would this earn Daniel, The Carpenter brownie points on the score boards I wondered. I was in the zone. Ready to complete the task at hand. We were going to meet in Dun Laoghaire and then go to Dalkey. Only a short beautiful journey down the coast with the sun beginning to go down. I was liking this sober dating business.

The outdoors was stunning and right on my doorstep. The visual experience of the surroundings, and the handsome man at the wheel were so much better when all my senses were on red hot steamy alert. I imagined I wouldn't appreciate the simple pleasures if I was in an intoxicated state. He pulled in at the side of the road. There were benches to sit on.

We climbed up on them, and we placed our feet on the seat part, with our bums on the top of the back support. This gave us the extra height advantage. From there, the burnt orange hue of the sun cast a firey glow on the sea. He noticed the tiny hairs on my arms raise. There was a cool breeze. He put his arm around me and pulled me closer. He tilted my chin up to his and looked directly in my eyes to tell me a romantic story about one of the Martello towers we could see. Originally this was designed against invasion from the French but served as a rescue point, and place of refuge for secret lovers of rival families. The story and historical building worked some magic on me.

From there we hopped in his car, there was still enough daylight for reasonable visibility, and he took me around various houses he worked on, so he could show off his craftsmanship. To me some were truly beautiful pieces of art, as opposed to functional pieces of wood, which were just aspects of somebody's home, used for daily living. He drove down the coast heading towards Bray, he was telling me stories of the sea and of the mountains. I loved this, this was wonderful. Apart from the fact that I loved learning, he was so knowledgeable and I found it oh so appealing.

We pulled in near the train station at Dalkey, I had no idea where we were going. His wisdom gave me comfort as we held hands along the road tracking the edge of the sea southwards.

"We are going just up there by the Cat's Ladder" he pointed with both of our hands, fingers entwined towards some steep, stone steps.

I smiled, loving his local knowledge. I followed him by the hand up the hill to the summit. From there he pointed out the Sugar Loaf mountain, the Wicklow Mountains and Dalkey Island, with its very own Martello Tower.

"I will take you to all of the places your eyes can see," Daniel whispered in my ear.

"Ha that would be a very long date!" I laughed.

"Why do you have to kill the moment Laura, I'm trying to tell you that I like you, and I want to go on more dates with you."

Wow, he sounded quite pissed off, angry even. Well that was plain blank, angry admiration if ever I heard it. I didn't really know what to say, I reached for his arm, "I have enjoyed your company too, we have had such a great time on our dates."

"Nope, too late, you ruined it."

Gosh how quickly his temperament turned, I really didn't know what to make of it.

A few minutes staring out to sea and he seemed to return to the pleasant version of himself.

"You know this is Dublin's answer to the Bay of Naples," he looked all gazingly into my eyes. He knew what he was doing, this was such a romantic setting, and the sun was slowly lowering against the mountains.

"You know this is a local spot for marriage proposals too," he winked, and we laughed.

"You'll have to take me back here again on another day so," I said chuckling and sticking my tongue out at him.

Our conversation veered towards serious again as we drove back to Dun Laoghaire. He informed me that he has been in two four-year relationships. This was something I was starting to learn was a good thing. This meant he had the capacity to be in a relationship. He should, with his experience, know there was going to be give and take. He should, with his experience, know certain things about a woman's way.

Suddenly the car jolted to a halt. His window was down.

"Hey, hey, do you want me to pull you by the neck like that!"

Faintly in the distance I could hear another man shout back.

"Get lost, and mind your own business!"

Daniel opened his seatbelt. Oh God please do not let him get out of the car I prayed. We don't need to be getting into a fight with perfect strangers at night!

Daniel twisted around in the car. More shouting. I could feel the heat radiate off him.

Apparently the man walking his dog, was pulling too hard on the leash. I hadn't seen what the supposed bad man had done to the dog. So I couldn't comment. There were other people out walking their dogs too. No one had said anything. Why did Daniel have to get involved? Was it really that terrible? It must have been for him to react like that. The poor little dog.

We were driving down the main village street. It was
fairly well lit up with street lights and not too far from my car.
There were lots of people around as it was a beautiful, mild
evening. A man staggered out of a pub. He was very well
dressed but not quite in his prime. He looked a little bit the
worse for the drink. He stumbled over and 'face planted' the
pavement. By this point we had gone passed in the car.
Without warning I was flung forward. The car had come to a
sudden and complete stop. Daniel had the indicator on and I
thought he was parking for us to go somewhere.
"Did you see that?" he asked.
"The man falling over drunk?" I enquired.
"He was hit, that other man hit him, I think he is trying to rob
him."
Daniel jumped out of the car and began shouting at the two
men.
Jeez twice the one day, within an hour, this was surely
something out of the ordinary.

The younger man did seem very close to the older tipsy
gentleman. The view from the rear view mirror and the
windscreen mirror was poor. I was at a bad angle and too far
away to really see what was going on. Daniel got back to the
car, and told me how aggressive the younger man had been,
and all he wanted to do was protect the older man, who was
clearly in a vulnerable position. I agreed that we must protect
the more vulnerable in society. I didn't really know what else
to say, but I couldn't wait to get out of his car, and get home! I
only had to try and follow through with one more date with
him. We quickly agreed upon another date as a hike up
Glendalough, which melted my heart enough to give him a
quick peck on the cheek, before leaping from the car and
heading on home.

Date 3 with Daniel, The Carpenter

The weather had taken a turn for the worse, so we decided it best to reschedule our Glendalough date. I was far from disappointed with the weather, and rescheduling our date when he suggested we do an alternative, and he would meet me outside my apartment later.

"You know I was thinking; you know how we both enjoy the walking. The scenery brings us a sense of calm, and we are chilled and relaxed in our mind?"

"Yes, it does", I agreed but I had no idea where he was going with this.

"Along with that we also get our buzz from, what did you tell me they were 'happy hormones'?"

"Ha yes! Endorphins giving us our happy moods post physical exertion. It is a great mix!" I still had no idea where he was going with this or what he was going to say next.

He nodded in agreement. He paused in motion holding my gaze. With a devilish look in his eye like he was up to something, he began to walk towards me in slow motion. He stopped shy of his chest touching mine. His hand traced my temple, tucking stray hair behind my ear, then gliding his hand down my check, down my neck and he paused. He looked like he was calculating something in his mind. His thumb glided across my collar bone and down my arm to my waist and planted his hands on my hips.

"Well," he said, "my alternative date suggestion is, to do that a different way."

Well now, this was not what I had in mind, was he about to say what I thought he was going to say?!

"Em, Daniel, I'm a bit concerned you are going to say something you can't take back, where this is going?"

He rolled his eyes. "You always assume the worst! We are going somewhere special and I will raise your heart beat, but not the way your mind is going, get it out of the gutter!"

I pulled a face, and wondered was it going to be a haunted house or something, if it was I already didn't want to go. "We are going somewhere special to raise my heart beat?"
"Yes, though I would like to think I was doing that already," he winked chuffed with himself.
"So when, or where are we doing this?" I queried.
"Now, and it's a surprise." The only clue was we would be driving towards the city and not towards Glendalough. It really left me none the wiser. He caved and gave another clue, and said it would take about 30 minutes to get there. Calculating the driving, and the fact we were not going in the direction of the M50, that meant we were going city central-ish, or so I thought.

On the drive our chat reverted back to why we swiped right on each other in the first place. He knew the body, face and hair he liked. Apparently I ticked all those boxes for him. The only thing he said he didn't quite like was that I classified myself as a 'Princess' in my profile. He began to question my reasoning behind it.
"You really do not know yourself Laura."
"How do you mean?" I was all confused.
"Well I certainly would not call you a 'Princess', why did you indicate that as your personality?"

I had forgotten I indicated a 'Princess' personality. The thing you need to know about genuine personal profiles on dating apps is that they are tricky to actually convey oneself for two reasons. The first is you really have to have a certain understanding of yourself. The second is that some apps require a single word description of yourself. Does anyone have just one word?! I would like to think I was more complex than a single word. In trying to conform to the constraints of the app, and the need to identify yourself with ONE word, a number of problems arise; no one whole word fits quite right.

I didn't want to say I was a 'sapiophile' firstly, despite a PhD in medicine, I had to look up what that meant! I also didn't fancy attracting men who think they are super smart because they are well read, but more often than not, are not street wise, and minus craic on the chats front. Intellect, I have learned can be subjective in many ways.

I love to explore new places, I love travelling on trains, boats, bikes but flying unsettles me to the point it could ruin a trip entirely. Most people prefer to travel by plane so I didn't really feel like indicating my personality as the 'explorer' type. In the past this has led to invitations away to European cities which I had to politely decline due to my irrational fear of the safest mode of transport.

Another potential option was 'outdoorsy'. Although I love the fresh seaside air, and the invigoration of hiking, I have never camped and was not at one with nature in any true sense. Those pesky wasps made me dance around like a child practicing a shimmy! Greatest of all my irrational fears, let no one forget my paralysis upon the approach of a large eight legged creature! Therefore, the 'adventurer' option did not really suit me either. I would consider myself somewhat a 'foodie'. I love food but that was more my friend Rebecca's thing, so by comparison I am not a TOTAL foodie.

In a professional capacity I liked to believe I was the complete professional, fully trained, intellectual, open minded, imaginative, and creative - but did not wish to describe myself as a 'free thinker' as it had connotations with being a bit of a hippy. Therefore, I had to rule it out too.

I thought back to my selection of Princess, and knew exactly why I selected it. I wanted the man I would be with to look at me like the royal prince looks at his princess.

That non-verbal cue, where the intent is deep and meaningful, not the stare of a threat, nor the longing of physical lust, rather pure love. A look denoting a playful flirtatious affection extending beyond desire and passion to encompass a charitable and selfless compassion for another. This combined with pupil dilation indicative of interest in what the prince was looking at. In my mind, should I ever find a prince charming, I would wish he would look at me as his princess.

When I explained all that to Daniel, his simple, mocking response was that I should have selected the option for 'romantic'! Eventually he pulled over and parked the car. As a result of my prince charming speech along the way, he told me to wait in the car. He hopped out and came around to my side. He opened the car door, and held out his hand for me to take.

"You know you will have to get used to taking my lead" he smiled. "Do you trust me?"

"Ha! No!" I said mockingly.

"Ok, well come inside this building." It looked very modern, I could still smell the paint work in the foyer. The receptionist greeted us with a grin. "Sign in here please."

We obeyed.

"Do you trust me now?"

"A little bit more now I know you are not taking me to some dodgy warehouse to sell me for parts! Haha!"

"For goodness sake would you stop with the drama Laura."

We took two flights of stairs and then we stopped. He gently teased the scarf from around my neck and told me to close my eyes. He lightly covered my eyes with the scarf and tied it in a bow behind my head.

"Keep them eyes closed, no peaking." I did what I was told.

"This is getting a little BSDM, you know, you didn't tell me you were into kinky stuff?!"

He placed a finger on my lips and whispered "Shh, we are nearly there."

He led me a few steps forward. I heard a door open, he led me a few steps further and 'click' the door closed. His hand tugged mine, gently moving me further about ten more steps. "Keep those eyes closed," he whispered in my ear. I could feel the knot of the scarf loosen against my hair. Then I was free. "May I open my eyes now?" I asked politely.

"I will tell you, hold on just one more minute." His voice sounded farther this time. I heard another 'click' and his footsteps on a wooden floor coming towards me. He held my hands and said "OK now, open your eyes."

The first thing I saw was his handsome face, eyes twinkling in the dim lights, grinning. Was he blushing?! I twirled looking all around me, taking in the room. One side was paneled floor to ceiling with mirrors. A waist height bar surrounded the three remaining walls. The main lights were not switched on. Instead from a closed curtain rail on the back wall hung fairy lights like you would see at Christmas time. "This, this is really cool, it's a dance studio, right?!" I was ecstatic!

"Yes, it is. And Tony my friend is going to give us a lesson. He should be here any minute."

"How, what, why, what made you think of this?" I was so shocked that he would plan something like this!

"What do you think of the floor?"

"Ohhhh," I said as it began to dawn on me, "you laid the floor here?"

"I sure did, and Tony owes me a favour- see I haven't been paid yet so lets just call this interest on delayed payment. I asked him to set the room up for us, for a lesson tonight. I finished the floor the day we started chatting. You agreed to our first date when I was working right at this spot right here."

"This exact spot? Yeah right."

"Look between your feet and you will see why I remembered."

I looked down and on the floor board between my feet was a darkened knot in the wood that was remarkably shaped like a heart. I smiled. What were the chances?! If you believed in signs (which I don't) you could be forgiven for thinking that this was one.

"Ha, hmm that is pretty memorable alright. Something tells me I will remember this date for a long time."

CLAP CLAP "All riiiight, arrrre my students rrrrready to salsa?!

The doors swung open and a short dark haired Portuguese guy strutted into the dance studio. The rest of the night was blur of colourful fairy lights, music and dancing. It was so much fun! When we were making mistakes and tripping over ourselves I laughed so hard I could hardly breath at times. My stomach did knot at the beginning, when we were struggling to follow the routine. This, I thought would bring out Daniel's temper, but it didn't. It was actually a great night! For his gallant efforts he was rewarded with a kiss on the dancefloor, we were just caught in the moment. In the car on the way back, I realised how sweaty and gross I was from all the dancing. We danced for hours. Daniel went in for another kiss, but I stopped telling him the stink of sweat from the both of us was a bit off putting, in a jokey way. He sighed heavily, rubbing his temples with one hand and gripping the steering wheel so tight his knuckles went white with the other.

"To be honest, you are ruining the night, men don't care what you ladies smell like Laura. As long as it is not too strong or too revolting. You know, I could say, I like my women to smell like me, but you are such a prude that you probably won't see the funny side of it! Laura I think you need to grow up."

That was the final blow to crack the egg- there was no way I could stand being next to him for another second. He was turning out to be everything I hated in a man. His condescending, his mansplaining, his derogatory comments and his temper! I quietly got out of his car without saying a word. I left the girls a voice note, to try explain how the surprisingly good date, turned out surprisingly bad! Goodness knows how the overall scoring was going to turn out!

Phase 2 End Message from the Chief Advisor to the Principal Investigator

That night my brain was on overdrive. I just couldn't get to sleep, even though I was physically and mentally drained. It was 4.15 am, and I hadn't slept a wink. I know you shouldn't go to your phone when you can't sleep because it keeps you awake for longer, but, I knew I was already passed the point of sleeping.

The light of the phone stung like a B! I couldn't see the screen properly at first, for a moment I thought I had a new message, it could have been a half asleep phantom one! I don't know what I was clicking on, but eventually with one eye shut, I found Maria's number. It would be cruel to call at this hour, so I simply left a voice message recapping on Candidates 4 to 6 now that Phase 2 was complete.

By the time I woke up, half the morning was gone. I checked my phone and had a voice note from Maria. I boiled the kettle for an instant coffee, none of that fancy home brew machine stuff for me! Settling on the sofa with my caffeine fix, I was ready to hear whatever Maria had to say.

"Good morning lady, someone either had a lot of fun night last night, awake past 4 am, or some really poor quality sleep. Something tells me it was the latter. OK, so here are my thoughts on the Phase Two candidates.

The Accountant sounds like a dream, sure, a non-drinker would drive you anywhere! He was very respectful to you and to his mother. His relationship with his mother shows clearly that he has the capacity to be devoted. I probably shouldn't say this, but you know, the mother won't be around forever; and all you would have to do in the interim would be to fix the sister up with someone better!

Besides, whatever the issue is with the mother, sure no one completely *loves* their mother in law exactly, and if they do, it's a fine rare thing. You know it's the exception and not the rule. All you had to do was train him up a bit, and ignore the mother. It would be fine in the end. However, having said all that, I would be exactly of your mindset in firmly believing it would be more hassle than it was worth!

Now, for mister chancing his arm, treating you like some financial investment, he makes my skin crawl. Do not, I repeat DO NOT let anything he said to you be absorbed. He is so irrelevant on every level, and desperate to make a career for himself and failing epically. Not to mention he is the scummy leach type of creature! We are all about symbiosis, he really does not deserve to have the classification of human!" (I laughed at this! Check Maria out with her 'symbiosis' and biological 'classifications'. I wondered was she spending too much time listening to me, or was she interested in becoming a super scientist too, per chance? I didn't have much time to dwell on it as she launched straight into her evaluation of The Carpenter.)

"Ok, so I really don't know where to begin with Mister Angry, or should I call him Mister Personality Disorder, a.k.a, The Carpenter. Sometimes he seems super cool, then he is a complete psycho hot head. Then he becomes Mister Romantic and back to psycho hot head again. What can I say Laura? Except please stay away from him for your own safety. He sounds like a control freak. Of course people get annoyed and argue their points, but there is no need to raise your voice at people, especially at complete strangers, for all he knew any of them could have reacted a lot worse! I can't believe he got into **two** arguments, and even got out of the car to shout at people on one of your dates! Whoever he ends up with would be living on edge for fear of him getting violent, maybe not towards them, but you don't want to get caught up in any of his fights. I have to admit, it is interesting hearing these stories, but would you ever just take my advice and give the not so local guys a chance, they can be a lot more charming than the natives! I do hope you have much greater success in the next phase! Ciao!"

I rang Maria straight back just to say thanks really quickly!

"Hello young lady, did you finally arise from your slumber?"

"Hi Maria, yes indeed! Thanks for your comments. I couldn't agree with you more about The Carpenter! You're picking up a bit of the science-y lingo too. Thinking about a career change?"

Silence.

"Ha! No, no, Laura, I'm sorry I'll ring you later, I must dash, I have a client appointment, bye babes!"

I felt like Maria paused a bit long before she laughed and said no. Or was I imagining it? What did she do in her spare time, that she seemed to have very little of? Or why was it that she had such little spare time? Did she really work all those crazy hours like she said? She travelled a lot too. She mostly claimed that most of that was for work, for inspiration, she was sculptress by trade. I guessed that would remain a mystery for another day.

I was SO tired, if I didn't have the Review Board meeting with the girls to get dressed and up and out of the apartment for, then I would totally be back in my bed! The days were beginning to get noticeably shorter in length and after last night, all of the fatigue I was feeling from life in general, was being added to by the impact of the burden of this dating experiment. I gave Lisa a text, I hadn't seen or heard a peep out of her all morning! Then I asked the Review Board if they were still on for brunch at noon. All I needed was for one person to say they were not too keen and I would totally bail too!

Phase Two Interim Report
Review Board Meeting

I left the girls a voice message too!

"Girls, I won't lie, this is turning out to be mentally exhausting, I am starting to forget who told me what, about themselves."

"That is what you have your notes and review table for, and don't forget your trusty Review Board!"

This morning, the girls were in great form! A few funny video clips later, and I felt so grateful for my friends. It's so true, you really should surround yourself with positive people. These ladies were like my power plug, all the drudge immediately dissipated and I was glad to have the Review Board meeting today! The thought of the pancakes helped too! ☺

As almost regulars, we were getting cheeky with our orders at our usual spot just off Grafton Street, asking for more, and more, variations on the pancakes. This week we were in agreement that hot chocolate sauce, drizzled over the usual raspberries, mascarpone cheese with maple syrup on the side, would just give it that extra edge of what we were looking for!

"Ok ladies, I'm six guys in, so at least the end is insight. I am over the mid-way bump."

"Keep your eye on the prize! Focus on how great it will be to have arm candy at the wedding this once! Arm candy with excellent conversation skills, a sense of humour and nifty on his feet on the dance floor!"

"Sure we don't ask for much do we?!" We all had a giggle.

"Ha, ha! OK, OK," said Lisa settling us down, "right let's get this reviewing done, then we can have some food! Remind us briefly again who have you got for us to review today, Laura?"

"The Phase Two candidates, here we go! First up was 'Raj, The Accountant' who was the classic 'Mama's Boy', entirely devoted to his mother, but any lady in his life would always play second fiddle. The next candidate, who can only be described as an utter shambles of a human was 'The Personal Trainer and Health Nutritionist', his looks got him the date, but not even his looks could save him from everyone's derision! Finally, there was 'The Carpenter', who definitely has some underlying issues. To be fair, I think he would have good potential, if he ever sorted out his issues and perhaps attended some anger management classes. Let's look at the review tables for these guys".

Table 4 Raj, The Accountant

Candidate 4	Marks
Date 1	4.5 /5
Date 2	5.0 /5
Date 3	3.5 /5
Good Communication	4.0 /5
Good sense of humour	4.0 /5
Willingness to dance	4.0 /5
Confidence among strangers	4.0 /5
Personality +/- alcohol	3.0 /5
Trustworthy	4.0 /5
Punctual	4.0 /5
Total	40 /50

General comment form Laura: He was cute as a button, with a big heart, but, even the best lady would receive second place silver to his mother's gold!

Wedding guest suitability: Medium

The Doll was speaking rather loudly, "He does look pretty good. He definitely works out! Sometimes good looking men are a bit dim though, surely he knows at one point he would have to give some value to a woman over his mother. His pictures make him look a little shy, it's hard to imagine he has the full package, minus the mother of course! Speaking of package, any inclination on his? Is it full? HA! HA! HA! HA!"

"Eeeww, shush don't be saying that so loud! He is a perfect angel and you are lowering the tone! We'll get kicked out of this place, and we love it here!" I shrieked. "Although," I whispered, "I hadn't thought of that, maybe he is so wonderful in every other aspect of his life in compensation for you know what! Ha! Ha!"

The Doll, "Well if you don't want him, I'll have him!"

Lisa and Anne were too busy in convulsions of laughter at how loud The Doll had been, so I nodded at Rebecca to fire ahead with her input. Rebecca was almost frowning. You could tell she hadn't fully made her mind up about this guy. "I am finding it tough to limit this guy to just a dessert," she said. "In one way, it seems to me like he is a staple dessert that everyone likes, he is definitely a profiterole. You know you just can't go wrong with it, but apart from satisfactory, is it anything more?!"

She continued.

"From what I have learned of Raj, I think he is so much more than that though. He is so sweet and so pure of heart. He would also be an organic, hot, dark chocolate drink. He is soothing and good for you, but somehow not quite right. The reason behind this you see, is that we are not used to the good stuff. Our bodies are so used to processing salt, to get the flavor to hit the spot we need a teeny, tiny pinch of salt. And, for full-on satisfaction, I recommend you spice it up, and put some fire in your belly with a little nip of chili powder, otherwise, there is no chemistry there."

Table 5 Andrew, The Personal Trainer and Nutritionist

Candidate 5	Marks
Date 1	4.0 /5
Date 2	2.5 /5
Date 3	1.0 /5
Good Communication	4.0 /5
Good sense of humour	2.0 /5
Willingness to dance	4.0 /5
Confidence among strangers	4.0 /5
Personality +/- alcohol	3.5 /5
Trustworthy	1.0 /5
Punctual	5.0 /5
Total	31 /50

General comment from Laura: He is a user and a leach around whom I cannot enjoy my food. He claims to be ambitious but lacks imagination and creativity, and his only **UN**-original idea to do well for himself is by sponging off others. I wouldn't subject anyone to spending any time with him.

Wedding guest suitability: Very Low

"I had high hopes for The Personal Trainer at the start," said The Doll, "I would have gone into business with him. He is so smarmy and slick, I wouldn't have realised it until he had me bled dry of money!"

"Such a chancer, trying to ride on the back of Laura's hard work, that man child better think again! Safe to say he will not receive the golden extra five points from anyone!" proclaimed Lisa, who was evidently still on a bit of a man bashing streak since the breakup with Francesso, the Italiano.

Anne was in agreement. "Sure you couldn't allow him near any of your friends or family. He would be trying to swindle them out of every cent they might have! How did you not punch him? I am not sorry for suggesting it. I am so glad you have the confidence to know you are a hundred thousand times out of his league. My only concern is for some poor insecure woman, who believes his crap, and completely falls victim to it! He didn't come up with the idea himself. He is clearly not that smart, so unfortunately there are bound to be more like him out there!

We all looked at Rebecca to have the final say. "You know I was excited for you and this guy at the start. I agree he seemed kind of cool. It is refreshing to have someone talk about your work so animatedly. However, you want to be able to enjoy the food at the wedding, without your date eyeballing you! Ultimately though, this guy is mint ice cream; initially he seems cool and fresh, but it's a lazy dessert suitable only for convenience.

Table 6 Daniel, The Carpenter

Candidate 6	Marks
Date 1	4.5 /5
Date 2	4.5 /5
Date 3	4.0 /5
Good Communication	3.5 /5
Good sense of humour	4.0 /5
Willingness to dance	5.0 /5
Confidence among strangers	4.0 /5
Personality +/- alcohol	3.0 /5
Trustworthy	3.5 /5
Punctual	5.0 /5
Total	41 /50

General Comment from Laura: Attractive to look at, very thoughtful, questionable social skills, may have good potential if he went to anger management classes

Wedding guest suitability: Low

"Ok ladies, I think it is safe to say there was one factor which significantly lowered this man's suitability - his temper! Do you think I have been too hard score wise? Anything to add?"
"I think you have been as fair as you can be. You don't want to have to tip toe around someone in case they explode, he really should try some breathing exercises!" offered Lisa.

Anne's response was more about the system than The Carpenter. "In terms of accuracy I believe this scoring to be in line with the other charts you have sent on. At the end of the process we should review all charts to ensure weighting was attributed in an equal manner."

The Doll was half laughing at her own thoughts of him "Ha! Yeah he probably doesn't drink in case he punches a wall, and he needs his hands for work! On a more serious note though, he seems to have some issues, like maybe baby issues? Hopefully he will get himself sorted out because apart from that he sounded good."
"I don't know," said Anne, "he was an interesting and thoughtful one. Logistically it should have worked out, you like the same things, he even took you dancing for crying out loud, what guy thinks to that all on his own?! He was perfect apart from his rage."
"If you really liked him Laura, the rage wouldn't have got to you this much though," argued Lisa, "perhaps the magic x factor was missing?"
"Yeah, a few screws missing more like! Next!" replied The Doll.
"Ok, let's have your verdict Rebecca!"
"I don't wish to be mean" Rebecca said softly. "I'm sorry to say this, but it seems to me he is like a sharp rhubarb and ginger crumble, without the cinnamon! Without this secret ingredient to counteract the sour with a little bit of sweetness, it's painful and he is not the dessert for you!"

"Ha, ok cool, Becks I love your descriptions they are so funny, and yet so accurate! You really do know your stuff! Ladies, am I sensing some love in the air for one of these guys. Are there some extra 5 points being dished out at this meeting?" I asked.

"Upon reflection, oh gosh, you know apart from his temper, I could listen to Daniel's sweet romantic tales all night long, Laura! How were you not totally a smitten kitten with his stories?" asked Lisa.

"It's the temper, the quick temper, I can't describe it properly, it really is just like a switch that flicks on and that's it, his eyes are unseeing to anything, his ears are closed off and he is on a mission to right a wrong. It's like he wants to be a superhero, even when there is no one and nothing to save! I know that sounds sweet too but, it just did not feel right!"

"I don't mean to go on about it, but a lot of people benefit from yoga, and breathing exercises, I am sure we could take the edge off him just a little bit. He really sounds charming with his wise old tales and ghost stories. I am not resolute on this one, but so far my 5 points go to The Carpenter, let's see what Phase 3 brings!"

"Well we all know The Radiographer from Phase 1 had the pants charmed off us all, and yet by Date 3 look how that turned out. All talk, just words, it's the actions that really speak to me" beamed Anne. The Accountant is getting my 5 points so far, and no, before you all say anything, it is *not* just because he works with numbers, and I fantasize about any man who can balance the books! Let's just see what Phase 3 has in store!"

Phase 3, Man 1, Candidate 7, Nathan, The IT Guy

Ohhhh this guy's profile located him in Belfast, how on earth did he come up on MY radar?! Maybe he had been down South here visiting, or with work? Well, sure everyone knows the world's top ranked accent is the Northern Irish one. His voice alone might be worth the swipe right. I wondered if he was part of any extreme groupings up there, if he was more Nationalist or Loyalist? Maybe he was neutral? I guess that would probably NOT be a good conversation opener. Back at home when I was growing up there were only two subjects that one was not allowed to talk about, and they were politics and religion - funny how that has stuck with me decades later!

He worked in I.T. Much like the guys who worked for the MI5, to me what the guys who work in I.T. did was an enigma. What on earth would we chat about?

To be fair, I am a devil for preconceptions. It is really hard not to imagine what people look, or act like after the smallest engagement with them via text, email or phone. I was expecting him to show up dressed like the cliché young, professional, nerdy type, that doesn't see daylight. I was expecting faded navy-blue jeans, but with the good sports footwear (he was on date after all). My mind wandered to imagine what sort of coordinated upper body, this nerdy type could pull together as 'cool'. Perhaps a layered white t-shirt over a red, topped with a red and navy, checkered fully opened shirt. This would all be wrapped in a grey hoody, which would of course match the grey beany hat he would be wearing.

Date 1 with Nathan, The I.T. Guy

When I met him, I realised, I was so far wrong. My jaw would still be on the floor except I didn't want germs getting in! He looked clean cut. Certainly he was well-dressed, but not in a suit and tie kind of way. He looked like he knew how to put an outfit together. In years gone by that might indicate a man was gay, but with the metrosexual trends these days, well, you never can tell. He was skirting on the precipice of metrosexual for sure. Almost too groomed. Potentially the type of guy who would body check himself in the reflection of shop windows walking by. This was going to be interesting! Let's see what the vocal chords had to offer!

The Northern Irish accent has indeed been voted the sexiest in the world. The popularity of this accent comes as no surprise sure, with world famous actors, Liam Neeson from Antrim, and Jamie Dornan from County Down, appealing to women and men across all age ranges. These confident, assertive voices have the power to draw you in and retain your attention. Or maybe they are just downright, plain, old, sexy. There are high percentages of both men and women who go weak at the knees at the sound of the Northern Irish, Twang, Warble, Lilt, Brogue - whatever description you choose to put on it. A lot of the intrigue is largely due to the amazing vocabulary accompanying the dialect. How people confuse the Northern Irish accent with that of the Scots is beyond me, however so often, the BIG FILM industry gets it oh so very wrong! That's why it really should be left to the locals!

Our first date was a coffee date. He was rushing to get there on time. I actually think he did in fact run there. On pulling off his jumper, to help cool down, his once tucked in shirt raised up out of his trousers. His body was healthy for sure, but what really caught my eye was what I thought looked like some ink. A tattoo. I could only see the bottom of the image, but whatever it was on the left of his abdomen, was also mirrored on the right. I must have been oogling, because as soon as he sat down again he asked.

"So, do you have any tattoos yourself?"

"Oh gosh, I was staring wasn't I?" I blushed. He actually had a Derry accent, not a Belfast one, it was strong, rough and absolutely had a biological effect on me!

"No, no I don't think I could commit to liking the same pattern, or print for long enough in the one location to get a tattoo. I would love a bit of henna temporary artwork though. The patterns are so ornate. It would be so delicate and pretty. If you ever need a plus on to an Indian wedding, I'll make myself available!"

My inner voice scolded me for mentioning marriage on a first date. How stupid was I, he was going to think I was properly on the hunt for husband material! I knew I wasn't savvy enough to talk my way out of that blunder, and into making myself sound cool. At best, I could just pause and let the rush of blood to my head calm down. A rush I was sure he could see, as he smiled politely and chuckled just a little.

Gathering myself together I managed to get the words out to ask, "So what was that I saw on your abdomen? And I don't mean your belly button!"

"My what?"

"Your tattoo?"

"No I heard that bit," he smiled and half laughed, "what's the other thing you mentioned?"

"Belly button? Do you not call it a belly button? Your navel I mean."

"Ha, ha I was only joking, I call it that too, I just like your wee southern accent saying belly button, it's very cute."

Oh a compliment from this man was making me melt, and it was only over the words belly button!

"I have several tattoos, but you usually cannot see any of them when I am wearing a shirt and trousers. I like to keep a clean look for professional purposes."

"Oh, so there are more than the abdominal pointed prints? I really didn't see much." I said shaking my head.

Nathan turning his back completely to the rest of the coffee shop, lifted his shirt slightly to his waist. I could then make out that he had two Celtic Cross tattoos flanking each side of his tight abdomen.

"They have some really elaborate detail." I hoped I wasn't opening a can of worms but I was curious. "Do your tattoos hold a significant meaning to you? I mean these crosses and any others you have?"

"Ha, well if you are wondering if I have an ex-wife, or ex-girlfriend's name printed on me, no. Nor do I have a heart with Mum written on it. My tattoos do however bear meaning to me. The crosses, I got them when I was sixteen. I was very close to my grandparents, and they died from smoke inhalation in a fire."

"Oh gosh, I am so sorry, I didn't mean to bring up any upsetting subjects, I hope you are ok?"

"Yes, it was really tragic and very sad at the time, it was a long time ago now, and I am a bit older than you, I think."

"That was something I was going to ask. Your age didn't come up on your profile, but my settings indicate that you can at most be 5 years older than I am."

"Oh really?" he raised a brow.

"Really" I smiled back.

"So what age do you think I am?" he asked flirting.

"I think, thirty-three."

"Ha, Laura I am so glad you pronounced it like that and not 'tirty, tree' ha ha!"

"Ha, well am I right, what age are you? And tell me more about the ink."

"Yes, I am thirty-three, good guess, but I have a feeling it wasn't a guess. You were very sure of yourself Doctor Laura." I won't lie, when he said my name, I got chills.

"And the ink?"

"The Celtic Cross is important to me because it symbolizes, faith, honour, life and hope. My grandparents lived their best lives, with deep faith, and to honour them I intend to live the same. The circle joining the intersection of the arms and stem of the cross signifies the circle of life. Some people also say it signifies knowledge, strength and compassion to manage life's ups and downs."

With my phone under the table like bold school student, I conducted a little online search. "The internet says the Celtic Cross represents Unity, Navigation, Ascension, Temperance, Transition and Balance. Quite a lot of meanings I guess."

"Did no-one ever tell you not to believe everything you read online?" he smirked.

I laughed, I had no comeback, but I was starting to believe he was smart beyond I.T. and I wanted him to believe the same about me. Or at least have him recognize that I was observant. "You know that kind of artistic design is often in Cathedrals?"

"I guess that just means the design was popular then too, who knows, maybe it is pre-Christian." He was good, and he had a point.

I got brave, "You know somewhere I still have yet to visit is the Book of Kells, in Trinity College. Celtic Crosses were definitely a symbol of the Celtic Christians."

"What's that book again?" he asked.

"Oh my God are you serious? It's a world famous book! A total tourist attraction in Dublin! Artistic monks created an illuminating piece of religion, and art in the form of this book, like, around 500 AD. It's fascinating to try interpret it, you know it wasn't just a doodle, more like a craft. The knot work and spirals appearing in Celtic art have no beginning or ending. The spirals and circular lines never cross one another. The meaning of this type of Celtic pattern is to highlight how the circle of life is never ending. Some people believe that the spirals and circular lines in the Celtic Cross only connect between Heaven and Earth. Ha let's not do an experiment to test that out!"

"Hmm" he raised a brow, "I agree, although a low risk experiment might be to get an ouija board, and ask it, no?" I am impressed that he was quick thinking on his feet because this was an unusual conversation.

"Oh darling" I said with faux dramatics, "I am on a date with you, I don't want to tempt the devil out any further!" I winked, thanking the baby Jesus for letting my confidence appear finally!

"Now that you mention it, when I was getting this tattoo I remember being told something like, this symbolism is the indication of desire of humans to know and experience the unfolding mystery of life. This includes nature and the world around us, just like you my sweetie scientist, understanding and exploring to reach a wisdom of sorts."

Well I couldn't have my date teaching me everything. I had to give my tuppence worth of information.

"Actually as a scientist I have to keep an open mind to all hypothesis. Other theories associated with Celtic Crosses are mostly around the idea of eternity, like of course the sun for the pagans, but also the sacrifices of Christ for the Christians and, the lifelong never-ending circles are still reflected in wedding rings."

Oh my God I was mentioning weddings again - what was wrong with me!?!? He didn't seem to notice, though he did seem to enjoy the exchange of knowledge to which he wanted to add. Maybe he was one of those people who just had to have the last say about everything?!

"There are earthly connections to the Celtic Cross too, the four quarters of a Celtic Cross. North represents winter, stability and wisdom. East represents spring, learning and knowledge. South is for summer, strength, passion and vitality and West is for inner knowledge, emotion and intuition. The circle that connects the four arms of this cross reveals the rebirth, eternal cycle of life and unity. Maybe we can at least agree that there are a variety of different symbolisms associated with the Celtic Cross?"

"Ha, yes ok, that is fair but can I just add that the ancient Celts considered that the Celtic Cross had deep values. They had their own interpretation of the four points in a Celtic Cross and these four points represent different things, which include water, wind, fire and earth. So, this meaning of Celtic Cross is also associated with nature. Some others considered that the four points in a Celtic Cross symbolize four parts of a man - but maybe let's not get into that ha!"

"Ok agreed the Celtic Crosses are cool! Really artistic, some people design Celtic art in knot work, mazes or spirals within the cross, others design the entire cross in Celtic art. It is all so beautiful regardless of meaning!"

"Well, with all this interest and chat, we will have to go to the Book of Kells on our next date so!" he declared.

"It is in Trinity College though, you will come to Dublin again?" I queried.

"Yes, of course! Are you free Saturday?"

"In the morning, yes - does that work for you?"

"If you're there, I'm there." He winked again.

"I tried to visit the Book of Kells earlier this year, in the Spring time, but when I got there, there was an extremely long queue so I think let's book in advance online."

Pulling out his phone he said, "Perfect, I'll do it now - whooa the picture online alone looks impressive."

My inner voice was exclaiming oh my goodness! This guy is cultured, and kind, and quirky and intelligent and funny, and is booking tickets to go see the Book of Kells on Saturday!
"I think it is meant to be super impressive in real life," I assured him.
"Just like you!" he winked at me!
"I just let you walk straight into that one didn't I?!" I was beaming and genuinely laughing with him. On occasion, on a date I found myself laughing out of politeness but this was real.

He was really cool though. Never before had I thought guys with tattoos were anything particularly special. This guy was interesting enough so far, he had the map of the globe tattooed on his forearms when he held them out together. It was unusual - well unusual to me. It was almost cool. I think I was just dumb founded by the fact he didn't fit my brain-mould of the other I.T. types I had come across online. His hobbies were not gaming (my brain screams RUN, RUN, RUN when I see that, it's an automatic swipe left).

He was also not THAT into Bit Coin, which was refreshing- what the hell is the obsession with this Bit Coin thing anyway? If world currency was going to change forever, I just prayed it wasn't in my lifetime, because that was one band wagon I had not jumped on! Surely there would be some security hacker who would over run it all anyway? This was apparently not the best thing to say to someone who was keen on it, and who had invested thousands! Thankfully this was not Nathan. Or at least he didn't admit it.

I was excited to see what date two would bring. I just hoped there would be no more explanations of Celtic Crosses!!

Date 2 with Nathan, The I.T. Guy

I knew Trinity College was plagued by the death trap that is uneven cobble stones. Trinity College, and Temple Bar were not good for a girl in heels trying to elongate her muscular legs. Nathan was there before me, and he did not look at all like a nerdy I.T. guy standing sheepishly waiting for a date. Rather, when he clocked me trotting toward him, teetering in my heels, he approached with a broad smile, with his broad chest open and arms out to catch me should I fall. Thankfully I didn't! The hug on greeting was great though! He was so warm and snuggly!

There was a positive energy among the crowds passing through Trinity College. You couldn't help but be in high spirits. "It really is tucked away in a magical library isn't it?!" Nathan asked, he was being all nerdy, yet somehow looking very cool.

"Of course! Sure where else would you place a national treasure, one of Ireland's most prized possessions?" Today I was little miss confident, in spite of uneven pavement.

"Is it really THAT cool?"

"YES! Wait until you see the queues of people from all over the world coming to see it! It is supposed to be so stunning, and have exquisite decorations and intricate illuminations, it's a precious thing, you know. It's supposed be from the 9th century or even earlier!"

"You illuminate my day when I see you, you know."

"Oh my goodness, you dare to use my words against me?!" I asked, I liked this bit of banter. He knew how to take a phrase and flip it around. It was smart, and cute and I liked it.

"Not against you, the only thing I want against you, is me," and he stuck his tongue out, and laughed holding his hands up, he was only teasing.

"And just like that, my date went from Mr. Smooth and Slick to Mr. Sleazy," I laughed back at him.

"Can't blame a guy for trying!" He laughed and went red in the face.

This was unbelievably cute. It seemed like he really wasn't used to saying anything too bold or cheeky.

Finally, we reached the entrance to the world's most famous medieval manuscript. I had never been in such an old library before. We gained access to the Long Room, which to me seemed like the libraries in the fairytale stories I heard as a child. The extensive room held over 200,000 ancient books! I was totally mesmerised and spell bound by its beauty.

"I never thought I would mention Jesus and religion so much on a second date," Nathan laughed, "but the artistic nature of the monks and dedication to the delicate nature of creating this book is more than impressive. And to think this nice wee date came about because you noticed a tiny bit of ink on my body while I was taking off my jumper."

"The Lord works in mysterious ways," was my response and we both had a little chuckle. He followed my lead as we walked around.

Whenever I stopped, he stopped immediately behind me, and lowered his chin over my shoulder. I could smell his cologne. It was oh so good. His face was so close to mine each time, the very tip of his stubbly beard grazed my neck. It was a very satisfying tickle! I couldn't help but laugh each time. He knew exactly what he was doing. As our tour came to a close, he leaned in once more and said, "Doctor Laura, I think with all that laughter you may need a drink to sooth your throat, would you agree?"

"Ha, oh is that so?"

We went for a coffee and when he asked me what I did to keep fit, I nearly choked.

"Oh no, please don't tell me you have a side hustle as being a personal trainer or anything like that?"

"HA no, no, and WOW, that was some reaction to a simple question," he laughed raising an eyebrow knowing there must be a story behind it.

I told him about the brief date with the gentleman who tried to get me to be his guinea pig and his scientific support. Nathan laughed with me, and said there was another benefit to me not falling for that guy's tricks. It meant I was free to spend time getting to know him, and he was so pleased to be spending time with me.

"You know, I am not like that Laura, I just like you, I like you a lot. You said you like the water, how about we go for a swim on the next date?"

"Oh Mr. Confident and his next date!" I smiled, I would actually love to going swimming with this guy! I could easily get him a free pass to my gym. The pool was huge and there were no children allowed.

"I guess I could check my diary, seeing as it is you."

"Did you ever hear the gospel story of how Jesus turned the water into wine?"

"You know, I actually do think I heard of that one, and if it was good enough for the main man himself then it is good enough for us surely?"

"How about we go for a swim then have a few drinks? The other way around would be rather risky."

"Sounds pretty perfect to me!" I was on cloud 9. "It's a date!"

Date 3 with Nathan, The I.T. Guy

On the Sunday, I had a 4 hour extremely long walk with the girls on the Review Board in preparation for the Dublin City Marathon. Then Monday was intensely busy with work meetings, Tuesday was a blur of experiments and by Wednesday evening I had completely forgotten about any candidates. Regular life had just taken over, and I was completely distracted by a work conference coming up. That was until I got a text from Nathan.

Nathan:

Heya, are we still good for Saturday? You didn't reply yesterday so I thought I would give it one more go before I take the hint that you are not interested! ☹

Guilt waved over me, I used to think it was impossible for people to forget about their dates, but I guess it really is a thing. I had read his message yesterday, and I was going to reply but then I had phone call and needed to work on my presentation. I felt the need to over compensate to him to make up for it. I had to send him a sweet reply back.

Laura:

Ok I know you said you work in IT, but seriously, are you listening in to my conversations through my phone?

Nathan:

Ha ha ha! I wish! No why's that?

Laura:

I was literally just talking about you to my housemate, saying I wouldn't be here on Saturday because I had a hot date! X

I lied, but it was white lie. Surely in the grand scheme of things it wasn't the worst thing I could do. I set reminders on my phone to message him Thursday and Friday at lunchtime. He was travelling down from Belfast, giving him some attention was the least I could do!

The whole of Ireland was having an Indian summer, which meant it was tempting to go for a swim in the sea. Good sense did not prevail, and I agreed when Nathan asked me to meet him at the beach. Even before we got near the water the goosebumps were prickling my skin. My legs were changing from the road maps of blue and green veins against a white background, to a complete leg landscape of lavender purple.

Nathan was perfectly olive toned, and the chill made the fine hairs on his arms stick out, he looked really good. "The trick is to get in the water really quickly and keep moving!" he said enthusiastically.

I was not convinced. "You go on ahead in first, and test it out."

"Whatever happened to ladies' first? You women want it every which way that suits you!" he laughed. "It's ok I will be the brave soldier that goes in first!" and he ran in until he was waist deep before diving under.

"Ah! Eeeh! Ah!! Oh it's a bit chilly alright, you better come in and rescue me!" What an ordeal! "You better come in or I am coming to get you!" he teased.

"Ok, Ok I'm coming, I'm coming!" The thoughts of him trying to pick me up, and the absolute weight of me! No, no that would not be happening. I pulled off my dress and ran into the water next to him.

The benefits of being in the water meant he couldn't see my purple legs or dimples of cellulite, but for the first minute I struggled not to hyperventilate! He splashed me and I splashed back and then we swam and kept moving.

A few minutes later we had acclimatised and were floating on our backs chatting. I noticed another tattoo, was it Greek? He was cloud gazing, which gave me good opportunity to observe, I was NOT going to get caught staring this time! I swam closer to him to get a better look. Oh there were two bullet points, one after the second and fourth letters, or perhaps they were roman numerals across his shoulder? A date? It looked like a date. I wasn't a master of roman numerals, but if my memory served me well, those numerals were a date earlier this year. I wondered what it was about?

Flipping onto my back to float and cloud gaze too, my mind began to wonder, maybe I should just ask him out right what the tattoo is for? I mean he is half naked in the water, he knows I can see his upper body. Therefore, he knows I can see his tattoos. He was very open about the meaning behind the Celtic Cross tattoos. Though he did mention that every tattoo had a special meaning to him. What could happen that you would get a date tattoo? The birth of a child was very a popular rationale for a date tattoo. He did say he did not have any children. Well it wouldn't be the first time a man lied about that, or anything else for that matter. It could also be another death, in which case I didn't want to bring down the mood, we were having such a good time.

With our efforts to keep active in the water slowing down, our bodies began to chill.
"Time for some vino, and time to get warm!" Nathan announced smiling broadly.
I was definitely in agreement with it being time to get out of the water, "More like time for a hot whiskey!" I grinned.

Once in the warmth of the cosy old man pub down the road, Nathan ordered a bottle of smooth and supple Pinot Noir, and my goodness did it go down easy, it was pure heaven.
A glass of wine in, and I began to giggle.

"Somebody needs some food in their belly to absorb this fine wine."

"Yes, the seafood here is amazing, we should order!" I agreed.

Before the food arrived, my mind floated back to seeing his tattoo. Forgetting I didn't want to stir things on this perfect date, my curiosity got the better of me. Well, curiosity and a damn good red wine! Putting on a false posh accent I began, "Nathan darling, forgive me but my eyes did wander over your body in the water."

"Ha, oh really, did they now? And were they satisfied with what they observed," he was loving this.

"Well you know, it is quite an extraordinary thing, whilst in appreciation of every cell that makes up your frame, I did notice, a date inked across your shoulder in a beautiful font"….

He was silent. I was silent too. I wondered why he wasn't saying anything. He could hardly have forgotten the date was not that long ago.

Keeping up the charade I continued "I do believe the date was not quite two months ago. Good sir was that," I paused, "was that an important day for you?"

I was praying it wasn't another death, my gut told me it wasn't (always trust your gut - it is your second brain!), after all he would have mentioned it when he was talking about his grandparents and his other ink.

Nathan swirled his red wine in his glass allowing it to breath, he took a sip and pursed his lips, then simply stated, "That was my wedding day, well, that was supposed to be the day I got married."

"Oh no, did your fiancée die too?" I should have kept my curiosity to myself, what an idiot. Ruining everything with my questions, sometimes I wished my brain would just shut up and let me enjoy life!

"Oh gosh no! No, no!" He drew a deep breath in and exhaled. "I, well, things were not right for a long time but, I ended up calling it off."

The immediate relief that it was not another death evaporated when it dawned on me that he was supposed to have been married 7 weeks ago. How on earth did I end up on date with a man who must have believe at some point, that he was going to get married 7 weeks ago? Otherwise, why would he have got the date permanently imprinted on his body?! This did not make sense to me.

"Oh" was the only sound I could make at that point, as I let the information be absorbed. I was never in a situation like this before. I wanted to know more, but was it really rude and nosey and prying to ask? To probe deeper? At the same time, I needed to know what I was getting into here.

"You look like you have seen a ghost, Laura, it is not that big of a deal, I promise. Ask me, ask me anything you want about it. I can practically see the cogs turning in your mind, what are you thinking?" He looked concerned.

"When did you call it off, and why? And when did you get the tattoo?"

"I called it off 6 months ago, because things were not going well between us, and I got the tattoo when we got engaged three years ago."

I really didn't know what to say. There would be a lot of explaining to the girls on the voicemail later!

Phase 3, Man 2, Candidate 8
Larry The Guard

His photographs were of the outdoors. I liked the outdoors. He gave no indication as to what his intentions with his online profile were, which in my experience meant he was player. Ordinarily I would have swiped left, but in an effort to remain unbiased and keep an open mind, I should give him the benefit of the doubt. So I proceeded to swipe right, and it was a match! If the messaging went well, and he ended up being a candidate, I already felt like he would be trouble. My gut was already sending me signals. I feel like this had a potential to be a red flag. Always trust your gut, it is super connected to your brain! I shared my ill feelings with the Review Board via a voice message.

"Hey girls, I am just flagging up with the board that in my efforts to remain unbiased and keep my mind open, I may have landed myself hustling for a date with a potential man whore. This is based on his lack of profile information, and my gut. He said he was a Garda. I am not too keen on dating a Garda. Why do men in uniform always tell you their profession so openly? Is the 'man in uniform' really a thing? What I DO know about men in the Gardaí (the guards) however, is that they were of course one of the original 'Hat-fishers'."

Lisa responded with a voice message immediately.

"Hat-fisher? What's that? How are Guards hat-fishers?"

I explained.

"OK so, you know how a catfish is the term we use to describe a person who uses a fake online persona to lure a person into a relationship online, making their victim believe they are something they are not?"

Lisa indicated she knew what that was "Yeah…"

So I proceeded with my explanation.

"Well a hat-fisher, is a person who lures another person into thinking they have a full head of hair, but actually they have their head covered by caps, and hats in all of their online pictures to hide the bald patch. With Guards in the olden days it was worse, they also had the 'short back and sides' haircut, so you really couldn't tell if there was much or any hair growing underneath their cap or not!"

Lisa sent a string of the laughing emojis.

This Guard, Larry, was really quite friendly with all of his texts, he kept me occupied with text messages and funny video links when I was baby-sitting my nieces and nephews late at night. He did mention coming over for cuddles but sure of course he was joking, we hadn't even met yet.

He came across as the quintessential affable guard. I had come across his type before, not in my dating life but with Guards in general. My early life was intertwined with Garda tales, but that's a story for another time. "An Garda Síochána" are the Irish police force. The English translation is "the guardians of the peace", and are more commonly referred to as "The Guards".

He seemed super devoted and dedicated to his job, but in terms of dating or a relationship I didn't get the vibes that he would be a trustworthy fellow! He was coming across as the cheeky chappy type.

Date 1 with Larry, The Guard

We messaged for a week before he asked me out. For the first time in a really long time, I didn't pick the first date location or have any involvement in the planning of it. Oh a real proper date, now this would be interesting! In fact, I had no idea where we were going, except that it was for brunch. He really was keeping it a secret.

My inner control freak began to wonder if he actually had a place in mind, or was he just going to wing it on the morning. I wanted to know how to be dressed; smart, casual, super casual (yes that is a thing, it's a one-step upgrade from pyjamas, and completely acceptable in some places on a Sunday morning).

I love a good brunch. In the mornings I am always hungry. The body needs to be re-fueled. I wonder if he would be a good eater, a fussy eater, a one who watches you eat so intensely it puts you off your food eater; or the devil incarnate - a noisy eater.

Or would he order something like poached eggs with nothing, while I horsed French toast drizzled with wild berry coulis and hazelnut spread into my big gob. There is always more to brunch than you might think!

The way he picked a restaurant for brunch, and managed to keep it a secret under such stringent interrogation, was actually quite romantic. I was impressed he didn't falter or cave with my grilling. The place was perfect. It wasn't too much, too common or too creepy, it was just right. I felt like goldilocks. How did I get so lucky?

Well, apart from one thing. The only downside was that he was horribly hung over from the night before. This was not exactly ideal. He knew it himself.

He apologised for his state of near death, due to alcohol poisoning. Of course I said it was ok and not to worry. He promised he would make it up to me the next week and take me out to dinner in a swanky restaurant on Kildare street. I suggested perhaps he should walk some of his hangover off. He said so long as I walked with him, he would walk anywhere! His charm offensive was switched back on again, and we enjoyed a flirty walk in Marlay Park.

Date 2 with Larry, The Guard

A whole week later, and cancelling on me twice in that time with little notice, Larry assured me repeatedly that on Wednesday, we were definitely going out! He had the restaurant booked and was eagerly anticipating our date! I text him on Wednesday afternoon to be sure, and he replied in confidence that he would not let me down.

He was to pick me up from home at 7 pm. I really wanted to get a gym session in first after work. I would be cutting it tight but I needed those happy endorphins! I knew I was going to have to change my gym eventually. Days like this reminded me of that. As I headed southbound on the M50, I passed the chock-a-block traffic on the other side going North. This was such a bad idea. The time, and the corresponding traffic was not on my side!

I parked far from the entrance to the gym so I wouldn't have to go around the stupid one-way system that took FOREVER on the way out. Walking briskly (more like trotting) to the gym, I checked my phone for the time, it was bang on 5 pm. The half sprint from the car to the gym, with my gym bag, would have to count as my warm up. I had 800 calories to burn and 40 minutes to do it! Was this possible? Larry sent a message while I was at the gym saying he was looking forward to seeing me soon. He was really sweet like that. Once on the bike, I repeatedly checked Google maps to see how the traffic was doing, it was improving slightly. If I increased the resistance on the bike, and peddled faster I could gain a few minutes on reaching my target before hitting the shower!

In the shower, I did not need to worry about time. This, I had to a fine art, shampoo in and rinse out, conditioner in, and mild exfoliation after the gym sweats. Finally, wash off the conditioner and body wash simultaneously. Showering at the gym was quicker than any other location, largely aided by the power-hose force of the water. This was not an exaggeration. Through naivety I had stood face front to the spout the first time I showered there, and nearly lost my nipples with the dangerous force! An arm and hand always protected them now, anytime I moved in the gym showers. The force of the water however, got all the suds off one's body in record time, every time. Today this was something I was grateful for!

Makeup on and with my squishy rollers neatly stacked in my hair, I trotted back to the car, I would have plenty of time to change my shoes and paint my nails - provided traffic didn't get worse. Once home, I raced inside to tend to my talons. No little message from The Guard. I topped up my makeup. By now it was after 7 pm. Hmm, he was late, I looked out my bedroom window to where he had parked before to pick me up. Not a single blue car with a Kerry registration was outside. I decided to text him.

Laura:

Not like you to be late, everything ok?

I knew before hitting send that I was being stood up.

Larry:

I'm caught babes, have to go into work.

A fireball of heat rumbled in my core, rage thumping, my heart began pounding in my ears! I breathed out and began to cry. I was torn between anger, and disappointment, and shame. Why did he think so little of me, not to let me know? He didn't strike me as the sharpest tool in the shed, but he was digitally competent to use a phone. He was a PRICK! URRRRGGGGGHHHHH I hated men like him. I hated people like him! Even if someone was so ugly, or so horrible, or so dumb that you couldn't bear to even breath the same air as them, the most basic common courtesy was to let them know you couldn't spend time with them!!

Should I be sad, or angry or annoyed with him? Or should I just let him go? Maybe he had a child he had to tend to, because I just plain didn't believe the last minute call into work story? Hmm nope, I had definitely asked him if he had any children, after he had asked me the same question. I wondered at the time if he thought I had a Mom bod? Hopefully not! I would definitely never rock up in a pair of Mom jeans. At best, for now I could only describe him as a chancer. At this rate we actually had clocked up more planned and cancelled dates than the three real ones I needed to mark him on.

I would love to do a background check on him and see how much of what he has said is true. Can't a friend of a friend recommend someone for me to date instead? He was from Kerry, to a woman from the North East he might as well be from Azerbaijan. I wracked my brain to think of anyone I knew from Kerry. In my 30 years of life, 10 years of international work and I couldn't make a connection to Kerry?! Maybe those Kerry folk were shy and kept themselves to themselves? I had heard that Limerick was an up and coming city so fewer people in their 20s, 30s and 40s were migrating to Dublin. That must be it, the Kerry folk were staying local.

What a waste of actually perfect makeup! A millisecond of feeling like a deflated balloon and my mood flipped once more.

I just can't believe someone would be so careless with my time. It was infuriating. Texting is quick and easy. If you are in a place where you have to be quiet or discrete it is a great way to communicate. Do you know what else is great? Phoning someone, you know if you look a mess and you don't want to video call anyone, you can just phone and communicate with your voices to each other. You know what else is great? Voice messages, you don't have to actually engage with the other person, you can just leave your message, this is particularly handy if you are busy with your hands or trying to walk etc. You know what isn't great? Is leaving someone hanging! I was beginning to hate the candidate trial process. At this point I just wanted to go to the wedding and have fun, on my own with the people I knew, and if they wanted to bring plus ones, who cared, I knew they would be fun.

I was livid at him, at myself, at the situation, at every stupid f-ing relationship that never worked out before that led to this point! I hated my stupid cousin's wedding, and that god dammed plus one written on the invite. If my cousin actually liked me, you know the decent thing would be not to write "plus one". Then, at least I could half bitch about not receiving an invitation for a plus one, while secretly being delighted there was not an expectation for me to have one!

Luckily I had the best housemate! If by magic or telepathy, or karma for the few good things I had done in my life, my housemate Lisa text.

Lisa:

Heya, I'm in Dundrum, do you want anything home?

Laura:

Are you coming home via McDs?

Lisa:

Is it hot in hell?

Laura:

Add an ice cream to your order, to mend my broken heart!

Lisa:

Your wish is my command! Ha so long as it doesn't give you a cold heart sweetie pie!

I was well pissed off. All this cancelling business was killing my spirit, I was losing morale. It wasn't a real experiment. I didn't have to finish it if I didn't want to. I could just stop. Forget the whole damn thing. At the rate I was going at, even with all my efforts, it was unlikely I was going to have a date for my cousin's wedding anyway. This stupid Guard really slowed the process down- BIG TIME. What I should be doing was thinking of smarty-pants-answers for when my half-drunk relatives would ask:

"Is there a man on the scene?"

"You've been back in Dublin a while now, and we don't see you home too often, is there a mister up there keeping you company?"

"Were you not asked to bring a plus one?"

"What's wrong with you that you can't get a man, are you too fussy?"

The answer was simple, Lisa explained it to me one time. Yes, we are on the shelf, but we are on the top shelf. The pool of men who are as smart, as successful, as wealthy, as witty, as kind and as decent as us are limited. We don't suffer fools gladly and we can pick up a hot guy for a few days, weeks or months as we desire, till they bore us, their novelty wears off, or something finer comes along. The trouble is explaining that to your 60- year-old aunties and uncles! Ha, ha, ha, ha!

I hadn't the will to chat to anyone else on the apps, I was suffering dating fatigue. I just needed to tough it out and get this Guard to go on three dates with me in total. Then I would be able to include this mess in the ranking table.

Why was trying to date this one man so hard, was it because he was a Guard? You know there was one person I could ask about this; Auntie Rose. My Auntie Rose was married to a guard more than 40 years and counting. No time like the present, I'd send her a voice note- Auntie Rose was super tech savvy.

"Hi Auntie Rose, you may find this a strange question but I promise I will explain everything the next time I see you. In your opinion, you know the way the Guards do shift work, and have emergencies and all that, well do you think it is hard to date a Guard, or be married to one? Obviously not too difficult, you are still married! I mean more like in the beginning. I don't necessarily mean specific to just your own experience, but was it hard for women in general to date someone in the Guards? How did guys and girls meet back in the day?"

Auntie Rose was a gem, always got a speedy reply, via voice note too!

"Well, you know it was very different back in my day. There was none of this online dating, less drinking and no mobile phones. Showbands! Showbands were very popular particularly on a Sunday night".

Ok so going out on a Sunday night was not too popular now, so I had to ask.

"Were they like the descriptions people give of the dances in the school halls, with the priests chaperoning them, men on the left, women on the right? How could you tell if you were going to be asked to dance?"

Speedy as ever Auntie Rose explained it.

"Ha, ha, ha, no, no. You would go into town with your friends about 10 pm at night. You would all stand over at the wall chatting. You would be looking for a guy to take you out jiving, but he would have to be good like. Ah sure you easily could tell what was happening, the guys would be eyeing up who they were going to ask for ages before they made the approach. You could tell by the walk too, which was handy. If you didn't want to go dancing with a particular fella, you had time to start making your way to bathroom, or try find a chair to sit down, to say you were sitting that dance out."

"Ha, ha Rose you're a dark horse! So seeing as you didn't have phones how did you know when to meet someone, if you were not really going out together?"

"Well everyone went to the Showbands on a Sunday, I just had to wait for the Sunday nights when your uncle would be off work for him to be there, and he could really jive."

"Ha so uncle Joe was wanted for his moves on the dancefloor?"

"Yeah, he was a fine man, tall, square shoulders, straight walk, you'd know he was a Guard a mile away."

"Was the appeal because he was a Guard?"

"Well being in the Guards was a government job, steady, and you know back then there were the girls who liked a man in uniform, like the postmen, the Guards, and the customs men."

"So if he was such a good jiver, was their competition for him?" I couldn't help but wind her up.

"WE were great jivers, though we were giving it loads on the dancefloor one night and your uncle being so tall, his elbow knocked out a girls' contact lens and it fell to the floor. There were seven or eight of us then, on our hands and knees for a few minutes looking for it and after a while your uncle crawled over and asked me whispering......What are we looking for?! He was a funny one. Things were very different back then. When a Guard was getting married, neither he nor the bride could live within a 30-mile radius of the girls' parents. This was in case he was coerced into "squashing" fines or summons, but the less said about that the better! There also was the height requirement where the Guard had to be over 5 feet 9 inches in height, but to be sure most were 6 feet 2 inches. You pretty much knew who was a Guard by looking at them. Does any of this answer your questions?"

"Thanks Auntie Rose! That's plenty for now!" I replied.

He had the cheek to text at 9 pm that night asking if I wanted to call over to him. When I said no, he offered to call over to mine. Was he serious? Did he think I would let that happen? I had to be clear in my next message.

Laura:

I don't know how to make this any simpler for you, I do not want to call to your house. I do not want you to call to my house. I am only interested in going on a date.

Larry:

Look, let's leave it off all together

OMG was he ending it? Relieve washed over me.

Laura:

Oki doki

I replied, delighted it was over. That was it, the only snag was I was supposed to go on three dates not just one, which meant I would have to find another guy.

Beep, Beep went my phone. Oh Christ another message.

Larry:

**Look, I am not going to mess you about xxx I like you xxx
You are a stunner xx Sorry xxx**

Oh, I knew this type of message. He just wants to have his cake and eat it too. I knew if I just waited two more minutes there would be more from him. *Beep, Beep* - And there it was!

Larry:

I do like you, but you are full on... I would rather take it slower

God he was so dim. I would enjoy seeing how this played out.

Laura:

One date is pretty slow, how would you like me to go slower?

Even a fool like him couldn't argue with that. He replied with,

Larry:

You are looking for something more than I am

Oh God not only was he dim, but he was also suffering amnesia.

Laura:

You text me to tell me I was the one for you, and that you wanted to know how I felt about a house and kids, I said that was a long way off for me. You said it was your plan in the next year or two. Please explain how THAT, is ME looking for more than you?

Larry:

Ah I know but you gotta realise my job is shift work and is tough on my body xxx and sometimes things will change last minute, it's not anything against you xxx

He was totally backtracking. What a flake. This man was a mess. It was very clear he was just pursuing me for you know what. I focused on my experiment. At least his poor scores would make some other man look exceptionally good. I decided I would have to try dumb myself down just to get through two more dates with this man. Perhaps a career in acting might not be off the cards.

I did my best to text like him.

Laura:

Yeah babes I know all about circadian rhythm

Woops. I knew he wouldn't know what I meant. So I followed it with another text immediately.

Laura:

The shift work can mess with your body but I totally understand. All good babes. Take it easy xxxx

I threw in the kisses at the end for good measure. He was back on side. What a simpleton.

I was trying to focus on the positives. As far as I knew the Guards couldn't have beards so no fear of him becoming a hipster. I had a niggling feeling holding out for a proper date with this loser would waste too much time.

The best way to get through two dates quickly with him would be to agree to sporadic random dates. He claimed his shift work was the reason he messaged at odd hours in the evenings, this I understood. However, this did not justify him looking for last minute "cuddles". Did he think I was stupid? Actually he was so self-absorbed, he hadn't asked anything about me properly, so he wouldn't know whether I was smart or dumb.

He was showing sleazy signs; a game I could fake to lock in the date. I agreed to meet him at 9.30 pm on Tuesday. He thought we were going for spin up the mountains. Ha! I let him think that! To me, he now only served the purpose of making other men's scores look good.

Right on cue he pulled up outside at 9.29pm. When he showed up, he was punctual.

He sent a message.

Larry:

Heya, I'm outside, are you jumping in?

It was time for me to bring on the Oscar!

Laura:

Oh gosh I am so sorry I really need to get to the shop before it closes at 10 pm, will we go for a romantic walk to the shop instead?

Larry:

Jump in, I will drive you!

There was no way I was getting in that car!

I phoned him. "It's quicker walking, really. Come on!" I said cheerily. He didn't know the area, so he couldn't really argue. So out he got and we walked to the shop. As we approached my apartment on the way back he asked if I was letting him in.

"Oh my house mate goes to bed really early, so we have a no guests after 10 pm on a school night rule, sorry!"

I lied, just like him.

"I'll be quiet!" he offered. I laughed "Ah nice try, but not tonight".

I attempted to fake a yawn - and a real one popped out! This dating was a drain. I really just wanted to sleep.

"Safe home!" I said and turned my back on him. Date two - tick!

"Laura!" He whispered after me "Ah Laura I want you so bad, can I not just come in for a minute!"

God, I rolled my eyes, he was worse than pathetic, and it made me mad to think he thought I would find this romantic, or worse again that I would fall for it!

I turned around and waved goodnight! Right I just had to tolerate him one more time and then that was it.

He was already sending me a message from the car.

Larry:

Babe I just wanted to have some cuddles with you xxxx

Yeah. Sure. If he knew anything about me he would know I absolutely hate being called babe, it is such a turn off!

"Cuddles" I laughed to myself.

Larry:

Can I come over Friday night?

Laura:

Hiya, oh I thought you were working Friday night?

…Because you are such a f&^king liar and a chancer to boot!

Larry:

Oh I am yeah but not til 11pm so I could call over for an hour or so

I hadn't planned to tell him it was my birthday, but there is nothing like a birthday to make a bad guy run!

Laura:

Oh great, yeah sure come on over, it's my birthday Friday, I'll just be getting ready to meet the girls in town

Silence. It made me sad in a way, to know how well I knew the dirty rotten men, and their nasty modes of action. The only positive was, that I knew I would never end up with one! My radar for this type of man was always bang on! I will say it again, ALWAYS trust your gut!

Isn't it funny though, with social media, those you are least connected to actually remember your birthday - or at least they acknowledge the fact that Facebook reminded them you still exist. I got a message from Padraig, The Radiographer, and Daniel, The Carpenter. I even got a message from a guy I went to French college with, almost half my lifetime ago! The birthday came and went and not peep out of Larry.

Beep, Beep A text from Larry -maybe he could redeem himself I joked to myself!

Larry:

Hey sugar, would love to call over for cuddles later!

OK, so no maybe no redemption. Maybe he was a total loser, good for nothing waste of space, who, with any luck would end up on his own. The alternative would be that some poor woman, with absolutely no self-worth would tolerate him.

What a PIG!! You know that name suited all meanings of the word. It applied to persons, usually in contempt, since the 1540's; the derogatory slang meaning "police officer" has been in underworld slang since at least 1811. It is quoted from the Dictionary of Buckish Slang, University Wit and Pickpocket Eloquence published in London that same year.

He was the type of fool to plague you with messages until he got a response.

I better text him back.

Laura:

Simple clue: 9 letters, Look in the mirror

Larry:

Huh?

Laura:

Complex clue: Noun; 9 letters, a slimey, untrustworthy person, usually male, especially in dealings with the opposite sex, used to carry things

Larry:

You know this smart stuff turns me on, you're such a nerdy weirdo

Laura:

It won't when you realise the answer is you, you SLEAZEBAG!

There was no way I could do the three dates with this guy. He was a complete and utter write off! I'd have to voice message the Review Board to let them know.

Beep, Beep Oh a new message, not from Larry thank goodness!

And my-oh-my! I might just have identified Larry's replacement in this process, he is a bit of an outlier, more of a Positive Control perhaps. The Review Board can have the final decision on it. First though I really need a day or two to de-stress before I meet Candidate 9, Bobby, The Teacher!

Phase 3, Man 3, Candidate 9, Bobby, The 'Teacher'?

His height was going to be a good problem. He was lovely and tall. The confusing brain fog of handsome or tall wafted over my eyes. I focused on his facial features, you know the part of him I should *actually* be looking at. This guy was definitely my type on paper. He was 6 foot 3, but you would be able to tell that from his pictures anyway. His lips were plump, all the better for kissing. His eyes were a light sea blue, so they would need to be protected from the sun.

He had a very light glow to his skin. Perhaps they were all holiday photos, he definitely had some sun exposure, but you wouldn't say he was tanned. Although I doubt he had the skin type that would tan very much. He didn't look aged, his skin looked good. He was either smart enough not to let his skin get sun burned thus speeding up the aging process, or, he was originally a pasty white and learned the hard way!

There was not much information on his profile, other than he was a teacher. He really didn't look like a teacher. His name was Bobby. He looked good, crinkles just at the very corner of his eyes suggested he has led a life of laughter to this point. Animals also featured in his pictures - no cats, thank god! Cows however, were plentiful. This was interesting, then it dawned on me, he was likely not a local. He was more likely to be one of those guys who goes home every weekend to work on the farm. For all I knew he could have a sweetheart back home, and be chancing his arm every night in Dublin. My inner cynic was raising her ugly head ever since my 'Lousy Larry' experience. There was a sincerity to this guy's face which swiftly wiped that thought from my mind. I had nothing to lose by swiping right, indicating I found him attractive, sure he might not fancy me, or he might not message first, or if I message him, he might not reply. Luckily it was an instant match. That feeling still gave me a high! He sent the first message a few minutes later.

Bobby: **I think you look familiar.**

I pulled up his profile to get a better look at him. Nope, no bells were going off in my head. I looked at the limited information on his profile. Back again to the profile pictures to see if I was missing something. Oh. He was wearing a Gaelic football jersey from my home county in one of his pictures, maybe he recognised me from back home.

Laura: **Oh really, maybe I just have that type of face, you know a friendly one? Ha, ha**

Bobby: **Nope, you are not that friendly, ha!**

Laura: **What makes you say that mister? I have hardly insulted you already, have I?!**

Bobby: **Nope, not today but you have made me wait in the past.**

Laura: **Me? Make you wait for what? When?**

Bobby: **Nope, I am not telling you, you are going to have to guess!**

Laura: **Guess! But that could take FOREVER for me to get right! Can you give me a clue?**
Bobby: **Nope, you are smart girl, you will figure it out!**
Laura: **Not very positive are you with all these 'Nope's'**
Bobby: **Nope, I am actually a very positive, happy chappy**

Communication ceased. I really wasn't in the mood for playing games but I was committed to the cause of trying to find a date for the wedding, and at this point the situation with The Guard meant my timeline was not great.

Laura: **Ok I will ask 3 questions, if you answer them honestly and I still can't guess, will you tell me or at least give me a clue?**
Bobby: **You can ask 3 questions to which I will answer yes or no**
Laura: **Ok. Deal! Right: Question one do you know me from outside of Dublin?**
Bobby: **Yes**
Laura: **Question two do you know me from school days?**
Bobby: **No**

I searched my brain, what did he mean by me making him wait in the past. Wait for what? God, was he talking about ten years ago when I worked in the nightclub in the next town over?

Laura: **OK. Question three: Do you know me from working in a nightclub?**
Bobby: **Yes - ha, ha, ha how did you guess?! You remember me?** ☺
Laura: **Eh I'm sorry nooo, but it was the one time in my life where there was a lot of people, a lot of faces, no names, just drink orders, and, I guess not everyone can be first in the queue! Ha, ha!** ☺

We exchanged messages for about the next hour. I learned he was from Wexford. Oh the strawberries - yum! I knew this guy was going to be good already! He worked for one summer in Dundalk, while staying with family in nearby county Monaghan. He used to drink in the nightclub I worked in, every Friday and Saturday night. It was always a great night out! He remembered me as the one barmaid who didn't let him skip the queue. I was a stickler for adhering to a protocol even back then! I had no recollection of him at all!

He said he was back in Ireland four months now, after a number of years working abroad. For some reason, based purely on his exotic profile pictures, I presumed he was teaching English abroad. I didn't have time to ask, he launched straight into his plan to meet for coffee.

Date 1 with Bobby, The 'Teacher'

We agreed to a coffee date high up in the mountains in a real old touristy bar and restaurant, that played live Irish music every night. We however, were planning a nice, quiet daytime date. It was to be a casual date, the type of date where 'jeans and a nice top' would suffice. However, I am one of those who simply never has a suitable 'jeans and a nice top' outfit. With jeans on the brain I opted for a casual denim dress and tan boots, they would have to do. My housemate joked that I was dressing appropriate for the country style venue!

I pulled into the carpark 5 minutes early. I checked my makeup in the rear view mirror, and saw this obnoxious 'look-at-me' Lamborghini car park up beside me. I rolled my eyes, the driver likely saw but I didn't care. Maybe I was just jealous? You really never know who you were rubbing shoulders with in touristy restaurants, but there is never an American too far away! I hopped out of my car and headed towards the restaurant.

"Laura, Laura, is that you?"

I stopped dead, and flipped my head around. Was the guy in the suit, in the fancy-pants-car talking to me?

I pointed to myself and asked, "Me?"

His face flushed red, I couldn't believe I had the power to make a grown man blush.

He walked towards me.

"Yes, Laura, I am sorry for shouting after you. I hope I didn't startle you?"

The closer he got, I realised it was him. It was definitely him. I thought he just looked tall because his car was so low to the ground. The car was really off putting. Not that you should ever judge a book by its cover, or a man by his car. Seriously though, what was he compensating for, eh? I scolded myself and instructed my brain to try to remain unbiased.

We made our way into the restaurant. He held the door open for me. I don't know why, but I curtsied in thanks. He laughed, so it was all good!

His face was boyish and handsome. He wore a three-piece suit which he apologised for. He had had a meeting with his financial advisor earlier that day. He hadn't time to get back home to change his clothes into something less formal, and then to make the subsequent journey out here.

The dark grey tweed suit must have been tailor made, it was millimeter perfect. The checkered shirt was not that of the typical country fella, I smiled to myself. Maybe he saved the farmer-boy checked shirts for the cows! The checkered squares were small dark grey overlapping grids on a pristine, almost glowing, white background. When he took the suit jacket off, his broad shoulders filled the shirt out perfectly too. My gaze followed his long arms extend full length, outstretched towards me. I just about managed not to full-on drool, when I realised he was holding his hands out to help me with my own jacket. His 5 o'clock shadow was apparent (though it was only 3 pm) and I couldn't help but think how good that would feel kissing my neck.

I blushed. I felt my skin go pink from my chest up my neck, to my face. There was no way he could have missed that! How was it that I was nervous *now*?! I had been on a ridiculous number of dates recently. I knew the drill!

We were shown to our table. He smiled politely, came over to my side of the table, and pulled out a chair for me to sit. It was a move that was so quick and smooth, it surely was second nature to him. Was he always this smooth with everyone I wondered? Or was he trained to be chivalrous? Mockingly, I turned my head to the side and dipping my chin towards my shoulder, looked back at him fluttering my eye lashes in recognition of this token gesture. He laughed again. "Oh now you flutter your eye lashes at me?! I saw you rolling your eyes at my car!"

That was his opener. Ok, well, this was going to be an interesting date!

"Eh yes, I, well I hadn't seen one of those in real life, I was not expecting my date to step out of it."

"Don't worry, my financial advisor did the same thing. He warned me of the depreciation as soon as the wheels hit the road. What can I say? When I saw it, I was in love with it and I just had to have it!"

I laughed, he was only teasing me. We ordered coffee, normally I would go for an Americano and milk, but I was feeling light and airy, a bit like froth, so I ordered a Cappuccino, and he did too. He called the waitress back to make sure we got chocolate sprinkled on the top. A man after my own heart, I thought to myself.

From there the conversation flowed. He was charming and delightful and I was at ease. He was an only child and spoke a lot about his parents. He lived at home when he wasn't away with work. We were having a great time, the slagging was good, and it was all lighted hearted fun. It was nearly time to go and he began to look a little bit shifty. "I have to tell you something Laura. I'm not a teacher."

To be honest, I did wonder when I saw the car. I thought maybe he just had rich parents, or was a scam artist, or had won the lotto. The scam artist theory was in the lead position I must admit, but I was going to let him tell his story. "I mean, I do teach. It's not really a lie. I teach people how to fly, but really, I'm a pilot. Well I'm actually a Captain. I didn't want to put all that online because all anyone asked was "Are you really a pilot?" and the first thing you see in their eyes is a dollar sign. For a while that's great, I mean come on, I am a young man, and women are beautiful. Sometimes I like to," he paused, "chat."

Chat my eye! I knew exactly what he meant! Though he actually was *really* chatty, I didn't realise how much time had gone by. The only reminder to leave was a text from Lisa, checking cinema times, it was girls' movie night tonight! "Ha well that's for sure, I like to chat too, especially with you, but you have been hogging the microphone all day"! I laughed and winked. He told me the floor was mine to say what I liked.

"Right, so mister pilot guy, I guess that partially explains the beast of a car, but you still kind of lied so that's not ideal. Just please don't be some sort of pathological liar, and we might get along!"

His face grew serious, then he raised a brow, and trying not to laugh he continued.
"Laura, I think we will do more than just get along. You know, there was a mirror at the entrance to the bar, on our way in. I saw us in it. We looked really good together. Like, we make a good looking couple. We would make really good looking babies."

He blushed again. On one hand, it was so endearing. On the other hand, what is it with guys and babies these days? This was starting to freak me out. I laughed and said,
"Ok, baby steps! We are only on a first date!"
"So let's go for a second one," he responded with confidence.

Health was important to him. Unlike the Health Nutritionist, who was clearly unhealthy but putting on a great façade for the sake of drawing clients in. This guy needed to have full health for his job. He explained if you had any physical injury - you couldn't fly. A cold or flu affecting your ears and you couldn't fly. Fail your medical, and you can't fly. Alcohol in your system, and you definitely can't fly.

I was thinking to myself. I could do with some more walking in preparation for the Dublin City Marathon. Glendalough had been on my mind ever since the failed attempt to go there with the Carpenter, which ended up as a salsa dance date. So I suggested with his enthusiasm for health and fitness we should go walking at Glendalough.
"Will I take you for a spin there in the car?" he winked.
"How about I meet you there, I wouldn't want anyone to see me in that yoke! I'm a respected super scientist you know!"
We laughed and agreed to meet there at 10 am Saturday.

Date 2 with Bobby, The Pilot

A Glendalough date, with a man who seemed perfect. Cue the gnawing feeling associated with the belief that if things seem too good to be true, they usually are! I decided I was just going to live in the moment and enjoy it! Glendalough was my happy place.

Unfortunately, the pre-date inspection, standing in front of the mirror was not. I took the advice from the Review Board ladies, on board. I went shopping and got myself some brand spanking new sports attire! Thank goodness there was beginning to be a decline in the pure white sports footwear. That trend was WAY too hard to keep clean! I selected black sports footwear with white markings. These were currently very trendy, and functional. Black ankle socks which were not visible - check! My feet were totally on point!

Gone were my long, oversized super comfy, grey, draw string tracksuit bottoms and matching hoody. These were replaced with black mid-calf sports leggings with white stripes down the side. Vertical lines are supposed to make your legs look longer and thinner, or so I was told. A fitted black vest top to match, was teamed with a dark green loose crop top hoody to bring focus to the smallest part of my waist. Dark, emerald green ear-rings completed my look. I wore my hair down but brought a hair tie, for when we began our walk.

He messaged to say he was leaving his house, and it would take him close to an hour to get there. I replied letting him know I was on my way out the door, but had to stop for fuel on the way, so we should arrive at about the same time. Note to self, put diesel and not petrol in the car!

I really enjoyed the drive down. Glendalough was my local paradise. It sparked joy regardless of my mood, or any situation I was in prior to getting there. When I parked I spotted I had a message from Bobby. I hoped he wasn't last minute cancelling on me!

Bobby: **I've arrived, abandoned the flash car for something more hill worthy** ☺
Laura: **I've just parked up, meet at the visitors' centre?**
Bobby: **Sure! Think I spot you now anyway!**

Oh, even in his chilled out clothes he was looking well! If anyone saw us eyeballing each other, looking each other up and down, I would be mortified! I'm sure it was obvious to all around us that we were on a date. He greeted me with a welcome kiss on each cheek. We commented on how well we timed our arrival, and how surprisingly hot it was for late October. The Indian Summer Ireland continued. We decided to walk down to the Miners Village, then up to the Spinc, and back down to get some food.

I told him how glad I was that it wasn't a crazy hot summers day, though. He was in stitches laughing at me as I explained my frequent, summer activity-date dilemma. You see, I would ordinarily insist that everyone wears their factor 50, or at very least factor 30 when the sun is out. So me, one hot sunny day, I would be lathered in the thick, sludgy greasiness of it. My concern then would be, that this, combined with mountain peak sweat was not exactly something I was aiming for! He agreed, my description of it was not quite oozing sex appeal, but insisted that it was better than looking like a half-baked lobster on top of a cliff.

I was glad he could see the sense in it, and the humour! He immediately then apologised for the overpowering scent off the antiperspirant he used. My heart melted a bit, he was actually a little insecure - it beats me why! As far as I could tell, he was a dream come true!

We walked over the little foot bridge that crossed the stream, then down by the lakes.
"Glendalough is where I find my peace from the chaos with work" I told him.
"Really?"

"I know it has lots of tourists in the summer, but it's calm and tranquil and even the drive here lowers my blood pressure, I'm sure. I guess it's because I don't get here too often. Do you know what I am trying to say?"

"That Glendalough is your odd weekend yin, to the workload yang?" He responded confident he understood me.

"Pretty much, ha!"

The lakes as always were a perfect calm. In fact, so still were the lakes, they reflected mirror perfect images of the colourful nature around them. It was spellbinding. The woody scent makes you feel so at one with nature. Through the still and the quite, a deer approached. He was gorgeous. So elegant, walking as if he was on a cat walk. Bobby took my hand and whispered to me not to move a muscle, while he took out his phone to get a picture of the three of us, him, me and 'Bambi' (yeah, we got all mushy and named him).

We continued on our journey, passing the Miners Village and up the side of the waterfall. Reaching the tip top, was a bit tricky, and a little slippery. Bobby held his and out to help me up. I loved this. For once in my life, I was not taking the lead. Instead, I had a guide. A strong, handsome guide at that. At the precipice there was one last big rock to climb up on. Bobby got up first then bent down to help me balance on my way up. In doing so he let rip a very, VERY loud fart. I swear it echoed! I tried, but couldn't hold in my laughter. It was so funny. I took a proper fit of the giggles.

Bobby asked what was so funny. Oh my god I thought, did he not know he farted?! I was laughing so much I couldn't get the words out.

"You, you, just ha, ha, ha you just farted REALLY loudly!"

Doubled over with laughter, I began to pray that my laughing wouldn't make me need to pee! I couldn't even look up at him to see his reaction for a moment. I didn't need to I could hear him laughing already.

"I did not fart," he just about managed to say.

I was in convulsions again! I knew he was joking.

"Then why, why," it was really hard to breath and laugh and speak at the same time. I tried again. "Then why are you laughing?"

This seemed to make him laugh even more!

"I'm laughing because of how you are laughing! It's contagious!"

Eventually we calmed down. Mostly because I thought if I didn't, then I would have to go pee in the woods! I really didn't want to do that! A few minutes later Bobby's stomach grumbled really loudly. He promptly looked at me and said, "I'm sure that noise came from you, are you getting hungry yet Laura?"

"Ha, are you sure that was not your stomach grumbling because, YOU, emptied it of gas from the other end?" I laughed, and he took it in good spirits.

"It's the hungry grass!" Bobby exclaimed!

"The hungry grass? I have never heard of it!" I shrieked, laughing.

"The hungry grass is the reason you have to keep some food with you at all times hiking through Ireland, especially these parts," Bobby explained. "Don't you know we had a famine back in the eighteen hundreds?!"

"I do know we had a famine," I was not going to be outsmarted by this dude. I knew my Irish history! "The famine of 1845 to 1849 was in part due to the blight of the potato crop, in part due to those British….. well I won't tell you what I'd like to call them, but those horrible Brits at that time who starved us, worked us like slaves, and stole our land! To survive, half the country went to America, only about half who stayed survived!"

"Yes" Bobby interjected taking over, "I like the patriotism in your voice by the way, and the other half are the reason we have hungry grass." He looked at me deadpan, as if that was all the explanation I would need, even though I was still clearly baffled. So he continued.

"The grass is haunted by the ghosts of those who starved and died, and are buried in the mountains all around us. Upon stepping on the grass, without some food, you will become tortured by hunger pangs of the ghosts!"

I smiled and laughed softly, it was a bitter sweet tale.

"That was such a cute wee story Bobby! I will surely pass it on! We don't know how lucky we have it, do we?"

"True, but, somedays we know just how lucky we are, and we enjoy it to the max, like today!"

He took my hand and twirled me around at the top of the mountain. "Sure you don't need music to dance!" he shouted! The rich smell of the flora and fauna was euphoric especially this time of year as the leaves began to change colour and fall. The smell of the birch, ferns and pine were a woodland retreat from the fumes of buses, cars, motorbikes, and industrial outputs in the city. It was a feast for the senses - there really were forty shades of green!

By the time we were down at lake level again we were famished. We were well after the lunch time rush and too early for dinner so the place was quiet enough. The food in the hotel never tasted so good! (Though to be fair, I say that for every meal after a few hours hiking). I noted he ate like a normal person, and I didn't hear a thing! He didn't slap the food around in his mouth, he wasn't a noisy chewer, or a loud gulping swallower, he was perfect! Or maybe I was just a smitten kitten with an overdose of post-hike endorphins? It helped I was in a place I simply adored, with views that would sooth anyone's soul.

Though I was really happy, I began to feel sleepy towards the end of the meal. Bobby felt the same. We decided we better order coffees before we drove off. Back on my usual Americano, with Bobby still on the Cappuccinos, I remembered for the first time since I met him that dating him was part of the process to find a date for the wedding. Maybe that's what a good date does? Maybe a really good date makes you thoroughly enjoy the moments you have together, and forget about the rest of the world? Bobby interrupted my thoughts.

"Penny for your thoughts Dr Laura? Are you wondering about our next date? How can we top this one?"

"Well hello Mr Smooth, welcome to the table!" We were giddy again, and were cracked up laughing at the silliest of things. We agreed we would be doing ourselves a disservice if we did not go on another date together. My only concern was the amount of time I was spending dating instead of prepping for the Dublin City Marathon, which was getting closer. I mentioned this concern to him. Lucky for me, Bobby was keen to get some more steps in too and suggested we go to Curracloe for another good long walk.

"Trust me Laura, I have the solution!"

"Right," I said, "I better get home before another sleepy wave washes over me, and you can phone me later about this Curracloe place!"

"You, my dear lady, have got yourself a deal, it will be great to have you in my neck of the woods!"

Date 3 with Bobby, The Pilot

True to his word Bobby phoned that evening, and the conversation was directly focused on going to Curracloe beach the following morning.

"Curracloe? It does sound familiar, where is it?"

"Wexford, it's a gorgeous beach."

"Well I guessed Wexford, because you said it was down home for you, and obviously it's on the coast, will it take long to get there?"

"About two hours, you'll love it, it's a blue flag beach! Good and long too, about 10 km, so if we do the full length up, and back, that will be a good distance to have covered, won't it?"

"It sure will, and you don't mind doing it with me? All that distance I mean?"

"Not at all, sure I might bring the dog, if that's ok?"

"The dog?!" my eyes widened so much it wouldn't surprise me if he heard them moving down the phone, "you have a dog and you left it until now to tell me! What breed? How old? Do you have pictures? How did it take you so long to tell me?!"

"Ah, he's still only a pup, we have him about a year." Bobby flicked through his phone and sent me some photos and videos of the dog, he really was a bouncy puppy.

"He is definitely no shepherd; he is useless with the sheep. We think he is half afraid of them, but we still call him Shep, and the cows respond well to him."

"Oh look! He is just adorable! Such a cute wee black and white guy! Is he a border collie?"

"He is yeah, but he's not like you, he's not actually from the border! Ha, ha!"

I laughed along, this was going to be the best date ever!

"So I'll pick you up tomorrow morning, we'll head to the farm to get Shep, and then get walking?!"

"Sounds perfect!"

I need not have worried about keeping the chat up on the 2 hour drive down to Bobby's home place. We tuned the car radio to a station playing classic hits from the 80's and 90's. With the music pumping, we belted out the songs at the top of our voices. Neither of us could be described as having the voice of an angel. That didn't matter. We knew the words and totally kept to the beat, swaying and shrugging our shoulders in our seats. Chair dancing at its finest!

I had searched online about Curracloe beach, how could a beach so beautiful and so long have not been on my radar after all these years! Maybe the internet photos were photo-shopped, but I didn't think so.

"So this beach we are going to is famous, I didn't realise it until I looked it up last night. It's the beach from the opening scene of the movie 'Saving Private Ryan'!"

"Ha, yeah did you not know that? And sure, our very own Enniscorthy was in the film "Brooklyn", we are no strangers to the big screen down here in Wexford you know!"

We pulled up a narrow road, more like a lane, with neatly trimmed grass growing up the middle, and with black berry bushes on either side. About one hundred meters from the farm house the small bundle of black and white energy that was Shep, came bounding towards the car.

"Hey gorgeous," I hunched down to pet him and scratch behind his ears, he immediately rolled on to his back for a tummy rub!

"Ha, ha, well he is clearly spoiled by someone here!" I exclaimed laughing at the dog and his tricks.

"He's like every man, knows where he likes to be rubbed!" winked Bobby.

My Goodness! My face flushed, maybe he meant that innocently and my mind just ran away with me. I laughed trying to conceal a red face.

A man hopped out of a jeep, and was coming towards us.

"Well he certainly wasn't spoiled by me! How are you? I'm Patrick, Bobby's father. I see ye are dressed for a bit of action. There's a few cows after getting out of the far field, will ye give us a hand."

I looked to Bobby who was looking questioningly back at me. "Sure of course, we will" I replied, "what do we have to do."

"You're a brave woman, Laura," said Bobby, "didn't think you were one to get down and dirty."

"We just have to show them the way back in to the field right?"

"That's it exactly," winked Patrick. We hopped in the jeep with Patrick, and two minutes later we could see the six cows on the road. The cows, I realised, were a lot bigger in real life when they were only a few meters away, instead of away off in a field. I was a little bit excited and a little bit afraid. We jumped out of the jeep. "So what's the plan of action here?" I asked

"H'uuup" roared Patrick, raising his arms and a small branch of a tree, almost like a stick. "H'uuup!" he said again, this time taking a little run at the cows. This time two of the cows started to move up the road. "Well are ye going to just stand there gawping, or are ye goin' to help me?!"

"H'up!" shouted Bobby putting his arms out as if to guide the cow up the road, "H'up! H'up!" The cow turned and slowly began walking up the road. I stretched out my arms and approached another cow "Hey up! Hey up the road you go! Up the road you go now!" and I took a little run behind the cow which began to trot and poop at the same time! "Waaahhhh, oouff" in my effort to hurry the cow along, chasing the cow I slipped on the poop. "Ahahaha" Bobby was cracking up laughing. "I think you were doing too much talking. Ha! They are nervous of you. If you make them nervous they start to poop!"

"Ah jaysus, you make one of them nervous, you make all of them nervous, they'll all be shitting all over the road now!" laughed Patrick giving me a hand up.

We all had a good laugh, at my expense of course, but we got the cows back in the field. My clothes were destroyed though. Back at the farm, Bobby gave me some of his clothes to wear while he put my clothes in the wash. We called for Shep, who was more than happy to jump in the jeep with us again, and we headed for the beach!

The walk was good and long. The sound of the sea was therapeutic. Shep messing in the water, kept us occupied most of the walk. The rest of the time we talked about our work, our friends, places we would like to visit, the pros and cons of living in different countries and why we would always pick Ireland at the end of the day. At that point we were nearly back at the jeep.

He told me he liked my hair, my face, my lips, my eyes, and my smile. He told me I seemed perfect to him, that I was the type of woman he would marry. He continued with flattering me but in my mind I was imagining the wedding invitations 'Captain Bobby and Dr Laura cordially invite you to their little blue book wedding venue'. Snap out of it, I told myself, I could feel the 'but' coming.

"The thing is Laura, I need to tell you something." Ok, this was going to be big, I just knew it.

"OK, fire ahead, is this where you say, no, I'm actually not a pilot, and I teach people how to shear sheep, I am a farmer? Because you know that would be grand."

"Ha, no, unfortunately I am a pilot. The thing is, I am going to be based in the States for the next 6 months, during which time I will come home twice, a week in January here, followed by a week of skiing, and then 2 weeks at Easter, would you be up for that?"

What happened next was what I could only describe as a "moment" in time. He stared into my eyes and it seemed like he was quite serious about me, and I thought my goodness, this is what I wanted, wasn't it? … Or was it? My mind darted back to the plan, those calendar dates did not allow for him to attend the wedding with me. My gut spoke before I did, and I knew I couldn't wait for him while he swanned off to another country like! I politely explained all this to him, and he took it well, well kind of, he said he understood, but he was silent the rest of the way back to the farm dropping Shep home. In the car, on the way back to Dublin, the only sound came from the radio. It wasn't awkward, we just no longer had anything to say. He left me a voice message later that night to say he didn't speak in case he would cry. My heart broke a little, but I told it to shush. No doubt he would be only 5 minutes in America and he would have another girl on his arm, particularly now that America is great again! Ha! Was I really supposed to wait?

Besides, I did have another potential candidate. He didn't fit the criteria because I knew him from outside of the dating apps, many years ago. However, I did figure a way to justify his inclusion to this method to the Review Board at the next meeting. I just had to date him 3 times between this and then! My confidence in him was so high that he would more than satisfy the role of the 'positive control'. Goodness knows, this experiment could do with one!

The Positive Control, Candidate 10, Cathal, The Engineer

Unique among my selection was the next candidate, The Engineer. He was potentially such an outlier for selection, that I shouldn't include him in this process, but, when his beautifully chiseled jaw line appeared on my screen, the natural response was to swipe right. He was the only man I had ever matched on a dating app that I had prior knowledge of, that I knew external to the dating app, from "real life" about 15 years ago.

Our initial acquaintance was brief, two weeks in fact. That summer between 5th year and 6th year in secondary school when I was sent to a French language summer camp. I giggled just remembering it. During the summer holidays it was very common (almost a rite of passage) in Ireland for secondary school students to go to the remote parts of Ireland where Irish was the spoken language, not English. Students would attend Irish summer camps called Gaeltacht's, this immersion into daily life with a different language was to improve their ability to speak, and understand the language to help with their school exams.

It wasn't long until people began to spend time at other language summer camps - though the one I attended for French, was not in France! Instead it was a two-week summer camp in the boarding school in the next town over. I was quite proficient with French, but it was my mother's punishment to me, for getting caught being disruptive in French class.

I could still remember my mother's words "No messing around in the Gaeltacht with your pals this year smarty pants, it's off to French college with you! Catch up on what you might have missed in French class when you were too busy yapping to your friends!" To be fair I hadn't protested too much, Irish was more my sister's thing, and it was only two weeks, surely I could tough it out - and I did!

But what now could I recall about this old friend? I remembered he was a talented musician. I remembered he fancied the glamorous Dublin girls at French college. I didn't get any of that type of attention, except from the music buffs. I loved to compose and create, but I would never make a living out of it, or so I was told. Yes, Cathal just like all the other teenage guys were into the rich girls with the underwired bras. These girls knew how to apply fake tan, and had bottles of it with them, along with hair straighteners and serum so their locks were always perfectly located and glistening. These girls were from Dublin so I aligned myself with the other non-Dublin or "country" girls from Monaghan and Galway and we became a foursome of gal pals.

We ironed our hair on towels, and the rest could like it or lump it. The Dublin crowd stuck together and Cathal was definitely a Dub. It's interesting how the geographic demographic instantly created an 'us' and a 'them'. This geographic disparity was evident on the dating scene too. Would you rather date someone who lived in the city, or far away?

I willed myself to remember anything else about him. I remembered I fancied him even then. However, I knew I would never have a chance with a cool guy like him, but we were friends. We liked each other's music. It was a bonus he was delicious to look at. His flair for music enthralled me, I wished I was as talented and as brave to perform like him, captivating everyone who could hear. On stage his confidence was beguiling yet he didn't have a cocky swagger.

Think harder Laura! I pleaded with myself to remember more....We had to get into groups at French college as part of drama classes to make a short video. As a bit of an odd ball (maybe kinder to say alternative rock chic) back then, it was no surprise I found myself among the group creating a horror movie. I was playing the role of the girl being chased and ultimately murdered and drowned in the pool. I loved playing a main character, I was partially selected as I had the ability to swim, and the other girls didn't want to get their hair wet.

I recalled running towards the pool and leaping in! Upon hitting the water and struggling, it dawned on me! It had been four years since I had been in a pool swimming on holidays, and I never had to swim fully clothed! Good grief, the clothes were dragging me down and I genuinely was panicked. Eventually I remembered – float! Just hold your breath, float on my belly for the video, then float on your back, I told myself. I was fine in the end and everyone commended me on my great performance, they genuinely believed I was drowning.........little did they know it wasn't acting!

The group Cathal was in made a video based on Rambo - an action thriller! Basically the guys seized the opportunity to show their strength and physique. It was funny, more action than language, but us girls loved it - it was a visual treat! Especially for us ladies who went to all girls' catholic schools! Ha, ha! Hello boys!

French college ended, and the remainder of summer went by too quickly before the dreaded Leaving Cert year began. It was a quick year really, and apart from the glitch of who to ask to the school graduation ball (a guy from my applied math class, I took external to main school classes; he was present for the photo at the start of the night, and the good Lord only knows who he spent the rest of the night with, but it certainly wasn't me or my friends) the male species didn't enter my mind at all.

The night before the Leaving Cert Exams started I was filled with butterflies in my tummy. Nervousness for the exams, but excitement that this was it!! Once these exams were over, nothing in life would ever be as hard again - or at least that's the crap they were filling our heads with at school!

I was on a mental high trying to get to sleep, even though I went to bed early the night before the first exam, which was English Paper 1. Over the previous few days and weeks people were wishing me luck, and I returned the well wishes to those in the same situation. Lying in bed however, with my old Nokia 3210 with a bright red Ferarri cover on it, I just couldn't sleep. Then I got a text from an unknown number.

Unknown:

Let's Rock This Bitch!!

It was the night before my leaving cert! I didn't have time to play guessing games. I replied with a straight up:

Who is dis?

The reply completely knocked my socks off.

Unknown:

It's Cathal from French college

I drafted a cool quick response.

Laura:

Best of Luck, see you on the flip side! ;-)

I couldn't fathom how I would ever lay eyes on him again, but it was the polite thing to do, and I needed all the good Karma I could possibly get! That was it, my focus was totally on my exams. That was until Maths Paper 2, I had some time to spare after going through all of my answers and was satisfied I had done my best. I noticed the faint etchings on my calculator…. "FiddleKits" … ha it was the name of Cathal's band! It was barely visible. I must have done that at the start of 6th year with a compass in my geometry set. I giggled away to myself, and forgot him again.

My next memory of him was at the Christmas exams in first year of university, which was over a decade ago. It was the last day of exams for all faculties before the Christmas break. Outside the exam hall, as I sat cross legged among my bag, and notes and energy drinks, (which in hind sight did nothing but up my anxiety before the last exam), I recognized the outline of his face and smiled. There he was, still blonde and blue eyed. He looked a little more mature than I remembered him before, but a smiling friendly calm face among the thousands at the Exam Hall.

At the time I was obsessed with a guy who worked at the nightclub back home. Yet, I found myself praising the baby Jesus, and the makeup scientists for creating 'Pan-stick makeup'! My reason: because my crush from years ago was coming over, and though my neck and décolletage were puce with the rush of blood, my face remained 'nude beige'. The usual "Good Luck, Enjoy the Christmas" pleasantries were exchanged and voila, that was it! We entered the exam hall and parted to opposite ends for different exams. There was just 2.5 hours of a pharmacology exam keeping me from the fun and freedom of the Christmas holidays! I could taste it in the air already. Not a single thought of Cathal entered my head again, until now.

There he was, no longer a boy, but a man. His musically talented face captured in a still shot of him mid-motion, belting a song down a microphone, guitar in hand, strumming away. His profile picture of course. He was still clearly show casing his talents. Something stirred inside me. Was it jealousy? Jealousy that he continued with music and I didn't? Was it admiration of how he kept it going all this time, while maintaining a separate professional life? Could I do that too? Or was it too late? Gosh he was a handsome devil still. Maybe I just thought he was good looking. His creative side though…it was doing something to me. Where had my own creative beast been swept away to? And at what point in my life? Had I become so practical, so streamlined in my actions that I forgot, and shut down that part of my brain? Was this it, this strange feeling hammering in my head, screaming to be let out?! I couldn't ignore it and went in search of my own guitar!

The next day I had Dublin City Marathon training with the Review Board ladies. The five of us were going to walk 25 km, then go for dinner and maybe just one drink! It was mad craic, none of us really wanted to do it, but we didn't want to give up either. It helped alleviate the Sunday fear. When I got back home that evening I nearly lost my life when I had a message from Cathal! Four hours ago! How did I miss that? He was his normal pleasant self. It was really a case of, long time- no see. We decided to meet up for a catch up.

I felt my mind racing, I didn't know how to approach this thing, this meet up. Or was it a date? Was it really a date? Could I really count this as part of my plan to find a plus one for the wedding? I couldn't decide, or I guess I didn't know if there was a line between the real world people, and the online people that you shouldn't cross??

In this tech savvy society we are now in, surely everyone online was fair game, and yet there is still this underlying feeling in my gut that people we meet for the first time "in real life" are more special??
I had not experienced this strange feeling, what was it? Was it guilt?

None of these men know they are part of a competition of sorts, or do they? Isn't everyone who goes on a date in competition against every other man to win your heart? Your mind? Your body? Your soul?

Or was this feeling something else? There felt like an extra pressure on this date. As if this date succeeded there was actual potential for it to evolve. This couldn't be the case; I couldn't allow that feeling to be correct, surely? Otherwise, did this mean that all of the other dates meant nothing? Were of no significance?

No that certainly was not the case. My feelings were real for each and every guy. I could not detach from the process - nor should I.

Date 1 with Cathal, The Engineer

Many skill sets, trades and qualifications allow people to work anywhere in the world. Some people think that when that opportunity presents, that you should travel far and wide. However, in spite of the rain, one of the many reasons I choose to remain in our little island is that it is an ancient land full of opportunities to explore old castles and ruins, discovering legendary tales of love, rivalry, war, and so much more. For my first date with Cathal we were venturing in daylight to an infamous location, historically associated with occult practices, but with a lovely view over Dublin City.

We were going for a walk up to the Hell Fire Club. Notorious tales surround this location. However, in day light on a fresh sunny morning, this location was ideal.

It was important to counteract the nervous pre-date eating with an active date. Similarly drinks dates with the extra calories would have to be counteracted. I regularly checked in with Rebecca to know best how to achieve this.

After the decline from the Hell-Fire Club walk, we went back to Dun Laoghaire for some flat surface walking to even the legs out. Half way out the pier was a band stand. We climbed up into it and looked out to sea. Nostalgia sparked in our eyes and Cathal started singing

"I remember that summer in Dublin, and the Liffey as it stank like hell"

I smiled, it was **Bagatelle –Summer in Dublin**-a remix of it was my favourite song from years ago, when I first met him.

"And the young people walking down Grafton Street, everyone looking so well"

"I know you know the words Laura join in!"

He took my hands, placed one on his shoulder and held the other out as if to dance. I couldn't help but start giggling as his free hand landed on my hip and we began dancing, or rather repeat some sort of step and sway motion.

"I was singing a song I heard somewhere called rock'n'roll never forgets, when my humming was smothered by a 46A and the scream of a low flying jet"

Goodness he really hadn't lost it; his voice could surely melt ice.

Ha! *"So I jumped on a bus to Dun Laoghaire, stopping off to pick up my guitar"* I half whispered.

"When a drunk on the bus told me how to get rich, I was glad we weren't going too far", we finished in unison laughing.

It was such a good date, zero complaints from me. I had laughed lots, got plenty of fresh air. It was so long since I was beyond comfortable on a first date with someone! It was so long since I had spent time with a true male friend, and just had fun! I had forgotten guys were not all sleaze bags trying to get into your pants!

After Dun Laoghaire, he took me for a drive to the site where he was planning on building a house. In theory, I liked the idea of building a house in the countryside, however, the idea of not being able to walk to my local amenities was off putting. Not to mention the isolation. I have always felt much safer in an upper floor apartment than in an isolated house; who would hear you shout for help if you needed it?

His site was up a road with no road markings, though it was just outside the city. How was this possible? It was a dream home location! Surely it was a secret treasure that allowed country living on the doorstep of a buzzing city. There were a few bungalows on the left and right. It was not isolated by any stretch of the imagination, and yet there was a privacy to be had from your neighbours. How on earth did he secure this coveted piece of land, it must have cost an absolute fortune?! Not to mention obtaining planning permission to build here? Unless…unless being his wife, living in this idyllic setting would come with a catch. The mother-in-law next door, type of catch. It was right next to his parents, he informed me. Hmmm how many excellent mother-in-laws are there out there?

He pointed to his family home where there was a freshly laid pavement, boarded up with wooden planks. Freshly laid by him! Was there anything this man couldn't do?! He was smart, funny, up for a bit of day drinking on the rare occasion too. He had a great sense of music. He knew what he wanted from life and he was getting it.

Ticking one box off for himself at a time. He would be handy to have around a house, clearly. He was family orientated. He was tall-how was that not at the start of my list? Oh yeah, because he had so many other amazing attributes that his height was actually least among them! He had it all planned out. All that was missing was his future wife.

The life he had planned sounded really good. A house built with taps that were my height because he was taller than me too, and no way would allow standard low down taps be in your custom built house. It wouldn't be my house though. He had his own design in mind. It wouldn't be my ideal location though either, it was a plot of land he had selected years ago, in proximity to his parents. His life had structure and like a jigsaw puzzle he was filling it in. The main character, the leading lady was all that was missing.

Oh, he wanted it to be just so. Just a perfect little lady to fit in his perfect life. Well what if the lady he selected did not conform to sample? Would she forever have to second guess what he wanted to keep herself in line for him? That was not something she or anyone would be willing to do, surely? Perhaps there were women who do, and would, but that was just not my approach to anything. If I didn't fit the mold, I was out of there on my own terms.

I began to wonder; would any lady do? Did this de-value me? For all my credentials, was this really all I was to him, just going to be the wife, his wife, Mrs him.

Maybe this was not for me. I could feel the change in my perception of him brewing inside. He was tall, check! Handsome, check! Smart, check! Had his life together, check! Was financially independent, check! Friendly, social and someone you wouldn't have to babysit at a wedding, check, check and check! So why was there this gnawing feeling in the pit of my stomach that something was just not quite right? Was he settling? Or wanting to settle down? Did he know the difference? Did I? Was there a difference?

Date 2 with Cathal, The Engineer

I was starting to get a bit attached to chatting with him on the phone in the evenings. It was fast becoming the favourite part of my day. His clear way of talking suited me. He knew a lot about a lot. He was balanced. We were talking about everything. Most of my friends share common interest but not so much on the music side of things. This was a real draw in to this guy. He introduced me to bands I hadn't heard of before and what's more, I really liked them!

Not only that, but even listened to me whining about how my car was giving me trouble, it was well past it's sell by date and time for an upgrade. There were a lot of scrappage deals going across many brands. The only thing is, I don't really know that much about cars, what I did or didn't want, or need for that matter. As I rattled on about this to Cathal, he suggested he go with me to test-drive some cars. He was free the next day and suggested we could make an afternoon of it.

This felt like I was striking gold, how perfect! Why didn't I think of it as a date option myself?!

He asked if I wanted to be economical in my selection or if I wanted to splash the cash on a flashy model that screamed: look at me in my car compensating for something! He was funny like that. He also still cycled most places, and I reckoned his car was not the latter type.

We started at a car dealership of a very economical brand. I didn't really know what to say to the car sales man. I wasn't intent on actually buying that day. I just wanted to look at the cars and get some information. I commented to Cathal about how the sales people were really pushy. "Ah, you haven't been car shopping often before, or around sales people much, have you? This is par for the course. You are not misleading them by asking questions. You are just doing your due diligence on researching your motor investment. I deal with sales people all the time, I won't let anyone convince you to buy anything today. It is a fun day, let's play?" he winked and delivered the question in such an inviting way that appealed to my mischievous side. "Let's play" I nodded with a big grin plastered on my face in agreement.

We bid our farewell to the economical cars and moved on to a more luxury car dealership. On entering, Cathal took over. He told the sales woman we wanted a car for spinning around on Sunday drives and for a road trip around Europe next summer, a young couples dream tour! He paused only to add some flavor by turning to me to say, "Oh, baby you know, I would buy anything for you." Gosh he was a good actor. We got to take a heavy piece of German metal out on the road and it was fun, but there were more dealerships to try!

Though it wasn't the main car brand sold at the next dealership, the Mustang outside caught our eyes! "Let's go try that one" I enthused. "Oh sweet heart I am already impressed," was Cathal's response. Inside there were even nicer cars, in particular a 911 Carrera. It was my turn to act, the plan was to convince the salesman that Cathal was hell bent on buying this car, and that I was trying to talk him out of it. I channeled my inner sensible Anne, what would she say to someone in that situation.

"Babe, please I know you deserved your compensation, but do you really want to spend a quarter of it on this car? (This let them know he had money). There is not enough room for the kids seats in the back. I thought we wanted the same thing?"

"Honey, honey, we just want to have one more amazing year spoiling ourselves before we start having babies. This car is the dream, and I could definitely see myself picking you up from work in this beauty!", Cathal grinned at me.

"I think we should take her for a test ride," as he raised his eyebrows questioningly to salesperson, who nodded and went off to get the key.

"You are very convincing Cathal," I cooed in his ear. His smiled broadened clearly taking it as a compliment. I however, was not so sure it was a good thing. The thought entered my mind about all the times a man had ever lied to me. Cathal certainly had the capacity to do the same. I brushed the thought aside and hopped into the car, it was a blast! But there was one more German dealership we had to go to!

"Put your blingy ring on your left hand ring finger" Cathal instructed in my ear. Gosh he was very close to me; I could feel the heat radiating from him. "Ok, why, what's happening?"

"Just do it, and follow my lead."

We entered the very fancy foyer and began to walk around the cars. Cathal headed towards a stumpy sort of a guy. I was close enough to hear him say.

"You know I always drive around in a big old SUV, but the lady here, gets her dainty work attire all muck getting in and out, so I am not allowed to drop her off anywhere. Thing is, that fine young woman there, took some convincing to agree to let me put that ring on her finger, in the hopes that one day she will marry me! Now I've got a problem, there is a….gentleman….for want of a better word, who works with my prospective wife to be, who is all too keen to pick her up and drop her off. I am going to put a stop to this nonsense with whatever fine automobile you are going to sell me today. I'm going to pick her up in something a little classier."

To be fair, we were treated like royalty there, so much so, we were very tempted to sign for payment that day! They were some damn good sales guys! Luckily it was so far beyond what I found acceptable to pay for a car, we were just about able to say no!

Date 3 with Cathal, The Engineer

Driving around in cars we didn't own sure was thrilling! We didn't agree to another date that day. However, Cathal text the following day at lunch time to see if I would go to a Halloween party with him on Friday night as his date! It was fancy dress, and sure I couldn't say no to that!

Friday night came around rather quickly. The house was only a 15-minute taxi ride away, but I walked there, and it would be easy to escape from if needs be. I was super excited to get to the party, until I was walking down the street to the house it was at. Gawd, the looks I was getting! The small bit of cleavage might be a wee bit too much for this location. It is so unfair. If I was a flat chested woman, this top would be completely acceptable. It's not my fault others were not as well-endowed in that area. It came with the rest of my shape, they were not gawping at my lack of thigh gap! Once at the party my excitement returned, and I accepted a glass of fizz while leaving my own bottle on the kitchen table. For once, I actually believed Lisa on my way out the door, I *was* looking good. My chin was out, my shoulders were back and down. The bubbles may have gone to my head, because I was really feeling sassy!

"Tits and Teeth girls, Tits and Teeth!" my drama teacher used to say! By the grace of God, I knew better than to let my confidence run away with me, and break into a strut! My opinion began to change, I decided I was looking fierce good, so maybe just once the glances from the men and women were noticing my whole fabulous ensemble.

I probably downed that first glass of fizz a bit quickly. You see Candidate 1, Padraig, had text to say he missed me, and was going to this party too. How though?! In a city of over 2 million people, how was he going to the same Halloween party as me?! OK to be fair, we had a number of 'friends of friends' in common, but those people are acquaintances, and not the people whose houses you rock up to for a Halloween party!

This could get awkward. He said he was going with his brother as the Batman and Robin Duo!

Cathal hadn't told me what he was going as, I hadn't told him either. It was going to be a surprise. It would be like a game of hide and seek. Which was fitting giving it was Halloween. It would also test our vanity, maybe he would think my outfit was stupid and embarrassing, or vice versa. Did we like each other for who we were or what we looked like?

And just like that my heart stopped! There Padraig was as Robin chatting to the same dark haired girl I had seen him kissing at Poolbeg. They were standing so close. I tried to assess their body language but costumes and angles made it difficult to really define the context of their particular closeness. Did they come together? Did they just bump into each other? Were they whispering sweet nothings? Or having a lovers' tiff through gritted teeth?

He totally caught me staring! I was right in his line of vision and he was acting oblivious to me! Men, and their stupid attention span, he clearly wasn't missing me that much! I turned on my heel in the opposite direction.

I wasn't there to see him anyway. I was there for Cathal, and the fireworks he ignited in me, well the fireworks I hoped one day he might ignite in me. He really was such a good friend. Out on the patio I stood with my drink (blood punch) complementing the girls around me on their costumes. There were a few cat women, so I was glad I didn't opt for that in the end!

"Laura! Hiya!"

I turned around to find a Batman behind me, reaching for my hand. It didn't sound like Cathal.

"Cathal?"

"Who is Cathal? It's Padraig, I told you I was coming as Batman and Robin with my brother."

"Your brother is Robin!? I thought you were Robin, take of your mask a second, I don't believe you!"

Padraig slowly took off the Batman mask. "See! It's me, why wouldn't you believe me?"

"But your brother, your brother is just like you! I thought you were ignoring me! You said your brother was younger than you!"

"He **is** my little brother, he's my twin, I am four minutes older."

I didn't know what to think. All the contempt and rage I had held against him. All the curses and swears I let out on the way home that day from Poolbeg were all a jumble. Was this guy actually a good one? A nice one? A truthful one? "Laura!"

That WAS Cathal's voice. I spun around and there he was. Was he wearing fake tan?! I flushed. I had a flash back of him telling me his fantasy!

"Is that who you are here with?" asked Padraig quietly out of earshot of Cathal.

"Yes," I quietly hissed through a beaming smile.

"Padraig I would like to introduce you to, ha, well (Crap I drew blank on his name at the worst possible moment! My head was spinning!) I would like to introduce you to Tarzan, obviously, as you can see!"

The three of us laughed thank goodness, it was buying me some time. What on earth was happening here. Who did I see at Poolbeg that day? Was I wrong about Padraig? Did it matter, I was having a great time re-connecting with, with Cathal - there we go that's his name!

Oh! There was gasps all around as the lights went out and we were immersed in darkness. Then the whistles from the firework display kicked off.

Thanking my lucky stars for a moment to have a
chance to think and process what I had just learned, I tried to
assess the situation. Padraig hadn't been lying to me. He was
good. Actually he was great! The perfect candidate. Although,
if he really liked me he would have tried to stay in touch
surely?

However, I was at this party with Cathal who has been
the perfect friend all along. He was also the perfect candidate.
This was a mess! I knew the right thing to do when the
fireworks stopped and the lights came on was to focus on
Cathal. It was his date. It was his time.

The first round of fireworks began to slow down and I
felt a tug towards a man to my right, the muscular frame did
not belong to his costume suit. I recognized his scent. He
smelled so good. I knew it was Padraig. In the darkness he
tilted my chin up to his and planted the softest kiss as another
round of fireworks kicked off.

Once the display ended and everyone finished cheering
the lights came back on. Padraig was still standing beside me
to my right as he had been before the display. Oh no, Cathal! I
turned to my left, he wasn't there, and twisted around in
circles trying to find him, my Cathal, my friend! Where did he
go? Did he see me kissing Padraig? Surely not it was so dark!
"Cathal?!"
"Laura, I'm here I got you some more 'blood' to drink, are you
ok? Ha! you look like you have seen a ghost!"
"Oh I just thought I lost you!"
I reflected on my behaviour; I may have been dressed like a
fairy angel, but right now I felt like the devil.
"You seem very worried, you are the sweetest fairy, I am right
here, I am not going anywhere, you have me."

I took the drink from him and he slipped his hand around my waist. We tipped our paper cups together and said cheers! Thankfully the hosts were eco-friendly and not a single piece of un-recyclable plastic ware was in sight! We wandered around the house admiring the crafty decorations. It sounded like some rowdy shenanigans were going on outside. An unfair result in beer pong or some of the Halloween games that were set up outside, no doubt! I looked over my shoulder, I couldn't see Batman, or Robin for that matter, and the only villain present seemed to be me!

"Laura, I don't mean to keep bringing up ghosts here but you do look pale, like you do look as white as a ghost, are you sure you are ok?"

"Yes I think all the fun and excitement has just gone to my head, I might head on home soon, but please stay and have fun I don't want to cut your night short!"

"No way, I am going to make sure you get home safe, the town is mad and there's all sorts of creatures on the streets tonight, and I know you." He squeezed my side tickling me so I laughed and shrieked, then he stopped.

"Laura I know you are a chicken, so you will be scared stiff going home alone. Tell me I am wrong?" he smiled knowingly and followed it up with an even cheesier line.

"Let me feel like the protective Tarzan I am tonight?"

I gave him a weak smile back, then a giggle. It was so cheesy. My head was spinning but he was right. Though he didn't know the reasons why, I did need to get out of there and I would be scared going home on my own! I blame watching too many horror movies as a teenager and an overactive imagination.

Once inside the apartment, I found Lisa on the floor doing her best night time yoga poses. I filled her in on the night's events, then left a voice note for the Review Board, and for Maria.

Phase 3 End Message from the Chief Advisor to the Principal Investigator

"**Hello**, little cousin, thank you for the voice note, it made for a good bed time story! OK first of all, did I count properly, there were 4 guys this time? Because of Larry the louser?! Well, I will get to him in a minute.

First, The I.T. guy, straight up, he sounded lovely! Though, I can't believe you spent that long banging on about Celtic Crosses on your first date! I know in the past I was a little anti-the tattoo thing, but it HAS grown popular in recent years! I have revised my position on this, if tattoos are on a really muscular body, then it's ok. Ha - yes I know I am terrible! You know I would give him a chance, but you and your gut instincts, I have to trust you on that. So fine, if you insist on it, I will support your decision to let the man with hot body, intellect and alluring voice escape you!

The Guard - girl there are no words. He was by far and away the absolute worst of anyone you have ever mentioned to me, EVER. You had me in stitches telling me about his one rotten tooth at the side of his mouth, that you only noticed when he was snarling, ha oops I mean laughing. I will not forget your description of his haircut too tight for his blobby face. You really were letting your inner nasty come out! If I were you, I would have been arrested for grievous bodily harm, because I would absolutely have taken off my stilettos and thrown them at his face! He was so mentally inept that you were mad at yourself for including him. I would be too if I picked an idiot, and everyone knows you cannot reason or be rational with a fool!

Next on the list was, the pilot, oh yes, the pilot on the hustle as a teacher. Interesting mode of action there. He seemed quite smitten. What is wrong with you? You don't have to stay here; with your job you can work anywhere! Get your bum to the U.S. of A! I'll come visit! Hmm perhaps upon his return in the distant future you can pick up where you left off? Or just store it in the think tank as time well spent. It seemed like a good experience, but you do want a wedding guest, and he won't cave on his career to come back for just one day, so you are right, just let him go. You would do the same thing, so we cannot really berate him on that point. I still think he will come looking for you when he comes back- just saying!

Now, I think part of the reason it wasn't too difficult for you to let the pilot go, was because you had the engineer to look forward to. Your little blast from the past! You see, that is one of the reasons I will NEVER use a dating app. I don't want to see any men I know on it!

Unfortunately, with regards to The Engineer, my comment is simple. No way, there is clearly no spark there. Romantically he sounds boring. What is it they say about engineers anyway…..they are scientists that lack imagination?! Ha! And he is a performer in his spare time, do you really want to date a performer? Someone who must be an egomaniac showing off all the time; and with acting skills as good as you say, could you trust him? He might just be a really good liar? And as for the Halloween party, I mean, what a dope, leaving a stunner like you unattended, of course Padraig was going to chance his arm! Do you even know where he was when you were with Padraig? Him there flashing the 6 pack as Tarzan; who does he think he is. If you ask me he got what was coming to him. If you were right for each other he would have shown interest in you when you were teenagers!"

Phase Three Reporting and Review Board Meeting

I had listened to Maria's message on Saturday morning when I woke up. My head was still in tangles, but at least I had no tears! I hadn't really processed my thoughts the last few weeks. I was in action mode, working my way through my 'to do' lists, keeping up with work, keeping up with training for the DCM, and going on dates. Maria's input was SO important; she was never usually too far wrong with things. I was having second thoughts about the pilot. She was right, there was nothing keeping me here, except my job, and I loved it! I wouldn't leave! So how could I condemn him, or any man for pursuing their career too? There really was nothing wrong with our dating experience, or him, except I would have to wait and see what happened when he came back to visit. That however, would not help with the task at hand, to find a plus-one for the wedding.

The real mess was the Padraig versus Cathal situation, I might leave the thinking on that to the girls in the Review Board. Without a further thought, I spruced myself up, and got ready for the final Review Board meeting, which was also our last catch up before the Dublin City Marathon! This time, we were officially allowed to carb load – or so we kept telling ourselves!

For once, I was the first to arrive, so I grabbed our usual booth. Lisa was the next to arrive in her Yoga gear, straight from teaching her new class.

"I have changed who I want to give my golden 5 points too, but I will wait until the others get here to tell you who it is!"

"Well hello to you too!" I smiled giving her a hug, "Ok lady, I can wait."

Anne, Rebecca and The Doll were pretty much in on her heels.

Lisa was actually giddy, she kicked off the meeting.

"Well this is kind of exciting, we are coming to the end and get to suss out the results, and then you will know who will be going to the wedding!"

Anne pointed out that whoever was selected still had the potential to say no to the invitation. This totally burst Lisa's bubble.

"Ah you're no fun Anne, you could have let me drag it out a bit longer!"

"The final trio, shall we begin the review process?" asked Rebecca trying to stave off a fight.

"Oh my goodness Rebecca, did you not hear the last voice mail from the Halloween party?!"

"No, well, eh, I only listened to the information on the first guy because he sounds perfect."

"Who, The I.T. guy? Really? Oh wait, is it because you are imagining his accent Becks?"

"Well maybe, but he does sound rather cool too. I mean come on, dreamy Northern Irish accent. Yeah, I know he has THAT tattoo, but like he didn't actually get married so what's the big deal? He is cool, fun, and Laura you cannot deny apart from THAT tattoo you were a smitten kitten!"

"You should have listened to the full voice message, because I have selected *my* Mister Perfect," said The Doll, "it is of course the manly pilot posing as a teacher!! I totally get him and his need to fulfill his dream, going to the ends of the earth… or well far away from here anyway ha! He wants you Laura, it's obvious!"

"Well until he finds some other woman on his travels, waiting around is not really where I want to be. Plus, you are forgetting he won't be here for my cousin's wedding, and that was the primary end point!"

266

"Well maybe you need to reevaluate your priorities and introduce a new endpoint of having an amazing future boyfriend, he is a flying teacher who farms on the side. He has all the perks. City living and country bliss, sure you would be in your element girl!" said Lisa. We all knew she was projecting though; a country lad is what SHE was after.

"What about the new addition, the old flame, now HE sounds like fun! Although apart from meeting him that first day, you didn't really get all gooey eyed about him, did you?" asked Anne.

"You know me too well Missus, yeah it was all fine, and he looks great or whatever, but I think I am so relaxed with him because I am not that into him," I said pulling a shamed face.

"Ha, ouch" laughed Anne, "did it really take Padraig kissing you to figure that one out? Do you not think Padraig was a bit cheeky planting a kiss on you when he knew you were there with someone else? He's a bit too full of himself if you ask me, and how do you know he doesn't always play tricks on girls with his twin?"

"Oh Anne, look I really don't know what to say about him, it's a bit messy. I suppose you are right; like, could you really trust someone who would do that?"

Lisa instructed me to play the voice note again so that we *all*, (she said looking at Rebecca), would have an overview of the final four to be assessed. Then, in a soothing zen-like manner, she suggested we go through the ranking tables to see if the scientific approach could shed a bit of light on what to do next. She reminded us that the whole point of the ranking table and the review board was to look at the facts, so that any messiness, like this, could be overcome in a simple, methodical way.

Table 7 Nathan, The IT guy

Candidate 7	Marks
Date 1	4.0 /5
Date 2	4.0 /5
Date 3	4.0 /5
Good Communication	4.0 /5
Good sense of humour	4.0 /5
Willingness to dance	4.0 /5
Confidence among strangers	4.5 /5
Personality +/- alcohol	4.5 /5
Trustworthy	3.5 /5
Punctual	5.0 /5
Total	41.5 /50

General comment from Laura: Lovely guy to date, however something tells me he has his own troubles to deal with. Grand dates, but my gut says no.

Wedding suitability: Low – well particularly when he even called off his own wedding!

"Ah ha ha" The Doll was loving the drama.

Lisa agreed with me. "Listen to your body when it's trying to tell you something. If your gut says no, trust it!"

Strangely Anne was in agreement too, but managed to put some rationale behind it. "If something doesn't seem to add up, there's a glitch somewhere, you just have to find it. It doesn't take a rocket scientist to know, it is not the tattoo, but the story behind it that is bugging you. Well actually the tattoo is a bit like him having a child, he has it forever also reminding you of his past." She paused, "Unless… he gets it lazered off, of course."

Rebecca was still arguing the case for this guy. "But you see, he *could* get it lazered and the story behind it might not be so bad."

"Unfortunately Rebecca, I will only ever hear one side of that story and you know there are always at least two!"

Poor Rebecca was getting ganged up on here, with Lisa jumping in. "Yeah Rebecca you are too nice. There is no nice way to call off a wedding. Maybe if you ever turned that engagement into a wedding you might appreciate it more!" Just as quickly, she said "Sorry, that just escaped." She really did look apologetic, as if she even shocked herself. She had been on this new liquid diet to enhance performance for vegetarians or something like that. Trouble was, she was literally not consuming anything else and the drop in sugar was driving her mental all week!

"Jeez Lisa you are so hot and cold, would you ever go and eat some meat or solid food or something! That liquid organic earth diet is making you all types of hangry!"

"To be fair," said Rebecca, "it is justified, I only had that same discussion with Teddy during the week, so The Doll what's your take on The I.T. Guy?"

Was it my imagination or did Rebecca look smug? Ordinarily, she would nearly be in tears with a snap like that from Lisa. Maybe she was just empathetic to Lisa's recent diet restrictions.

The Doll just seemed glad there were no tears from Rebecca, so she ploughed on. "You don't have to find the solution, just replace the guy! You are right though about lazer, it works wonders, on acne scars, fine lines, and our hairy legs and other regions! Ha! Ha! Long live the lazer!"

We couldn't help but laugh. Then we called on Rebecca to give her final description of him.

"It seems to me he is like a tiramisu. He has the sophisticated coffee blend against an alcoholic liquor, combined with a rich decadent mascarpone cheese," paying homage to his tattoos, she continued "the body of the tiramisu is also sprinkled with a decorative cocoa powder. He definitely would satisfy you, but such a rich dessert can only be tolerated in small doses, or it might just be too intense."

Table 8 Larry, The Guard

Candidate 8	Marks
Date 1	3.5 /5
Date 2	2.0 /5
Date 3	0.0 /5
Good Communication	2.0 /5
Good sense of humour	2.0 /5
Willingness to dance	1.0 /5
Confidence among strangers	5.0 /5
Personality +/- alcohol	1.0 /5
Trustworthy	1.0 /5
Punctual	0.0 /5
Total	17.5 /50

General Comment: Wonderful- ha not!! Very shady altogether, shows zero consideration for other people's time.
Wedding guest suitability: Low
"He could just be very relaxed about everything. I would give him a chance; he sounds like he is great in person but terrible on the phone. Is he just a dope? You know, actually he is a lot like a puppy. A lost untrained puppy. Ha! A puppy pee-pee-ing all over the place and maybe not knowing he is actually doing anything wrong? Maybe, he might just need to be trained up?" Lisa was now practically gasping she was so giddy to get her words out and bouncing on her seat. The sugar in the pancakes was clearly kicking in! She was so odd today.

Scrunching up her nose and shaking her head Anne was having none of it. "I totally disagree, he had plenty of chances and opportunities and repeatedly failed. I don't know how you tolerated him for the last date at all!"

The Doll was nodding profusely.

"Yeah he is a waste of space, next! I will need a few sedative jabs after hearing about this guy. How did you manage not to punch him in the face? Or the balls? Lisa I need you to show me some breathing exercises to calm down ha! And actually Lisa!? Is someone's head melted? Why are you soft on this guy? Are you in love yourself or something and seeing the world through cloud 9 glasses?"

"O.M.G," squealed Rebecca, giddier than usual, "YOU SO ARE IN LOVE! Look she is positively blushing!"

"Wow, ok Lisa, do you need some water, you are quite flushed, let's lower that blood pressure. Laura," Anne was gesturing wildly in the direction of the table with the jugs of water and glasses, "get some!"

Offering Lisa some ice cold lemon water I whispered "I swear I didn't tell anyone you were dating!"

Lisa nodded understanding and gave me a pleading look. She really is very private about certain things, but struggles to even keep her own secrets, secret! She wanted to keep her dating on the quiet for as long as possible until she figured out if they were something solid, or just having a fling. I gave her a reassuring wink.

"Let's not quiz Lisa too much, all this blood to her head, do we really want our interrogation to wind up with us in A&E after inducing a stroke or coronary event!"

Rebecca nodded knowingly and interjected too. "Fair enough, besides I want to give you my run down on this ghastly guard. He is like a no bake chocolate oat bar, he is what you want for something quick and easy in the morning, but you would never have him for dinner!"

Lisa, Anne, The Doll and myself all looked at each other, with our eyes wide at Rebecca as we erupted in laughter! Never had Rebecca spoken so boldly before - even in the context of food!

Table 9 Bobby, The Pilot

Candidate 9	Marks
Date 1	5.0 /5
Date 2	5.0 /5
Date 3	4.0 /5
Good Communication	4.0 /5
Good sense of humour	4.5 /5
Willingness to dance	3.0 /5
Confidence among strangers	5.0 /5
Personality +/- alcohol	4.0 /5
Trustworthy	3.5 /5
Punctual	5.0 /5
Total	42.5 /50

General comment from Laura: Amazing guy, for whoever he ends up with. He is polite, charming, endearing, funny, an animal lover who has multiple interests. Unfortunately, he is unavailable for the wedding.

Wedding guest suitability: High (for any wedding he might be able to attend), but low in this instance.

"Ladies, look at your faces, you're all somber and feeling sorry for this guy. It just wouldn't be feasible for Laura to pursue him at this point. The objective was to find a plus-one to bring to the wedding. Unfortunately, this candidate is not available at the time of the wedding and is essentially a non-runner." Of course it was sensible Anne who led with this opening statement.

"You need to look at the bigger picture though. For something long-term he seems perfect, no?!" queried Lisa.

The Doll closed her eyes and sighed, "Long distance, it doesn't work when it is at the start of a relationship. If they had been together for a year before parting then maybe, just maybe they might have had a chance. We all started as scientists, we all know the best bet for success is to stick with what is proven and known, and not to be reliant on a Hail Mary attempt. Or in this case, the probability of man to be the exception and not the rule!"
"But she didn't even ask him if he would take the time off to go to the wedding?!" Lisa was distraught.

Not meeting Lisa's eyes, I made my own final comment on the matter. "What sort of an idiot would I look like doing that?! I'm afraid this case is closed. Rebecca do you have anything to say?"
"This is definitely a case of the strawberry roulade smothered with raspberry sorbet freshly whipped cream and smothered in hot chocolate sauce. Everything is delicious, the perfect amount of hot and cold, zingy and creamy, fruity and chocolatey. There is no reason for anyone to avoid this desert."

There was silence until Anne reminded us there was one more Candidate to get through.

Table 10 Cathal, The Engineer

Candidate 10	Marks
Date 1	4/5
Date 2	4/5
Date 3	4/5
Good Communication	5/5
Good sense of humour	3/5
Willingness to dance	5/5
Confidence among strangers	5/5
Personality +/- alcohol	5/5
Trustworthy	5/5
Punctual	5/5
Total	45/50

"Ok," said Lisa, "If you are not going to get with the pilot then it is clear to me what's going to happen next. It's like something out of a movie, surely you are going to ask this blast from the past to the wedding?! You have so much history together compared to the other guys, and none of it sleazy like a few other candidates I could mention!"

"Did he see you kissing the radiographer?" checked Anne, "and, how do you know if the radiographer frequently plays tricks on girls with his twin, or not? Having said that, this Engineer guy seems more like a friend."

"For goodness sake!" exclaimed The Doll, "he wasn't playing a trick on her, it was an unintentional case of mistaken identity. I'm routing for the radiographer. This friend guy is too in love with himself. If he wanted you, he would prioritise you, and he would have behaved a bit more like the radiographer, and kissed you when he had the chance."

Rebecca was getting fidgety and chimed in. "We should focus on the task at hand, critiquing The Engineer! It seems to me that he is Sunday morning pancakes, the ones that put a smile on all our faces. He is delicious pancakes with blueberry goodness, interesting mascarpone cheese and drizzled with a Canadian maple syrup. The thing is, it's a happy friendship, you can dress pancakes up or down, sweet or savory crepes are available too, but do they really excite you? You see, I suspect, The Engineer will be the winner and that you would have a great time with him at the wedding, but long term, deep down, you know he is just friend material."

The Doll looked impressed, Rebecca was coming out of her shell today. "Well said Rebecca! How's the training been going for the marathon everybody? Pull out the ranking table there Laura on your Tablet, and we can eyeball it while we eat and chat."

"OK ladies, this is your last chance to change your mind and reallocate your wild card, golden 5 points. Here, add it to the Bonus Point column!"

Ranking Table

Candidate	Mark	Bonus Points	TOTAL
1 Padraig	44.5	5 Lisa	49.5
2 Pierre	40		40
3 Laughlann	38.5	5 The Doll	43.5
4 Raj	40		40
5 Andrew	37.5		37.5
6 Daniel	41	5 Rebecca	46
7 Nathan	41.5		41.5
8 Larry	17.5	-10	7.5
9 Bobby	42.5		42.5
10 Cathal	45	5 Anne	50

"So there you have it, with the added golden points included, your winner, by the skin of his teeth, is the lovely Cathal, the blast from the past!"

"Yeah", I agreed but my focus was on Candidate 1, The Radiographer. I only really liked Cathal as a friend. Yes, it was great to feel comfortable with someone. Yes, for attending a wedding it is great to know that you will have a laugh with the person you would be there with. Now here is the "but", is there not supposed to be butterflies in your tummy too? Where were my butterflies?

I said nothing, the experiment was designed to find the most suitable plus-one guest to bring to the wedding. I had identified the correct person based on the inclusion and exclusion criteria. I would ask Cathal to the wedding, and, he being the lovely fella he is, will say yes.

The Doll interrupted my thoughts. "Could I tempt you to a bit of Botox, your forehead is fine, but I do see the fine lines around your eyes there!"

"What?! No way! Do you want me to stop laughing altogether? Holy divine hour, are you serious?!" I was in shock!

"Well it's all the go, sorry, as soon as I hear of an event it's just what pops into my mind." She proceeded to inform us of all the events you might want to "improve" yourself for, listing them on her fingers and paused after each one for effect. "Wedding, gala dinner, fashion shoot, holiday, that special date, I just think of the treatments my clients come to me for, and you ladies haven't booked me for anything, not even once!"

"Ah The Doll, I only get my eyebrows done and you know how fussy I am about that! I'd kill you if they ended up too dark!" said Rebecca.

"My pet peev is my tash and I do that at home, there is no way I am forking out your lavish prices, but maybe someday as a treat I will, it's not that I don't have every faith in you to keep my honker hairless," laughed Lisa.

"After all this I definitely need a massage, maybe an Indian head massage, will that help me to de-stress and keep my hair growing in case I want an up-do for the wedding? I'll book into your salon," I said.

"I've been meaning to try out some reflexology, I'll book in for that," and with that, Anne was booking in too.

"Is business OK?"

"Ah yeah, it's going grand, in the sense that I am kept busy, but in my business, being an entrepreneur, you might start off as a Makeup Artist, but you just have to keep adding to your skill set because the market is saturated. The salon is just about running itself. People much prefer to have their beauty technician come to them at home. For some reason the only profit I make is from the home visits. Don't get me wrong, profits are good, it is just eating up all of my time. Meeting up with you girls, and training for the DCM is my only down time. I love this candidate selection process. I'd love to try it myself! I will have to hire an assistant to free up some time."

"You know what" said Rebecca starting to look a bit shifty in her seat. More than shifty, she was squirming, and beaming, "that would be a really smart move, because, I have some news.....You will all be receiving a plus-one to *my* wedding!"

"Wow, that's the first time in AGES we have heard you mention your wedding, does that mean you have set a date?!"

"YES!!!!" shrieked Rebecca! "It's the August bank holiday weekend next year!"

"Congrats!", "That amazing!", "Great news! So excited for it! How did this all come about?!"

"Well, it was actually thanks to this candidate selection process. I was telling Ted about your method to find a date for your cousin's wedding. That got us talking about weddings and long story short we decided it was *finally* time to set a date!"

"We did get a cancelation for Valentine's Day, but," and she threw her head and eyes to Anne, "yes Anne I can feel you rolling your eyes! Valentine's Day would be easy for Ted to remember, so in a way it would have been worth all the eye rolling of the less romantically minded folk, ok!" She put both hands up to keep us silent, and she continued.

"However, the couple that cancelled, re-booked within the three-day policy the hotel had, mind you they had offered it to us the very next day!"

"We had fallen in love with the hotel décor. Ok I did, Ted agreed. He couldn't deny the garden outside, even on the rainy day we visited, was like a piece of art! The layout and landscaping were so ornate the pictures would be beautiful no matter what the season. So we asked for their next weekend availability and they said the bank holiday Monday in August."

She put her hands up to keep us silenced again. (I can totally imagine her doing this in the classroom keeping the noising secondary school students quiet.) This time she looked defensive.
"I know, a Monday is not ideal, but people will be off, and the venue is so perfect, and it means we have the whole weekend to get ready. If people want to, they can take the Tuesday off. It really is no worse than people getting married on a Friday. You would have to take the Friday off to attend, but I guess then you could enjoy a few drinks and stay up late and not have to worry about work the next day. Oh gosh!"

Rebecca was starting to spiral. Her face, which two minutes ago, was the happiest I have seen her in such a long time was beginning to look fraught.

We all intervened to assure her, no one would say anything to her about the Monday wedding situation. No one would care. All of her friends and family are going to be just so happy about the wedding going ahead. Everyone will be extremely delighted to have a wonderful event to attend, in what sounds like *the* most picturesque venue. We laughed and joked about having another good reason to keep fit after the DCM. Our new focus was to have lovely wedding bodies!

"That is so true," agreed Rebecca, "I will have to find, and order a dress by early next year! There is so much to think about and plan!" Her inner organized self was emerging as she reminded me not to forget to actually ask Cathal to my cousin's wedding. This was followed by instruction to the rest of the ladies to do their best to have a plus-one by her wedding. She didn't want to be fretting about unequal seating arrangements!

"Wow, Ok. Let's get just through the marathon first, and re-convene for a healthy brunch in a couple of weekends?" Anne was going to do her thing to restore calm.

That settled the wedding panic, and focused our minds on when and where we were meeting for the marathon. The rest of the brunch was spent discussing the weather forecast and if we should wear light rain coats, how much fluid and electrolytes should we bring, or if we needed any at all!

The Marathon

The marathon started off brilliantly. The atmosphere
was exhilarating. We were in a crowd of thousands. There
were so many of us bunched together, all running from the
beginning. Our plan was to run the first 10 km, then walk, but
with the buzz and the excitement we powered through
another 5 km. At the 15 km point, we were in no fit state to
keep running. Another 20 km and we were starting to curse
the stupid idea to take part in marathon in the first place, we
thought we were farther than we were.

We began to moan and groan. We even stopped at one
point to stretch out our sore, aching legs. The first to hit the
wall was Lisa, she became very quiet for a while, and then
tears started to flow. Silent tears fell. Then The Doll was
wiping away *her* silent tears. Before I knew it, my eyes were
streaming and the relief was wonderful. I looked at Rebecca
who was smiling through her tears, and Anne was a mix of
crying with laughter, or laughing through her tears. Our cries
grew louder before turning in to roars of laughter. There was
7 km still to go. We were happy. We were chatting to all the
other stragglers like ourselves. We thanked every remaining
supporter still out there, clapping us on.

At 2 km to go, we picked up the pace. A light
refreshing drizzle hit our faces, we became giddy. My ankle
gave way on me, but I picked myself up and hobbled on, I
was numb to the pain. Our first marathon ever! This was
amazing. Nothing would stop us! Well, except for the
photographer who shouted at us.
"Are you ladies in a tooth paste advertisement?! You have the
most beautiful, biggest, whitest smiles I have ever seen! Give
me a wave for the camera!"

And we posed and smiled bigger and brighter than we had all day.

Arm in arm we crossed the finish line. A few steps later and we all collapsed in a heap on the ground. Laughing hysterically, we eagerly accepted our medals and finishers tops. A shameful number of selfies and posts on social media later, we realised just how hungry we were! The surrounding restaurants were all very busy with post marathon customers. With a knowing look and hungry smiles, we all knew where we were going. With our medals around our necks, worn with pride, we navigated our way to the Luas (Dublin tram). A few stops out from the chaos and we were a short walk from our favourite Mexican food house.

In the history of any of our meals out together over the past 10 years, the Mexican dishes were *the* most divine! There was no guilt associated with the deep fried ice-cream in batter, drizzled with chocolate sauce for dessert. Undoubtedly, the post-marathon meal was the tastiest we could recall! The rest of the day was a blur of happiness, and quite a bit of a high. We were already talking about signing up again for it next year!

A few days later, and I was still hobbling around the lab with my ankle more painful than it had ever been. I decided it was time to do something about it. I went to my doctor and he referred me for a scan on it. At this point I was hobbling along using my umbrella as a walking aid. It really did feel like it was getting worse with every step and my post-marathon high was dwindling.

The Conclusion

Fortunately, I got a call for an appointment early the next week. Cathal would be happy. He had phoned me straight after the marathon to say he took photos of us as we passed him! I didn't even know he was out cheering us on! He is so sweet! He said he thought I was limping with an injury on my left side, and wanted to check if I was OK. He had been on at me constantly since, to get it checked out, so at least I could tell him I was taking action.

I told Cathal about my hobbling umbrella situation and he laughed. He said only I could do a fund raising event and end up needing hospital myself. I hadn't even thought about hospital! My mind was on getting the scan to know if it was ok to start physiotherapy. Cathal seemed to think it was more likely a scan to know what surgery I would need. He assured me he would write something lovely on my cast should I need one, but only if I was nice to him! Otherwise he fully intended draw something indecent! He was making me laugh for sure. He said he would pick me up later and take me for a mint chocolate milkshake, and you know what, that was exactly what I wanted. He was such a good man; how could I ever have doubted the results of the experiment.

While we were sitting in a booth, with cheesy music playing in the background, drinking the most top quality milkshakes ever, I asked Cathal to the wedding. He was chuffed, honoured in fact, and graciously accepted. I knew it would be fun. He jokingly asked if it was his dancing skills that got him the invite? Or was it his voice of an angel? Did I want him to sing a saucy number from a pew in the church and have it go viral? He was so comical, a pure tonic, laughter really is the best medicine. I completely forgot about my sore ankle until it was time to stand up again!

The night before my scan, I couldn't sleep a wink. I really didn't want to find out I needed surgery, although if it helped ease some of this ankle pain which was now radiating up my leg, it would be a welcome relief! The hobbling had slowed my movement down, resulting in having zero time to do my hair or makeup in the morning. My face was clean, my teeth were brushed and I was off to work before the hospital clinic. (Again if I was a lad- this would pretty much be my morning routine complete? Equality check-please!)

On arrival at the clinic, I had a few forms to fill out and then it was time for the wardrobe change. Off with my flowy top and leggings, and, into the not so flattering blue scrubs as I waited my turn. The nurse came out with a wheelchair for me, much to my dismay I couldn't take my umbrella walking aid in with me. I was beginning to feel like an invalid, but that was the furthest thought from my mind when I entered the scanning room.

My heart skipped a beat. The nurse asked if I was ok. I knew why, I could feel the colour drain from my face and she probably thought I was about to faint. It was him, I knew his side profile like the back of my hand, it was The Radiographer, as in MY radiographer from the experiment! He hadn't noticed me yet; his eyes were on my chart.

"Ok Laura," he turned around, "Laura," he paused for a millisecond, if I hadn't been waiting for it, if I hadn't been searching his face for some reaction I am sure I would have missed it, but a tiny curl of a smile formed. "We are going to get you up onto that bed, the bed will act like a tray to pull you into the machine and we will have a good look at that ankle. You look frightened, but I am sure you know that you won't feel a thing are you OK?"

"Yes," I said rather unconvincingly scrambling onto the bed/tray contraption. My timid voice was not because I was frightened but rather because I wanted the ground to swallow me up. I hadn't anticipated seeing or hearing from him again. More than anything I had not anticipated seeing him without my hair and makeup done, and in scrubs hobbling along!

I was told to keep very still, and that the noise would be loud. Good I thought. I didn't want anyone else hearing my thoughts. What would I say to him when my tray/bed pulled me back out?

He was unbelievably smooth, a super professional. He hardly flinched. I was so confused. I guess I had unresolved thoughts about him. Was this smooth nature really just him portraying his ability to be completely fake. Was he two faced? Or did he just have two sides to him? Was he a trickster? Or had my prejudice obscured the reality that he was just a guy, dating a girl, who miss-judged him? He had been extremely confident the night of the Halloween party though, quite literally stealing a kiss. I couldn't very well ask him about that here and now. I felt I should say something to him. I was holding some guilt for not responding to his last message. Maybe I could begin with an apology. That would probably be the right thing to do whenever the machine finally stopped making noise.

To my surprise however, the only person I saw once I was sitting upright again was the nurse, but no sign of Padraig. Again, my face gave me away. The nurse interpreted my confused expression as disbelief that it was all over, and responded with a statement that everyone is surprised at how quick and easy the scanning process was. All I could do was agree as she took charge of the wheelchair and pushed me back out to the ladies changing area.

I was told the results would be sent immediately to my consultant. I left with my umbrella crutch feeling a bit disappointed. I had not made it home when I received the phone call to say I needed surgery, a simple procedure apparently, and I was put on a waiting list.

What a day. First I see The Radiographer with no makeup on, and in very far from fetching scrubs, then I find out I needed to get a pin in my ankle. As soon as I hung up, I changed the direction in which I was hobbling, and I phoned Maria to meet her for coffee. Well, she couldn't help but laugh at poor old me down the phone. With her chuckling away, I guess I could start to see the funny side of it.

Maria had the coffees and cake ordered when I arrived. She greeted me with open arms and warm smile.
"Laura, you really are in the wars aren't you? When is the op?"
"Two weeks, unless there is cancellation."
"Let's hope for sooner then so, as much as I get a laugh looking at you hobble along with your funny little walk, I want you fit as a fiddle for the festive season, Christmas won't be long coming around and there will be plenty of socializing to be done!"
"I doubt there would be a cancellation, I mean why would someone put off their surgery? Unless someone dies or has some other urgent matter. OK I hope no one dies but maybe puts off their surgery to do something more fun! Or miraculously they get better!"

"Laura, you are ever the optimist!"

Maria proceeded to interrogate me about seeing Padraig at the hospital, and scolded me for not looking pristine when I was going there. She was right. If I had to be thinking properly I would have remembered that he worked there! His ears must have been burning, because while chatting about him to Maria, he text!

Padraig:

Hi Laura, I know you didn't reply to my last message but I just wanted to see if you were ok? That ankle looked nasty, I placed it as a high priority. With your age and otherwise good health, with a timely surgery you will make a full recovery. About the Halloween party, I'm sorry, can we meet and talk about it?

Maria snatched my phone, and typed up the response so fast, not pausing until the message was sent, to say I would thank her for it later.

Laura:

Padraig, your behaviour is confusing. I am facing into a surgery but perhaps after you might like to shed a bit of light on the situation.

Wow, I didn't know Maria could be so abrupt. She was right though, there was no point in me mulling over anything to do with him right now. I had asked Cathal to the wedding. The experiment was over. I had to figure out how I was going to tell my boss I would be having surgery, and therefore would be out of action for a while. I had to plan my actual work experiments around it all too. Padraig was the least of my concerns.

When I got home that evening I noticed another message from Padraig:

Laura, I'll admit I want to see now, but I respect your decision. I don't want to do anything to annoy you but if you need help with anything until your ankle gets better please let me know.

I put my phone on silent and went to bed.

Good fortune must have been on my side, a few days later I received notification of a cancellation and would have my surgery a week ahead of schedule - if I could make it. I responded that I would definitely make it! I would need some help after the operation. I phoned my parents to come to rescue me post-op. They were only too happy to help out.

My boss was not too happy with my impending absence from work, not in a mean way, just in the sense he would miss my input (ha or rather my results output). He was so sweet, said I was irreplaceable and to get back to him ASAP. He wished me all the best and asked if I needed help with anything. I'm sure he meant get back to working ASAP- ha! I told him I was fine and would be in touch soon after the operation once cabin fever set in!

A storm was brewing the day of my surgery, not only outside but in my interaction with Cathal. He was so fickle, his friend from his band had hurt her hand, and while I was waiting for him to pick me up to take me to hospital he text to say that he was instead going to her with some ice packs. He assured me she was just a friend and would come to the hospital to check on me. My annoyance was that I now needed to sort out a taxi who would not be able to find my apartment in the jungle of apartment blocks where I lived. I would have to hobble to the main road to be sure the taxi would get to me on time.

In the taxi, despite my pre-surgery fear, I was still managing to develop some sort of hanger while fasting pre-op. Cathal was really doing my head in recently with stupid things. Yes, he was easy breezy and a laugh, but you know what they say "easy come, easy go" and I wanted him gone. Part of me hoped he was more than just friends with his 'female friend' because then I would have good reason to end it.

When I reached the hospital the storm was getting worse. I was torn between hobbling in to the hospital with my umbrella as my walking aid, or as an actual umbrella. With my overnight bag slung over my shoulder, praying the umbrella wouldn't be blown inside out, I hobbled in as fast as I could. My mind was focused on getting in and out hospital seamlessly and looking forward to my recovery.

I giggled while I tried to hold a conversation with the anesthetist. Then there was nothing. I opened my eyes a fraction, there was someone at the bottom of my bed. I asked if my parents were here yet. A lovely voice said no. It was Padraig. I couldn't see him clearly but it was him. My heart was racing.

"What are you doing here?" I asked trying to sit up.

"Hi Laura, I hope you don't mind me being here, I will leave if you want?"

"No, no it's ok."

"Don't try to sit up just yet, take it easy. I was finished my shift and I saw you come in. Most people were looking like drowned rats but not you, you were beautiful. I guessed you were in for your surgery. I'm on-call and was called back in so I decided to see how you were. The roads are lethal with the storm at the moment so I figured it would take your folks a while to get up here, and I didn't want you to be on your own when you woke up."

Out of the corner of my eye I saw a Get Well Soon teddy. Padraig saw me looking and he said, it was just something to keep me company while he went back to work, and I was waiting for my parents. He was so good. He asked if I remembered the consultant coming around. I said yes, the doctor had told me it was success, I just have to do as I'm told for the next six to eight weeks.

"Exactly," said Padraig, he squeezed my hand, said he had to go to work and leaned over and kissed my forehead.

"So that means we have reasons to go for some cocktails and celebrate," he winked.

"Don't worry, I will mind you don't injure that ankle! You can lean on me, or your crutches, but promise me no more umbrella walking?!" We both laughed at that. Thankfully I was so out of it my body did not react with a blush, but I'm sure it would have!

I nodded and smiled, as he left to go back to work. I felt amazing, so warm, so happy, then I realised it was likely the anesthesia, but I didn't care, this felt good and I was enjoying it. It's so rare to have joyous butterflies in my tummy anymore. I closed my eyes for a second or maybe an hour, who knew?! When I opened them again though, the butterflies in my tummy turned to dread, and then a full on constrictor knot! I had forgotten I had asked Cathal to the wedding!

Could I really go for drinks with Padraig when I was supposed to be going to a wedding with someone else in 6 weeks? He didn't say it would be a date, it could just be as friends. Could I really go to the wedding in 6 weeks with this cast on my leg? Maybe that could be my get out of jail free card?

I turned my head and noticed my phone ringing in my bag, on the bedside table, it was Cathal. If he had any sense he would leave me a message, did he not know that people usually are not in their right mind after general anesthesia, and why was he not here as promised? I didn't want him with me now anyway. I was just nit picking at his flaws to justify what I knew was coming. I didn't want to talk to him, because right now, the only thing I had to say was that it had been fun, but now it was over.

My own thoughts frightened me, what if I had imagined Padraig being there? I looked over at the table, the teddy was still there.

Beep, Beep It was from Cathal:

Hey, how did you get on? Can I come see you?

Beep, Beep It was from Lisa:

Hello my dearest friend! How are you? How did the surgery go? Are there any handsome doctors or nurses where you are? Should I do a full face of makeup to come see you later?! Something has arrived for you at the apartment, I will bring it over to you later ☺ I have made a list of TV series for you to watch over the next while. LOTS of HUGS!! See you soon! Xoxo

I was still a little groggy so I just sent a short reply:

I miss your face! I won't miss Cathal. Surgery went perfectly! An angel appeared at my bed when I woke up! Will fill you in later! Puddles of Cuddles xoxo

  I felt so tired. I didn't want to think about the Candidates anymore. Thankfully at that moment I saw my Mam and Dad with wet hair from the storm, and big smiles. They never could go anywhere with one hand as long as other, so naturally Dad was gripping a bag of apples, and a wee nip of dark chocolate, while Mam held out our favourite chain store coffee. Not all heroes and heroines wear capes!

The END

Printed by Amazon Italia Logistica S.r.l.
Torrazza Piemonte (TO), Italy

12860264R00166